THE FAMILY SECRET

AN INTOXICATING NEW THRILLER

NJ BARKER

'Perfume'

from the Latin
'per fumus,'
meaning
'through smoke.'

THURSDAY 4 JULY 2024

1

HOUSE OF MARCHAM OFFICES, SHOE LANE, LONDON

6:30 PM

'You have a great nose.'

Jesse Marcham had heard that comment all his life. Why so much fuss about a nose? The answer, in a word: Perfume.

It was his first memory, and it had infused his life ever since. For each of his twenty-six years on the planet, it had meant everything to Jesse's family: financial security, a heart-warming backstory, and the dynastic promise. His undoubted talent to wake up and smell the flowers had inevitably landed him in the family business and led him to this moment.

His parents had eschewed the top floor boardroom and arranged for his interview panel to be held in the private suite of the company's flagship London office. Only Jacqueline and Richard had the black key card to access the basement suite. Few people even knew of its existence, with the room only accessible through a revolving bookcase from the main office and a discreet service lift. That evening, they were in the lounge area. The wooden table in the centre of the room was surrounded by a collection of designer chairs, from the Arne Jacobsen's Egg his mother was sitting in, to the Hans Wegner

Papa Bear, with its studied angles and padding that made it, in his father's opinion, the most comfortable chair in the world. Beyond the seating area was an open-plan wine cellar hinting at a more relaxed end to many evenings spent there. But not today.

Jesse had delivered his pitch and was now being pressed on what he'd said. However, only one question mattered— was it his time?

He was standing in front of the five people who would decide. He'd expected three of them to be there: his parents, Jacqueline and Richard, and Kath Newman, but the other two had been a surprise. Neither of his aunts had any role within the business, nor did they hold any shares, but he'd had no choice but to push his surprise at their attendance aside and hope it didn't affect his balance.

Both his parents were looking at him. They were implacable, whereas Jesse had only managed to remain seated for a few minutes before rising to his feet. He'd paced around the room as he outlined his vision for the company's future, pivoting for emphasis, his arms conducting an imaginary orchestra, and his fingers continuously tapping against his palms as if listening to music.

Jacqueline cleared her throat. 'If we were deciding on Kath's replacement, your nose would be the only thing we'd be interested in, but our decision today is who to appoint to the top job.'

She didn't mention Chloé, but Jesse knew his sister had delivered her pitch an hour before him. Chloé or Jesse? Daughter or son? Businesswoman or perfumer? However their parents viewed the decision, it was a choice of two.

Kath adjusted her glasses. Jesse had first met Kath when he was sixteen. A straight-talking American, she had been the first and, by a distance, the most important recruit of House of Marcham when she was enticed away from a large industry multinational to become the in-house perfumer. If there was ever a perfect role model for Jesse, it was Kath. She took her art seriously and treated Jesse with respect, not because of his parentage but rather because, as she had confided in him early on, she saw something of herself in him. When it became clear that he would hang around the firm's laboratory over that first summer, whether she wanted him there or not, she challenged him to re-create, from smell alone, the signature House of Marcham perfume, *Evocation*. The following summer, he finally got close enough, so she gave him a second challenge, then a third. He inhaled every molecule of his unofficial apprenticeship.

Jesse stood still, fighting the urge to respond to his mother's unspoken question. Jacqueline turned to look at her fellow panel members. 'Are there any final questions?'

At that moment, Jesse heard three simultaneous chimes, and his phone vibrated in his pocket. He pushed away a wave of irritation and looked around the panel, ready to deal with any questions.

'My God,' Kath's hand was over her mouth, and her face was pale. She turned to Jacqueline. 'I think you need to see this.'

Frowning, Jesse pulled out his phone. There was a text from an unknown number. It contained a link to an online article entitled *Sour Perfume: A Secret Threatens to Corrode House of Marcham's Foundations.*

Jesse slipped his phone back in his pocket, momentarily forgetting his presentation. The last thing he needed was a distraction, but it was too late—his parents bowed their heads as they read the story, and even Jesse was guessing what the article might say.

'Where the hell did they get this from?' Richard said.

'I don't know,' Jacqueline replied. 'But right now, we need to focus on our response.' She looked up at Jesse. 'I'm sorry, I need to make a call.' Without waiting for a response, she dialled and held her phone to her ear. 'Hi, Angie. I'm forwarding you an article. Have the PR team draft a response for my review in thirty minutes. Thank you.' She placed her phone on the table and looked at Jesse. 'Okay, then. Shall we continue?'

Aunt Rosie cleared her throat. Jesse barely knew Rosie, and he'd never really known why his immediate family had so little to do with her. She was seven years younger than her brother, Richard, although seeing them together, the age gap seemed larger. Her black hair was pulled into a ponytail, the scrunchy matching her pale green summer dress. 'Are you sure it's okay to carry on?'

'Yes. It's fine.' Jacqueline responded before Jesse could speak.

'Very well.' Rosie turned to Jesse. 'I was interested in what you said about synthetics. I would've thought that the company should focus on natural ingredients. Wouldn't that be more appealing to the consumer?'

Jesse nodded as he listened to the question, but the article's headline was echoing around his head. He tried to focus on his aunt. How much did she know about the perfume industry? He couldn't recall his father saying much about her, which was a problem when judging how to pitch his response. He opted for a question of his own. 'What percentage of synthetic ingredients do you think is in a typical perfume?'

Rosie shrugged. 'I don't know. Not much. Five percent?'

'It's nearer to 80 percent,' he replied.

'Okay, so I was close,' she said, smiling.

'People are instinctively drawn towards products advertised as natural.' Jesse paused before moving on to a familiar theme. 'The challenge we face, which I believe we should meet head-on, is that the preference doesn't stand up to scrutiny.'

'How do you mean?' Rosie asked, wrinkles appearing above her nose.

'Think about the risk of allergies. A natural product, such as sandalwood, contains over a hundred different molecules. Each one is potentially an irritant, yet synthetic sandalwood is a single molecule with a significantly reduced risk of irritation.'

'Huh,' Rosie tilted her head, 'that's the opposite of what I'd have thought.'

'Exactly.' Jesse started pacing again. 'The intuitive response is one hundred percent the wrong answer. Factor in cost, sustainability, and the range of scents available, and it's clear synthetics are the future.'

'And you think we should be open about that?' Aunt Elaine had already asked a few questions. Mainly softballs for Jesse to bat away. Unlike Rosie, Jesse knew Elaine well, or at least he had for the first ten years of his life. Elaine's son, Cameron, and Jesse had been not just cousins but best friends growing up. Jesse had spent as much time in Aunt Elaine's house as his own during those years.

'I do,' Jesse said. 'Transparency should be a key driver for the next stage of the business's development.'

'The truth, the whole truth and nothing but the truth,' Elaine said, glancing at Jacqueline as she did so.

Jesse wondered whether that was an oblique reference to the article. Everyone in the firm would have read it by now, and he had no doubt that the whole industry would be quoting paragraphs to each other before long.

His mother shuffled forward on her lipstick-red chair. 'Well, I'm not sure we should go *that* far. After all, secrets have always been at the heart of our industry.'

There was a slight edge in the interactions between his mother and her sister-in-law. Jacqueline's older brother, Philip Marcham, had married Elaine, and soon after, their son, Cameron, had been born. When Cameron was approaching his sixth birthday, Philip died of a heart attack. Elaine eventually remarried, although she and her son kept the Marcham name. The two families had stayed close, and after Cameron finished his business degree, Jacqueline had given him a job at House of Marcham. Cameron had lasted only a year, and Jesse had never got to the bottom of what had prompted his cousin to leave. Once, he'd thought his cousin was about to explain, but at the last second, he'd clammed up, seemingly caught between wanting to tell his side of the story and not wanting to trash Jesse's parents.

Secrets, indeed, he thought.

Jacqueline picked up her phone from the table. 'If we were to share our recipes in full, we'd be ripped off in a heartbeat.'

Jesse frowned. Did she believe that? Lab technology meant competitors could shoot a new juice within days of its release and generate a better than ninety-nine percent accuracy blueprint of the rival perfume. The law allowed it—a company could protect the name, the bottle, and the packaging, but the scent itself was a free-for-all, hiding in plain sight. Everyone knew everyone else's formulas, yet the world of perfume kept turning as if each recipe was a well-guarded secret. Jesse had always found it bizarre.

He looked directly at Elaine. 'I believe in transparency. Before we close, I'd like to share something with you.' He clasped his hands together and smiled. 'I've been working on my own perfume, a product which embodies my philosophy.' Kath raised her eyebrows, but Jesse pushed on. 'It's wholly synthetic and highly sustainable. It comes in a refillable glass bottle, and the recipe is fully detailed on a paper insert included in the cardboard box packaging.'

Jacqueline's lips were thin, and Richard tapped his fingers against his mouth. 'Does this radical new perfume have a name?' he asked.

The emphasis on the word radical made Jesse hesitate, but at this stage, his only choice was to be all in. He nodded at his father. 'Yes, it does.'

'Well, perhaps you will share it with us,' Richard said.

All five interviewers were staring at Jesse. He'd agonised over the name, wanting to capture something that gave a nod to the firm's heritage whilst suggesting a future direction, but it also needed an edge. He'd finally settled on the name the previous week. It was perfect. He cleared his throat.

'*Legacy*,' he said.

His aunts smiled. Kath, however, was frowning. Jesse couldn't afford to have her offside, not right then when her support for his tilt at the top job was crucial. 'It's just a concept,' he said, trying to catch Kath's eye. 'If we proceed with it, I'll need everybody's input.' He was rewarded with a half-smile.

'Maybe you'll be proved right,' Richard said. 'After all, the industry is changing in many ways. Arguably, though, it's moving away from the idea of an in-house perfumer like you.' Jesse swallowed. His father was still challenging him. 'So, my final question for you is this: If we appoint you to take over from me as our CEO, how can we be sure you'll be objective in making decisions about our perfumes? We exist to make money, not win prizes.'

When Jesse had first raised his sights from the laboratory up to the leadership of the family firm, he'd seen a horizon of pain. A future that required sustainable and responsible fragrances, combined with the downward spiral in the target price per kilo of perfume compound, could slash the perfumer's palette in two. But the more he'd studied, the more fear had given way to hope. He began to envisage an industry that would embrace biotechnology and, in a hyper-competitive market, properly value a brand which championed authenticity.

'Whichever way it moves,' Jesse replied, 'the perfume will always be at the centre of the industry. Even if you want to transition the company into a broader-based luxury brand, perfume's profit margin and distribution will ensure it continues to be the business's financial heartbeat. Lose focus on our fragrances, and we lose our business.' Neither of his parents nodded, but Jesse knew he was right. 'So, in answer to your question, you would never want me to be objective about our perfumes. And I never could be.'

He scanned the panel, trying to judge how well he'd recovered from the interruption of the article crashing into everyone's inbox. He leant down and rested his hands on the back of the Barcelona chair in front of him, bouncing on the balls of his feet, pleased that he'd finished with a statement core to his pitch. He hoped he could count on Kath and Elaine to vote for him over Chloé, and Rosie looked as though she might have been convinced, but he had no read at all on his parents.

'Thank you, Jesse,' his mother said. 'We'll let you know our decision on Monday.' He'd long since given up trying to second-guess her. All he could do now was wait. 'We have cars waiting outside to take us to the party. You're welcome to use one of them. I need to return to the office to deal with this story.'

Jesse shook his head. 'Thank you, but I'll walk.' He wanted to read the article, and he wanted to do that alone.

'Very well,' Jacqueline said. 'In that case, we'll see you there.'

———

JESSE TOOK a deep breath as the bookcase rotated back into position behind him. He walked along the corridor towards the hub of the floor, holding his phone, before stepping into an empty meeting room. His heart hammered against his chest as he closed the door behind him and clicked on the link to the article.

Rumours abound that industry powerhouse Jacqueline Marcham is considering her options for a new CEO. Husband Richard has been in post for nearly a decade, but we all know Jacqui M wears the trousers. Whatever the reasons for Richard standing down, the main question is: Who's in line to take over?

The usual answer is Jacqui's son and heir, Jesse Marcham. Jesse is popular, and everyone says he has a great nose, but can he run the business? No one knows. There is, however, a next-gen Marcham who is business-savvy. That's right, younger sister, Chloé. She's in the running for the top job, too, and according to our sources, she might even be the better bet.

However, it's not the sibling rivalry that has our noses twitching. Our spies tell us there's a damages claim about to be filed against House of Marcham. We don't know the basis of the claim, but we're told it's material enough to rock the House, and we all know that if a house isn't built on firm foundations, it collapses.

Jesse's mouth was dry. Who had been speaking to *Scent?* And what the hell was the suggestion about a threat to the firm? He hadn't heard anything about a potential claim.

He closed his eyes and tried to reset his mood. After a couple of deep breaths, he stepped back into the corridor. The air was thick with scent as Jesse's co-workers milled about in evening dress. The last few hours might have been about the choice for the next CEO, but the rest of the day was about the company. If Jesse could bottle the excitement that had even squeezed through the vacuum seals into Product Development, House of Marcham would have a new best-selling fragrance. *Heritage.* Or perhaps, *Number 25,* because that night was the company's twenty-fifth-anniversary party.

He flinched as his phone vibrated in his hand. Chloé. He let the phone ring as he walked down the stairs. Chloé had worked in the firm's finance team during her college holidays, and she'd returned with a first-class business studies degree and a six-month internship in a marketing firm under her belt, ready to build her career. Their parents rotated her through the core departments to give her rapid exposure to a range of real-life business experiences before she returned to the finance department.

Jesse's head spun whenever Chloé talked of debits and credits, money market swaps and revolving credit facilities. He had nothing against the finance team, but he didn't speak their language, and he never could understand how to apply a smell test to a monetary transaction. On *his* first day as a permanent employee, Jesse had burrowed down in the product development team, and he'd stayed there ever since - extended exposure to one narrow specialism, the perfect course for his nasal horse. There was no doubt that he had a gift. Kath was still what the industry called the firm's 'nose,' but Jesse was building a name for himself as a perfumer with flair and taste, and he'd hoped that would be enough to put him in pole position to step up to the CEO role.

He answered Chloé's call on the sixth ring.

'Where are you?' she asked. Of course, she wasn't interested in his location. She knew about the pitch and would be listening for clues about how he thought it had gone.

'I've just finished. I'm walking over now.' He forced himself not to say any more. After all, he didn't have to justify himself to Chloé. At least, not yet.

There were less than one hundred hours until the deadline their parents had set for the announcement, but this wasn't like the CEO transition for a mega-cap, with detailed processes and procedures. Things worked differently in private companies, and family-owned businesses had practically no rules at all. Jesse knew he didn't have a divine right to be appointed. Their parents were choosing the next CEO of the family perfumery business, and they had a genuine choice: their daughter, who had business savvy running through her veins, or their son, whose ability to create perfume was a rare natural talent. It was a perfume business, but it was impossible to know which way they would lean: towards the perfume or the business. Jesse reframed the choice in a way that made more sense to him. Paris or New York? Paris had been the only winner for a long time, but recently that had changed.

He shook his head as he pushed through the revolving

doors of the office and glanced at the coffee shop opposite. A waft of citrus with a hint of spice delivered a Columbian-style hit to his nose. Jesse didn't buy into the use of coffee beans as a 'nasal palate cleaner,' but he was down with a double espresso being a hell of a way to reboot his day.

'So, how are you feeling about Monday?' Chloé asked.

Jesse mentally unpacked her question—concern, expectation, trepidation, and a hint of bluff. 'What's happening on Monday, Chlo?' He tried to deliver it as a throw-away, but the tightness in his throat made it sound defensive. He decided to reach for some common ground. 'Rosie and Elaine were there.'

'Yeah,' she said. 'Quite a surprise, that was.'

'Any idea why? I didn't know Dad was even speaking with Aunt Rosie.'

'Your guess is as good as mine,' Chloé said.

He hadn't realistically expected any other answer. Even if she did know, she wouldn't tell him until after their parents had announced their decision. 'Okay. Well, I'll get there as soon as I can.'

He checked the time before putting away his phone and stopped momentarily, running his thumb over his fingers. His phone buzzed again. What did Chloé want now? He pulled the phone from his pocket, but it wasn't a text from his sister. It was an email from an unknown address with the title, WE NEED TO MEET.

Jesse hesitated. It looked like clickbait. Was it a coincidence it had been sent shortly after the *Scent* article was published online? He tapped his fingers against his leg before opening the email.

JESSE MARCHAM,

WHEN YOU KNOW WHAT I KNOW, YOU WILL DO THE RIGHT THING

I WILL BE IN CONTACT.

Jesse stared at the message. His nose twitched as a woman walked past, leaving a trail of a rival's perfume in the air.

He shivered, deleted the message, and walked into the coffee shop.

2

THE DORCHESTER, PARK LANE, LONDON

7 PM

Jesse glanced around the Dorchester Ballroom and wondered whether it was like this every night—day after day of hosting *the* highlight of the season. The round tables weren't exactly squashed together, but if someone was coming in the opposite direction, you had to stand aside or risk the awkward synchronised twist, sway and smile as you squeezed past. It was like riding a corporate fairground Waltzer. The evening would be so much better if he'd been able to attend with Grace, but their relationship was still under wraps, and that night wasn't the time to go public.

Jesse's parents were sitting together, each turned away from the table, engaged in separate conversations with people he didn't recognise. Their respective conversational partners would be either competitors or suppliers, although it was sometimes hard to tell them apart. Industry parties brought out overly enthusiastic applause and gushing praise even from the fiercest new start-up competitor. A fist bump, slightly too hard, when meeting face to face and a whispered quote to a journalist the moment you turned your back.

Whoever those people were, they weren't part of House of Marcham because Jesse knew everyone in their business. They were like family. Except maybe the finance team, he couldn't vouch for them.

Jesse loosened his collar. He tried to avoid wearing a suit, but tonight, there was no option other than to don black tie. At least it allowed him to blend in. A few men had opted for coloured neckwear, but when pressed into formal wear, Jesse always went back to black. Plenty of glitz and glamour was on display, but he'd noticed a definite shift from the previous event five years ago. The serving staff were predominantly male, a change from the cocktail waitress vibe, and whilst there was wine on the tables, the drinks in early circulation were mocktails.

Jesse scanned the people seated at his table. His parents' table. The hosts faced the main stage. Jesse and Chloé, already dubbed 'the next gen of House of Marcham' by the compere, sat opposite their parents. There were four other places set at the table. One was empty but was earmarked for Daniel Kane, who had messaged earlier to apologise for his no-show. Daniel was a long-standing family friend, the company's external legal counsel and recently, the firm's only non-executive director. The other three seats were taken by Angie, one of the firm's assistants, Ben, a recent recruit to the security team and Stan, who had joined accounts a couple of months ago, fresh from university—at least, that's what Chloé had told him.

All three had secured their tickets to the top table through a ballot. Three seats were allocated randomly amongst whichever employees wanted to enter.

Jesse glanced at Angie. She'd been with the firm since before he'd started. She was tall, quiet, and stunningly efficient. Even the way she spoke was almost robotic, so seeing her doubled over with laughter as Ben whispered in her ear was a surprise. Angie glanced at Jesse, which caused the security guard to look at him. Ben's face stretched into a wide grin.

'How you doin', boss?' he asked, offering a fist bump.

As far as Jesse knew, Ben called everyone boss. He seemed unshackled, one of life's freewheelers. 'I'm looking forward to the evening.'

Ben nodded. It was an open secret that there was a marquee announcement to help celebrate the anniversary— the launch of the latest House of Marcham perfume that Jesse and Kath had worked on for an entire year. Kath, Jacqueline and Richard had made the final selection from the last ten offerings, but they'd gone with Jesse's number one choice. In an important sense, *Distraction* by House of Marcham was Jesse's first perfume.

'Yeah. It's going to be a fun night,' Ben said.

Jesse took a sip of water. He turned to speak to Stan, who was busy cleaning his glasses with a napkin. When he saw Jesse was about to talk to him, he excused himself and headed for the toilets. Jesse wrinkled his nose. Lavender, mint, cumin, and vanilla. Stan was playing away from home with Jean Paul Gaultier's Le Male, but at least he'd gone iconic. Perhaps there was hope for the finance department after all.

The compere finished his slightly off-key jokes and then called for the audience to focus on the screen behind him. The stage light dimmed as Jacqueline's and Richard's faces appeared, enlarged on the canvas backdrop. They were both immaculately attired, blue-eyed, glamorous, and clean-cut. Sapphire and steel. When they'd married, Jacqueline had kept her maiden name, Marcham, rather than take Richard's surname, Ford. They were a team, but Jacqueline was, without question, the captain. Regardless of any corporate title, the company's name and Jesse and Chloé's surnames made that clear.

The room erupted into applause, with Richard leading the cheers. Within a few seconds, everyone in the room stood and clapped, facing their table. Jacqueline smiled as she walked over to the stage. Her outfit gave a nod to Coco Chanel's Little Black Dress, and she wore it well. She stepped into the spotlight and gazed around the room, waiting for the applause to subside.

'If someone had told me when we secured the bank loan to launch House of Marcham that twenty-five years later, we would be celebrating the continued success of the business with over two hundred employees and many more friends from the perfume industry, well, I would have said,' she paused for a beat, 'that sounds about right.' The room burst into laughter. Jacqueline used the moment to take a sip from her champagne flute. 'If anyone could bottle the sense of pride that I feel, standing here, knowing that all of us have built the company into what it is today, I'd recruit them as our head perfumer.' More laughter. She looked towards a table on her left. 'Don't worry, Kath. I think you're safe. Actually, Kath, perhaps you could join me up here.' Jacqueline stretched out an arm, and Kath made her way from her seat onto the stage. The two women embraced.

'You smell great,' Kath said, her rehearsed words picked up by the podium microphone and broadcast to the room. 'Is that a new perfume?'

'How funny you should ask,' Jacqueline said, facing the room. 'I was lucky enough to be given the first bottle of a new perfume from House of Marcham.'

'How lovely. What's it called?' Kath asked, playing along.

'It's called,' Jacqueline paused again, '*Distraction*.'

That second, all the lights in the room blacked out, and three white strobe lights above the stage kicked into action. The sound of a music tape winding backwards filled the room before giving way to a heavily distorted Hendrix-style guitar line. Then, the abrasive beat of 808 State's Cubik dropped from the speakers, and the backdrop to the stage was filled with a massive image of the round, light pink glass bottle emblazoned with the word *Distraction* that faded away with each letter. Some of the audience were standing and clapping. Others were already dancing to the music.

Jacqueline's voice cut in over the instrumental. '*Distraction* launches in our stores this weekend. Richard and I want to thank Kath, her team and all of you for what we think will be a milestone fragrance for House of Marcham.'

For a moment, Jesse forgot about the CEO battle and soaked in the atmosphere. Kath was looking at him from the stage, moving her head in time to the music, hands in the air, and although he was too far away to be categoric, he was pretty sure she winked at him.

———

JESSE WAS STANDING, enjoying the atmosphere, when he noticed a gaunt, late middle-aged man dressed in black tie shuffling towards the stage. The man's outfit was dated. With a turned-up collar, a plain cravat, crisp white shirt, dark waistcoat, and trousers that were cut short and elasticated at the knee, he looked positively Victorian.

The man stepped up onto the stage and moved towards Jacqueline. She stopped dancing, a frown darkening her face.

In the pause, the man unfurled a banner and held it out in front of him. Jesse craned his neck for a better view as the strobe light pulsed. Ben, the security guard, was now approaching the stage, moving fast but not yet running. Jesse blinked and tried to focus on the message daubed in black paint on the white banner. The strobe lights froze the words.

The Marchams must pay.

Jesse didn't know what the hell that meant, but it couldn't be good. He stood up, his head throbbing. The compere was now striding towards the protestor. He was only a few yards away when the man reached inside his jacket. Jesse started running, screaming at his mother, as the man threw something down towards the floor. Jesse instinctively covered his ears as a loud bang reverberated through the ballroom. Thick smoke billowed through the air. Jesse struggled forward. Nausea clawed at his stomach as he struggled to breathe. Shouting echoed around the room as the evening pitched from the bonhomie of a corporate event to the terror of an unprovoked attack. People flooded past Jesse, surging towards the exits at the back of the room.

He waved his arms in front of his face, trying to clear the air to see what was happening, but it was impossible. He guessed he was perhaps only two metres away from the stage when there was another series of loud bangs. He ducked down and pushed himself forward, crawling towards his mother. The ballroom was in chaos. Some people had dived under the tables, others were running. Jesse blinked, but the smoke was still thick, and he was too far away.

'Mum,' he shouted out. He burrowed through a group coming the other way to reach the stage, felt for the edge, and climbed up. 'Mum,' he shouted again. The smoke was starting to clear, and he caught a glimpse of people huddled together on stage. Ben had already made it to his mother's side. Her face was drawn, and she was shaking, but she was alive.

Ben beckoned Jesse over. 'Stay with her,' he said. Then he nodded at Jacqueline before running across the stage and disappearing through a door at the back of the stage. The banner lay discarded on the floor, but the protestor had vanished.

Jesse swallowed. 'Mum, are you alright?' he asked.

Jacqueline coughed but nodded. 'I'm fine.'

'You're not hurt? You haven't been hit?' Jesse put his arm around her.

'No. I couldn't see, but I don't think he came close to me.'

'What about the gunshots?'

'I don't know. Is that what that was?' Jacqueline shook her head. 'Nothing hit me.'

Jesse turned to look around the ballroom. The smoke had dispersed. People were crowded together, but he couldn't see any blood. No one seemed to be injured. He took a deep breath. 'Hopefully, Ben will catch the guy. Or the hotel security will get him.' He took a deep breath and closed his eyes, trying to process what had happened.

Then, his sister's scream filled the room. He spun towards Chloé, who was squatting down close to their table. Their father was lying on the floor. Jesse's heart thumped against his chest. *Oh God. Please, no.*

'Get a doctor,' Chloé's voice cut through the air. 'My dad's been hurt.'

Jesse and his mother rushed over to the table, and within a few seconds, they were next to Chloé.

'I can't see any wounds,' Chloé said, holding her hand

against her father's face. 'Dad? Dad, can you hear me? Dad, answer me.'

Jacqueline was kneeling next to her husband. Jesse remained standing, staring at his father. He saw Richard's hand flex. 'I saw him move,' Jesse said, pointing.

'Richard?' Jacqueline rubbed her husband's hand.

His eyelids flickered, and he opened his eyes, squinting and blinking. He rubbed his head. 'What happened?' he asked, his voice thick and slurred.

'Have you been hit?' Jacqueline asked. She ran her hands across his torso and then down his legs.

'I banged my head,' Richard said, gently stretching his neck. 'There was a loud bang. Someone shoved past me, and I lost my balance. I think I hit my head on the table.' He brushed his fingers against his temple.

'Okay, okay.' Jacqueline touched her husband's face. 'Thank God, you're alright.'

Chloé stood up and leant towards Jesse. 'What just happened, Jesse? What the hell was that?' She kept her voice low. Despite events, her one-shoulder magenta minidress trimmed with ostrich feathers looked untouched. She rested her hand on his arm.

Jesse shook his head. 'No idea.' The citrus note of Sicilian Mandarin fighting its way through the sulphur afterglow of the smoke told Jesse that one of the bottles of *Distraction* wrapped as a table gift had smashed.

'Did you see that message? *The Marchams must pay.* Pay for what? What does it mean?'

'I don't know, Chlo.' The words on the banner had buried as deep into Jesse's brain as the sulphur in his nose.

'An animal rights protestor, maybe,' Chloé said. 'I mean, they think we're all the same.'

'Maybe,' Jesse said, but it didn't feel likely.

Usually, a group with an agenda would make their view clear. Raising awareness was a key point, often the only point of the protest, but this hadn't been like that. This was cryptic. The message was that the Marchams had done something wrong. He paused. Marchams, not Marcham. The slogan wasn't aimed at the company. It was targeted at them. It was an attack on their family.

His mind flashed back to the email he'd received on his way to the Dorchester. Was the protest the contact the anonymous emailer had promised? Jesse rubbed his hand over his face. The hit piece from the journalist had come first. Then the anonymous email, and now the protest. They were all beating the same drum. There was a story, a family secret that would be exposed. Something that could jeopardise the company.

But Jesse had no idea what it was, what his family should have to pay for, or who they should be paying.

FRIDAY 5 JULY 2024

3

HOUSE OF MARCHAM LABORATORY
8:30 PM

JESSE CARRIED THE CUP OVER TO THE SINK, THE BITTER ALMOND after-taste of his second coffee still on his tongue. It'd been a long day, but he'd enjoyed losing himself in perfume to escape from everything that was happening. He yawned and glanced at the clock on the wall. Grace would be there any minute and the lab was deserted.

He'd cried off going to Grace's flat last night once it became clear the interviews with the police and the subsequent discussion with Chloé would push well into the early hours. The protestor hadn't been caught, and there'd been no CCTV footage that identified him. In short, there was little prospect of the protestor being found. The police had confirmed that the man had used a smoke grenade and bangers designed to incite fear and panic, but nothing that could have caused injury itself.

Jesse had promised to make it up to Grace by giving her a personal tour of the lab. He tapped his fingers on the table as memories of his CEO interview pushed their way into his mind. The more he'd thought about the panel interview, his parents' facial expressions, various odd phrases, and the fact that Aunt Elaine and Aunt Rosie had been invited, the more he feared the answer. He tried to imagine how he'd feel if they announced Chloé as the next CEO. There was some truth in *Scent's* throw-away line about Chloé being the favourite—Jesse might be five years older, but his sister was a lifetime smarter. Jesse was the past, the romantic. Chloé, twenty-one years old and with the world at her feet, was the future, the visionary. She was the captain of a ship constructed in New York that was navigating around France and would shortly set sail to the East, with her gaze locked onto the investment horizon.

He looked up at the sound of footsteps to see Grace standing in the doorway to the lab, scanning the room.

'So, this is your kingdom?'

'Well, one of them.' Jesse laughed. 'You've really never been in here before?' Whilst she wasn't an employee of House of Marcham, she'd been heavily involved in their firm-wide training programme as an external consultant for the last couple of years, and she provided one-to-one mentoring to their senior executives.

'No. It's my first time. I've never seen so many bottles in one place.' Her lips twitched. 'How many of these can you identify by scent alone.'

'All of them,' he replied without thinking,

'You sound very sure of yourself, Mr Marcham.' She walked towards one of the cabinets. 'How about we play a little game?' Jesse didn't speak. 'Five scents, five guesses.'

'What's my prize?'

'Get them all right, and you'll find out.'

'Careful. My father could walk in any time,' Jesse said, smiling.

'Your father is on a plane to China.'

'How do you know that?' he asked, but he knew she was right. Richard was negotiating a potentially massive contract. It was the firm's first real push into the Far East.

'I have my sources.' Grace opened the cabinet and started to pull out bottles. She used her body to block his line of sight, but he could still tell she had taken two from the top shelf, one from the middle, and two more from the bottom. Jesse turned so his back was to her.

'On the desk next to you, you'll see a jar full of blotters,' he said. Each five-inch-long strip of stiff, unscented, absorbent white paper was easily foldable due to its central groove. 'Take one, dip it, put the lid back on the jar, and then pass me the strip.' He listened as Grace unscrewed the top of the first bottle.

'Okay.' Her footsteps approached him. 'Here we go. Test number one.'

She rested one hand on his shoulder as she passed the strip to him. He closed his eyes and inhaled a buttery, woody smell with a tinge of sweetness. Sandalwood. Easy. 'This one's an aphrodisiac,' he said. 'Give it a try.'

'Focus, Jesse,' came the stern response.

'Number two?' He held out his hand, and Grace handed him the second strip. His guess of Cedarwood was confirmed the moment the molecules hit his nostrils. It was the unforgettable scent of school lead pencils—softer than Sandalwood and with less sweetness.

'Ready for number three?'

'Yes.' This one would likely be from the middle shelf, possibly Bergamot. But it wasn't Bergamot's spicy floral scent; it was the sweet floral honey scent of Neroli. Three out of three, he smiled to himself.

'Here's the next one.' Jesse heard the cap being screwed back on the bottle. He pulled his collar up to his nose and breathed in his own scent. He was confident in his nose, but a quick palette cleanse wouldn't do any harm. Number four was possibly the single most important perfume material. Jasmine.

'Oh, hold on,' Grace said. 'This one's empty. I'll choose another one.'

A few seconds later, Jesse was smelling the final scent. It was more challenging because he hadn't seen where Grace had selected it from. But she must have reached for the bottle on the bottom left because it was an Oud, the Arabic word for wood. Extracted from the fungus-infected resinous heartwood of the Agar tree, it was an incredibly expensive material, colloquially called *liquid gold*. It was also the Marmite of perfumery. The Ouds were Jesse's weak spot, but recognising it as Oud should be enough.

'You need more time?' Grace asked.

Jesse turned round to face her. 'Sandalwood, Cedarwood, Neroli, Jasmine and Oud.'

He saw Grace frown as she studied the bottles lined up before her. Surely, he hadn't got one of them wrong, but her frown gave way to a laugh.

'Very good. Five out of five. I'm impressed.' She placed the bottles methodically back into the cupboard. 'So, Mr Marcham, you've passed my test. As a reward, I'm commissioning you to make me a perfume.'

Jesse blinked. 'No problem. Give me two years, and I'll create your perfect scent.'

Grace scratched her nose. 'Two years? I thought you grabbed a few different bottles, mixed them up, and voilà?'

'Yeah,' Jesse drew out the word. 'Something like that.' He

paused. 'Okay, what's your favourite perfume? For these purposes, I'm prepared to accept perfumes other than those made by House of Marcham.'

'*Daisy* by Marc Jacobs,' Grace said.

'A classic.' Jesse was already scanning the bottles on the turntable. He selected three bottles. 'Perfumery is like music. You produce your symphony with chords. We start with a base chord.' He reached for another bottle, picked up a blotter, dipped it into the solution, and handed it to Grace. 'Try this.'

Grace lifted the strip towards her face and immediately wrinkled her nose. 'That's ... not great.'

Jesse laughed. 'That's patchouli, a classic raw ingredient of perfumes. Base notes need to last for hours; they help determine the chief characteristic of the perfume. It needs to have low volatility and high tenacity.' He used a glass dropper to add the first ingredient to a beaker as he spoke. Cleaning the dropper with rubbing alcohol between each selection, he mixed the three selected base notes.

'Tenacity sounds great and all, but not if it smells like that,' Grace said.

'Smell it again in an hour or two, and you'll find it more appealing. But we need to help it, so we add other notes. It's not important whether you like the individual smell; it's how it combines with other notes that makes or breaks a perfume.'

'So, what are you going to add next?'

'A middle chord, made from Violet, Wild Rose and Apple Blossom.' Jesse carefully measured out the ingredients and mixed them in a separate bottle. 'Nearly all middle, or heart, notes are floral.'

'I love the smell of violets.'

'I hate to be that guy, but it's synthetic. Violet is one of a handful of flowers that can't be rendered naturally. But don't worry,' he grinned at her, 'you won't be able to tell.'

'But now I know,' she said, pretending to pout.

Jesse continued his masterclass. 'The middle chord is the bridge between heavy base chords and light top chords. A perfume is a classic example of the whole being greater than the sum of the parts. We chose the heart notes, partly for themselves but mainly for how they work with the other notes. A good selection will remove any unpleasant first hit of the base notes.'

Grace leant forward to read the labels of the next three bottles that Jesse had selected.

'I recognise the smell of raspberries from when I apply the perfume. I didn't know there was grapefruit and pear, too,' she said.

'These are the top notes or the head notes. They are the first scent to hit your nose before they evaporate and let the heart and base notes do their work.'

Grace reached out to pick up a bottle of rose absolute. 'What's absolute?'

'Concentrated perfume material obtained by solvent extraction. It's a little like dry cleaning. How many roses do you think were used to fill that bottle?' Jesse started to mix the top notes.

Grace scrunched her nose. 'I don't know. Maybe one hundred?'

'Close.' Jesse laughed. 'Twenty-five thousand.'

'What? Seriously?' Grace handed him the bottle.

'Yes. You need three hundred and fifty flowers for each kilo. And about seventy kilos of flowers to make one hundred grams of absolute.'

'Wow.'

'It's crazy, isn't it? But ingredients are everything, and they need a lot of investment. Take iris, for example. The iris roots are planted for three years, and then once they've been cleaned and trimmed, they're dried for a further two and a half years.'

'That's nuts.'

'*You're* nuts. You wanted your perfume made in a day.'

Kath's revelation of a House of Marcham meeting with Global Fragrances burrowed into Jesse's mind. 'We still do pretty much everything ourselves, but we're unusual.' His voice was hollow. 'Most houses send their brief to one or more of the large international fragrance companies. They each produce a range of different perfumes, and the house chooses the one it prefers.'

'That must cost a fortune,' Grace said.

'You'd think so. But, oddly, unless you choose one of their perfumes, you don't pay a penny.' Jesse shivered.

'Are you okay?' Grace asked.

Jesse nodded and dipped another blotter into the top note blend. Grace's hand was already waiting. 'Oh, that's lovely. It reminds me of ... Daisy.' She smiled.

'It's transitory. Come for the top notes; stay for the heart and base notes.'

Jesse closed his eyes. He knew the famous scent well but couldn't know the formula without shooting the juice, which would take time. Right now, he could only guess. After a moment of intense concentration, he decided on the proportions of the three chords. It probably wouldn't smell much like Daisy, but it would be in the realm of an approximation. He dipped another blotter and passed it to Grace.

She closed her eyes as she inhaled. She didn't say

anything for a moment, then took a second sniff. 'That's not bad,' she said.

'Thank you,' Jesse said, mock bowing. 'It's not good. There are hundreds of reasons it's wrong: different ingredients, the balance of each chord, and the proportions of the notes. It'll smell different on your skin, too. In fact, it'll smell different on my skin than it will on your skin. All perfume does.'

'Really?' Grace's eyes were wide.

'Really.' Jesse dropped his voice. 'Did you know that smell is the only sense initially processed in the limbic lobe, the part of the brain responsible for sexual and emotional impulses?'

Grace leaned closer to him. 'Now *that* is interesting.'

Jesse grinned. 'I need to tidy up here, but how about we go back to mine for a coffee.'

She kissed him before reaching for her bag. 'I'll go and get my coat.'

4

JESSE'S HOUSE, WAPPING, LONDON
10 PM

THE FRONT DOOR TO JESSE'S HOUSE WAS OPEN. GRACE WAS standing inside, leaning against the doorframe and watching him walk up the driveway.

They'd known each other for two years, and their relationship was informal and comfortable. They laughed together, and their conversations ranged far and wide, but there'd always been a barrier until that heady April Fools' Day. He still wasn't sure whether she was joking when she'd told him, long after he'd said yes to her dinner invitation, that she'd chosen that date to give herself an out. But, April Fool or not, their relationship had deepened over the early summer months.

'Hi,' he said.

'Hi.' Grace pushed herself up. She was as tall as him, and their faces were only inches apart. He caught her scent and tried not to grin. *Distraction* was well-named.

'You're...' Different words hustled for priority. *Here. Beautiful. The one.* He hesitated and started again. 'May I come in?'

She shrugged. 'Fine with me. It's not even my house.' Her smile made his heart tumble.

They walked into the kitchen. His mouth was dry. 'What can I get you to drink? Champagne? Vodka? Whisky?' he asked.

She tilted her head. 'What I would really like is a cup of strong coffee.'

Jesse had bought the Jura Z10 a few days earlier, and the machine still sparkled with the gleam of a new purchase. He reached for a jar of coffee beans, lifted the clear circular lid from the machine and tipped the beans in.

'Getting drunk is overrated. Coffee is much better. I think I'll join you.'

'That's what I thought the deal was.'

'The deal?' he asked, faintly aware that she was teasing him. He selected an espresso, smooth grind, and medium strength.

'Come back to my place for a coffee?' she said.

Ah. Right. 'You do know that when people say coffee in that context, they don't mean coffee?'

Her eyes widened. 'Well, I did wonder. Coffee seems very popular,' she said as she walked towards him.

SATURDAY 6 JULY 2024

5

JESSE'S HOUSE, WAPPING, LONDON

7 AM

GRACE WAS LYING ON HIS BED, HER HOOPED EARRINGS GLINTING amongst her black hair.

'Have you got used to the idea of us yet, or does it still feel weird?' she asked. She said it in such a way that Jesse thought she could live with weird a little longer.

'I think I'm getting there,' he said. She was the fourth woman he'd classify as a serious relationship. He'd never been sure that any of them were the one. It had been that way with Marina, and they had been together for nearly two years before Marina decided for them both. Their split, the slow disentanglement of their lives, had been painful, but eventually, Jesse realised Marina had been right to end it.

Grace rolled over and propped herself up on her elbows. 'Hey, any chance of that coffee you promised me? I think the one you made me last night will be cold.'

'Sure.' He moved his nose to within an inch of her neck, still able to smell the hint of chocolate with the vanilla.

'Admiring your own work?' she asked, tilting her head.

'I'm admiring lots of things right now.'

She reached out towards his bedside table and picked up the bottle of *Distraction* he'd brought home from the lab. 'May I?'

'Go ahead,' he said.

Grace sprayed her wrist and started to bring her hands together. He reached out and touched her arm. 'Not like that,' he said. Her eyes widened, but she was smiling. 'You'll crush the top notes. It's better to let it evaporate naturally.'

'Well, I wouldn't like to crush your top notes,' she said, spraying the perfume on her collarbone and shaking her head.

'Better,' Jesse said, his eyes closed, lost in the scent. 'You need to smell the perfume again in twenty minutes and then again in an hour. The scent changes over time.'

'I never knew perfume was so *personal,*' Grace said. Then she hit him on the arm. 'Don't forget about my coffee,' she said.

Jesse sighed and rolled out of bed. Her question about their relationship had lingered. Undoubtedly, their work connection was a complication, but he had no choice but to deal with it head-on.

'I was interviewed for the CEO role on Thursday,' he said.

She raised her eyebrows. 'Well, I heard the rumours, of course.' She bit on her little finger. 'How did it go?'

He'd never discussed his leadership prospects with Marina throughout the two years of their relationship, but as he was discovering, things were different with Grace.

Jesse shook his head. 'I don't think ... I don't know. I have a feeling my parents might decide to go in a different direction.' He stood in the bedroom doorway, his hand resting on the door.

'Is that what you really think, or are you worried about that trashy gossip column?'

'You read *Scent*?'

'The whole industry reads it,' Grace replied.

He shrugged. 'Well, it might be right about Chloé.'

Grace tilted her head, a frown creasing her forehead. 'Family business succession is hard, Jesse. In my experience, these things can blow up.'

'It's nothing new. Chlo's always been competitive, but we've managed to avoid falling out so far.' He was thinking about summer holiday pedalo races where falling out had a double meaning. Grace looked at him in a way that suggested his confidence might be misplaced. Or was her expression in response to something else? He knew she didn't have any siblings, and her parents had both died before she was twenty. 'I'm sorry. I didn't mean to go on about my sister.'

'It's okay.' Something in the way she answered encouraged him to ask about her wider family.

'Do you have any cousins?' Jesse asked.

Grace shook her head. Did she look sad? Maybe, just a touch. 'My parents were both single children. I'm the last one, the last Nelson.'

'Sounds like a film title.'

She laughed. 'Yeah, I'm not sure it would be a box office hit. How about you? I've never heard you mention cousins.'

'I have two.' He paused. He wasn't surprised that he'd never mentioned Isabelle. 'I've never talked about Cameron?'

'Nope. I've never even heard you mention the name.'

Jesse pushed away a twinge of guilt. 'Cam and I were close when we were younger. We still are, I guess, but I don't see him much.' He scratched his jaw. 'I can't believe I've never mentioned him. Are you sure?'

'Positive. Who's number two?'

'Isabelle.'

'Okay,' Grace laughed. 'You've never mentioned her before either, but judging by the lack of warmth in your voice, that won't surprise you.'

'It doesn't,' he confirmed.

'Would you say the Marchams are a close family?' she asked, trying to stifle a yawn.

Which was a question and a half. 'It depends greatly on when you ask me,' he said.

She frowned. 'I'm sorry. You don't have to answer that.'

Jesse scratched his chin. 'Right now, the last Marcham sounds appealing.' He caught her expression at the same time as he heard the self-pity in his own words. 'Sorry, I don't mean that. Chlo and I get on well enough, but we're very different.'

'How do you mean?'

'I don't know,' Jesse said. 'Sometimes, when it's just us and our parents, I feel like I'm the odd one out. Not in a bad way, as such.' He smiled. 'I'm just not wired the same way they are.'

'And Cameron?'

'We're wired differently, too.' Jesse grinned. 'Thank God. But we get on. Everyone likes Cameron.'

'Sound like a typical family to me,' she said.

'Yeah. I don't know what life would be like without them.'

'Lonely.' Grace looked at him, but if there was sadness in her expression, there was something else too. 'When I graduated. When I was accepted for my MBA. When I got my first job. In those moments, I was happy, but I wanted to share the news with people. People who'd known me all my life. There's been no one since my parents died. Of course, I've got friends, but it still feels like a part of me is missing. Something that'll never come back.'

'I'm sorry.' He blew out a breath. 'Look, this doesn't feel right, talking about my family.'

'I asked,' she said.

'I know, but still, it feels weird. Can I change my answer to complicated and leave it at that?'

Grace nodded but said nothing. Jesse turned to head to the kitchen, not sure how to recapture the mood.

———

Jesse walked upstairs with two mugs of coffee. Grace wasn't in the bedroom, so he put the mugs on the bedside table.

'Grace?'

'In here.'

He walked along the corridor and into the spare bedroom.

'I'm sorry,' Grace said. 'I was coming back from the bathroom, and ... it was the smell. I shouldn't have come in.'

'No. It's fine. A bit embarrassing, but I'm sure you won't tell anyone,' he said, grinning.

'What are they?' she asked, pointing at the tiered wooden frames.

His mouth twitched. 'I'm making my own Jasmine absolute.' He walked over to the nearest frame and rested his hand on it. 'These frames are designed to extract the fragrance from the flowers. Each frame holds a glass plane. I spread it on both sides with grease that absorbs the scent of the flowers. Then I use my tweezers to remove the flowers every afternoon for a few consecutive days.'

'How many days?'

'Sixty.' Jesse said it quickly.

'Sixty,' Grace repeated.

'Once I've removed the flowers, I turn the frames over, scratch the grease with a metal comb and then lay fresh flowers on the glass. The flowers continue to produce scent even after they have been cut. It takes sixty days for the oil to absorb their fragrance fully.'

'That sounds intense.'

'That's only stage one,' Jesse said. 'For the next few days, I'll wash the pomade by mixing it with alcohol before leaving it to evaporate. I'm on day four of seven.'

'And on the seventh day...'

'God rests, and I produce Jasmine absolute,' he said. Grace stared at him. 'Don't say it.' A smile played across her mouth. 'Don't say it,' he repeated.

'Why?'

'You said it.' Jesse shook his head and covered his face with his hands. 'I don't know. I think there's something wrong with me. This is why you're not meant to go into people's spare bedrooms.'

He felt Grace pull his hands away from his face, and then she kissed him. 'Jesse Marcham, I think I might be falling for you,' she said.

SUNDAY 7 JULY 2024

6

AMERSHAM
11 PM

Jacqueline Marcham pulled her coat tight around her body. She didn't like taxi drivers dropping her at her front door, so she always asked them to pull over at the foot of the hill so that she could make the way up to her house on foot. It was spitting with rain, and although it was a mild night, she felt cold.

She'd stuck with fizzy water at the private gallery viewing, but now she allowed herself to imagine a glass of chilled, very dry white wine. Walking towards the house in her heels, Jacqueline cursed, not for the first time, at the choice of gravel for their drive. Pulling out her keys, she heard another footstep on the gravel. She spun round.

A man stood beside the house, swaying unsteadily on his feet. Jacqueline clutched her keys, holding them in front of her as a weapon. Her other hand felt for her phone and hit the button to call Richard.

'Don't come any closer,' she shouted to the man whilst holding the phone to her ear. He looked familiar, but she couldn't place him.

He held up a hand. 'I'm not here to hurt you.' Which only underscored the possibility that he could hurt her if he wanted to.

'Don't move.' The telephone line clicked, and she heard Richard's voicemail message. *Damn.* He was on a plane somewhere above Finland right now.

The man shuffled on the spot. 'I just want to talk to you,' he said.

Jacqueline's mind was spinning. Should she hang up and dial the police? No, not yet. Everything was recording on her husband's voicemail. She spoke clearly so the man could hear every word. 'Hi, Richard. I'm at home, and there's a trespasser on our drive.' She paused. 'The police? Yes, please do.'

The silence on the other end of the line screamed at her. She swallowed. 'Yes, he's about five foot ten, medium build, thinning dark hair. Silver stud earring in his right ear. Aged about fifty, I'd say.' The man still hadn't moved. He was blinking rapidly. 'Yes, good idea.' She pointed her phone at the man and took his picture. 'I'm sending it to you now. Yes, I'll stay on the phone. Two minutes until the police? Okay.'

She looked at the man. It was strange that he'd been waiting for her at her house in the dark, but it was just as odd that he hadn't reacted to her taking his photograph.

'I wanted to talk about House of Marcham.' His voice was slurred. It might have been just how he spoke, but he sounded drunk.

'Are you a reporter?' she asked, clutching the phone and her keys. The piece in *Scent* had triggered a few unwelcome press enquiries.

The man answered her question with a gruff laugh. 'No. This is a private matter. I can't hear any sirens,' he said, sounding genuinely confused rather than smug.

'They're nearly here.' She was processing everything, trying to evaluate the risk. She wasn't sure, but she felt he wasn't here to attack her, not physically. 'Who are you?' she asked. She didn't expect him to answer, but it might give her more time.

'I thought you'd never ask, Jacqui.'

Only Richard ever called her Jacqui.

'Who are you?' she repeated. She trawled through possible connections. What had he said? *A private matter.* What did that mean? She might have met him in a work meeting or at a function, but she didn't think so.

'My name's Martin.' He swayed on his feet and took a step towards her. He didn't move any closer, but his voice dropped to whisper. 'I believe you knew my father, Harold Baxter.'

Jacqueline balled her fists as blood pounded in her ears. The image of the protest banner crystallised in her mind.

The Marchams must pay.

She had dismissed the protestor as an attention seeker at the time, but now she knew that wasn't the case. She had never spoken to Martin or his father, but she knew all about them, and now she was sure that Martin Baxter had carried out the attack.

Richard had promised her he had dealt with Harold, that everything had been agreed, and that the issue was dead and buried.

But if that was true, why was Martin Baxter standing on their driveway?

'What do you want?' she asked.

'I told you.' He blinked, looked down the drive, and then back at her. 'I want to talk.'

The answer phone would have recorded their discussion, and she had emailed Richard his photo. Baxter would be crazy to try anything physical now, even if he didn't believe the police had been called. She ended the call.

Martin Baxter pointed at her. 'This, all this, it isn't right.' It took a moment for her to realise that he was indicating the house, not her. 'My father's dead.'

That wasn't news to Jacqueline. She'd wondered whether they might hear from Martin after Harold's death, but six years had passed with no contact.

His cheeks reddened, and his voice grew louder as he spoke. 'My mother died a month ago.'

Jacqueline's head was spinning. 'I have no idea why you're here.' She heard her own words. She sounded strong, sure of her position, but her insides were hollow. 'I think you should leave now,' she said.

He grunted and stumbled down the drive before pausing and turning around. 'You'll regret it. Now I know the truth; I won't let you get away with what you've done.'

Jacqueline reached up to open her front door, but she kept her eyes on him as he walked towards the open gates at the end of the driveway.

She was used to making decisions under pressure. She didn't know precisely what Martin Baxter was accusing her family of, but it was clear Richard had left them exposed, which meant she needed to take control. She needed to fix it. Now.

She pivoted and called out.

'Wait.' He turned back to face her. 'You're right,' she said. 'We should talk.'

MONDAY 8 JULY 2024

7

HOUSE OF MARCHAM OFFICES, SHOE LANE, LONDON

1:15 PM

JESSE WALKED INTO THE LABORATORY, LOOKING FOR KATH. THE firm's laboratory was largely open-plan, with workbenches, individual workstations, floor-to-ceiling cupboards, shelves and filing cabinets. As soon as he spotted Kath, he walked over to her.

'I got your message,' he said. She hadn't said what she wanted to discuss; she just said it was urgent.

Kath wrinkled her nose. 'Let's find a room.'

'What's going on, Kath?' She never suggested discussions behind closed doors. They spoke about perfumes openly. Was she going to share some feedback from the interview panel? The decision would be announced that afternoon.

Kath stepped into a glass-walled meeting room, waited for Jesse to follow her, and closed the door. 'You know I worked at Global Fragrances before I came here?'

'Yes.' Jesse said the word slowly, not sure where this was heading. 'Are you going back?' His stomach pitched. He needed her at the company.

'No. It's nothing like that. Well, not exactly like that.' She half-smiled. 'One of my friends called me about something they've heard through the grapevine.'

'What?' Jesse's mind was scrambling, searching for something that might make sense.

'Okay. I have no evidence of this, but my friend told me that House of Marcham recently met with Global Fragrances.'

'That's not unusual.' But Jesse knew there'd be something more.

'This was high-level strategy stuff.' She hesitated. 'The meeting was to discuss outsourcing the creation of our perfumes.'

Jesse sunk into a chair. 'Really?' he said. 'That can't be true.'

Kath shrugged. 'It absolutely can be true. It's how most perfumeries work, after all. Even if they don't start that way, that's where nearly all end up. There's no reason we should be any different.'

Jesse could remember when Kath had explained it to him —the industry's open secret. Most perfumes weren't made by the houses that sold them. They commissioned them and named them, but they didn't create them. A select few global scent-maker companies, the so-called 'Big Boys,' worked almost as hard at keeping their industry role secret as they did on creating perfumes for many of the leading brand names and perfume houses. The Big Boys had massive R&D departments, deep benches of perfumery talent and unmatched access to raw materials. They responded to briefs created by the houses, pitching their best ideas formulated within the budget set by their client, which meant, despite the impression given by virtually all brands, only a few houses had an in-house perfumer who created their perfumes. Houses such as Hermes and Chanel. And, for the moment, House of Marcham.

'Mum and Dad would never do that,' Jesse said, shaking his head. 'Our heritage is the perfume recipes created by our family. It's at the heart of everything we stand for. It would be like outsourcing our soul.'

'We're swimming against the tide, Jesse. I think you know that. Your parents definitely do.'

Jesse half nodded, thinking back to his father's challenge at the end of his pitch. Full creativity needed freedom, and that freedom cost money, which either took funding away from advertising or resulted in a price point too hot for the high street. Jesse, however, believed the more expensive 'private label' route was right for House of Marcham.

'So you think it's true?'

'I trust the person I spoke to. They couldn't, or wouldn't, tell me who was at the meeting from our side, but do I believe there was a meeting where outsourcing was discussed? Yes, I do.'

'My parents wouldn't do that to you,' Jesse said, looking Kath in the eye.

She turned away. 'I won't be here forever, Jesse. We would still have an in-house perfumer to create the briefs, manage the process, and select the winning juice. Also, at some point, I want to move back to New York.'

'When?'

'Not immediately, but in the next few years.' She smiled. 'The timing might depend on the CEO decision.'

'I just assumed...' He trailed off, trying to identify his feelings.

'I like you, Jesse. You're talented.' She leaned towards him.

'Most importantly, you're a perfumer. If you become CEO, my job would be safe.' Her mouth twitched. 'Although...'

'Although what?'

'I'm confident you wouldn't replace me with an outsourcing contract, but I'm guessing you'd have the final say on the perfumes.'

He frowned. 'Isn't that the same with Mum and Dad?'

'Not really, no. They have their opinions, of course, but they always trust me.'

'*I* trust you,' he said.

'And yet you've been developing your own fragrance behind my back.'

Jesse tried to analyse her tone. She didn't sound angry. If anything, it was delivered as a simple statement of fact, but she was clearly evidencing *Legacy* as a lack of trust, and he had the strong sense that she'd known about it before his interview. 'I'm sorry.' He scratched his head. 'I should've told you that I was working on it.'

'Damn right, you should. Although I understand why you didn't.'

'Do you want to try it?' He glanced involuntarily at the cabinet which contained his samples.

Kath shook her head. 'No. You're right. *Legacy* needs to be one hundred percent you. You have to make your mark. Just don't plan to make a habit of it.'

'I'm still not sure what you're saying. Do you want me to be the next CEO?' he asked.

'What's your view on outsourcing?' Kath said, by way of an answer.

'It's the last thing I would support.'

She nodded. 'I just needed to hear you say it.'

'Okay, then. Good.' He cleared his throat. 'So, what do you think we should do about the Global Fragrances meeting?'

Kath looked up to the ceiling, weighing her words. 'Nothing right now, but *Distraction* needs to be a hit, and we'd better ensure we smash the briefs for the next perfumes out of the ballpark.' Her hand rested on the door handle as Jesse's mind churned through the possibilities of the meeting with Global Fragrances. She was looking directly at him. 'My question to you is, CEO succession notwithstanding, are you ready to get back in the game?'

Jesse pushed himself out of the chair. 'Yes,' he said. He glanced at his watch.

'When's the announcement?'

'Chlo and I are getting a car to our parents in a couple of hours.'

Kath opened the door and held up her hand, fingers crossed. She nodded to him and walked back out onto the lab floor.

8

AMERSHAM

2:30 PM

J<small>ESSE AND</small> C<small>HLOÉ SAT IN THE BACK OF THE</small> S-<small>CLASS</small> M<small>ERCEDES</small>. The driver had headphones in and was chatting to a friend as they sped through the Buckinghamshire countryside. Chloé's phone rang, and Jesse saw the name Larry appear on her screen with a green heart icon replacing the letter Y. She grinned and hit the speakerphone button.

'You're on speaker, Larry. I'm with Jesse.'

'Oh.' There was a pause before the man spoke again. 'Hello, Jesse.' He had a Home Counties accent.

'Hi, Larry. Nice to finally talk to you,' Jesse said.

'Likewise. Chlo's told me a lot about you.' It was a stock phrase, but Jesse noted Larry had joined the select few permitted to call his sister Chlo. 'Chlo, I just wanted to remind you we've got a table at Core for eight o'clock.'

Chloé raised her eyebrows at her brother. The three Michelin-starred Clare Smyth restaurant was right up her street. 'I haven't forgotten,' she said.

Jesse pinched his nose. It sounded like a celebratory

dinner, booked in advance, for the evening of the CEO decision.

'Great. Have you decided what you're going to wear?' Larry asked.

'Yes, of course. I think you'll like it.' Her confident tone was interwoven with a tease.

'I usually do.' Jesse cringed while Larry laughed. 'Okay. Speak later. Good luck.'

Chloé was smiling at her brother.

'I've been meaning to ask,' Jesse said, 'when do I get to meet Larry? Strictly speaking, you shouldn't even have had a date with him before he goes through my screening process. It's been what, three months?'

'Seven.' Her mouth twitched. 'Your screening process hasn't proved that reliable in the past.'

'Well, how was I to know that Sebastian wouldn't be up to it *in stamina terms?* You do your own screening on that sort of thing. He ticked everything else off.'

'You have a checklist?'

'Oh, yes. Not strong enough to physically hurt you, not charismatic enough to break your heart, and not smart enough to steal all your money.'

Chloé laughed. 'It's so sweet how you just want what's best for me, bro.'

'What can I say? I'm a great brother.' He shrugged. 'So, how does Larry stack up?'

'He's strong, charismatic, and smart. As for his stamina, well, he—'

Jesse held his palms out. 'I don't need you to finish the sentence.'

'That's good,' she said, smirking, 'because I'm not sure I've got the energy for it.'

Jesse shook his head, but he was happy for her. Sebastian, whatever their jokey exchange, hadn't been good for her. She'd seemed muted, as if Sebastian had been leaning on her dimmer switch. So, even though Jesse hadn't met Larry, he'd give him a pass for his role in Chloé's reboot.

She frowned. 'Larry was at my birthday party. Didn't you meet him there?'

He shook his head. 'I left early.' He wasn't a great fan of parties. He didn't actively dislike them, but given a choice, he'd prefer not to go.

Chloé thrust out her wrist, showing off her watch. 'He bought me a Rolex. It's called a Lady-Datejust. It's from Highland Jewellers, the place in Princes Arcade. Isn't it lovely?' Jesse didn't wear a watch and wasn't a fan of the showy timepiece, but seeing his sister happy was worth the price of any watch—even a Rolex. She punched him gently on the arm. 'What about you, big brother? Are you ready to move on from Marina yet?'

He kept his face neutral. Chloé was more upset than him when Marina left him. The two women had got on like a firework factory on fire. In truth, that had been part of the attraction for Jesse, only a minor factor, but he recognised it was there all the same. His family *loved* Marina. Perhaps that had helped shift their perception of Jesse, elevating him to where they'd always wanted him to be, but when she'd left him, she'd lowered him back down.

Grace couldn't be more different. For a start, his family's initial reaction would be faint disapproval because Grace worked for them. They'd try hard to get over it. After all, they loved him; he knew that, even if they didn't always show it. Their struggle to accept Grace would, however, be clear to see.

'Yeah, I think I'm ready,' he said.

'Ooh, anything you need to tell me?' Chloé twisted on her seat to face him. Jesse kept quiet while trying to decide what to say. 'You have, haven't you? Tell me,' she said.

He grinned. 'You can't tell Mum and Dad, okay?'

She leant towards him. 'Your secret's safe with me. This is *so* intriguing.'

He waited for a few more seconds before speaking. 'Grace Nelson.'

Her eyes widened. 'Grace. Our Grace? Wow. How long has this been going on?'

'Three months.'

'Oh, so not as long as us,' she said. Her competitive streak was both deep and broad, but Jesse said nothing. She tucked a strand of hair behind her ear. 'I've always liked Grace. She's super smart. I'll have to take her out for lunch.' She paused. 'Although I wouldn't want to intimidate her.'

Jesse laughed. Grace wouldn't blink an eye at having a one-on-one with Chloé. As well as her role with House of Marcham, she was building up her consultancy practice. Grace was discreet about her clients, but he knew that she was the trusted advisor to a growing number of C-suite executives. She worked hard and was great at her job, and in the three months they'd been together, he'd not once heard her admit to any nerves.

'I'm sure she'd cope,' he said.

Chloé rubbed his arm. 'I'm happy for you. You're back in the game.'

Her comment carried a strange echo of Kath's closing question to him, and the Global Fragrances story bubbled into his mind. Someone from House of Marcham had arranged the Global Fragrances meeting, but only a few people would be granted such an audience. If it wasn't their parents, and it wasn't Kath, it could only be one of the other heads of department. But Jesse couldn't see it. Outside Kath's domain, the only one that made even a modicum of sense was finance. Yet the finance director wouldn't solicit such a meeting without a clear direction from either Richard or Jacqueline.

He glanced at Chloé, who had plugged in her AirPods and was talking to someone back in the office. What was his sister's view on in-house perfumers? He'd never heard her advocate in favour of outsourcing as an alternative. Still, she was focused on profit, and if she thought outsourcing was the way to achieve that, that would be enough—her brother would be a secondary consideration.

Could their parents be considering something more radical than just leadership change? Outsourcing the perfume-making would further break the link with the family's heritage, but a preferential contract with Global Fragrances or one of the other Big Boys could be clever positioning for a sale.

Was it possible that they wanted to sell out? After all, it had only been six months since their father sent them an article stating that only one in three family businesses successfully transitioned to the next generation. Beyond three generations, it dropped to one in twenty. Their parents had made a success of the business, but there was no guarantee that a family member could repeat the trick—whatever their respective skills, the objective odds were against either Chloé or Jesse being as successful as their parents.

Chloé sighed and relaxed back into the seat. 'Not long, now,' she said.

Jesse shrugged, feigning a lack of concern. They were driving down the country lane towards their parents' house.

In a few minutes, they would both know what the future looked like—for better or worse.

————

THE TYRES CRUNCHED on the gravel, and the petrol fumes lingered in the air as Jesse and Chloé stood at the front door of their parents' home. Their parents had bought the old National Trust property in an auction. It was too big for a family of four, let alone two, and its scale was suitable for live-in staff, although their parents had never gone that far. It had a wondrous vista of woodlands and farms that, on a clear day, reached out forever. The neighbouring properties were some distance away, hidden by an expansive collection of trees and shrubs, which meant there was no real sense of community when Jesse had grown up. Isolation had been the name of the game.

The doorbell sounded deep within the bowels of the house, and a few moments later, the front door swung open. Their father beckoned them in. Richard Ford was a couple of inches taller than his son, touching six feet, but his face was starting to show the signs of years of hard work. His hair had given the first warning of his approaching middle age when it turned grey almost overnight.

He'd never been a great one for shows of affection, and rather than offer his children an embrace, he gave them a cursory nod. Jesse spotted a pair of his mother's Jimmy Choo heels abandoned just inside the hallway as he followed his father down the corridor towards what they had always called the fire room. Jacqueline was sitting on the cream sofa closest to the fire, which blazed through the decorative screen, an odd choice for mid-afternoon on a summer's day.

She was wearing a suit rather than her usual home outfit of a jumper and yoga leggings.

'Don't get up, Mum.' Chloé bent down and kissed her on the cheek. Jesse followed her lead, trying to ignore the tightness in his stomach. Richard indicated where they should sit, with each place marked by a glass of iced water already poured and waiting on the table.

Richard cleared his throat. 'Thank you both for coming. We have some news we need to share with you. Bad news, I'm afraid.' He looked drawn.

Jesse thought the long-distance flights took more out of him these days, and it wouldn't have helped that the negotiations with their Chinese counterparts still hadn't concluded —China wanted more time to consider whether to open its shores to House of Marcham.

Jacqueline shuffled forward to the edge of her seat. 'I want this to stay amongst the four of us for now. News will spread, it always does, but I think we'll cope better as a family if we get on the front foot.' Jesse chewed his lip. The tone was off. It didn't sound like his mother was talking about the CEO decision, and the mood was sombre. Jacqueline carried on. 'We can't hide this news forever. At some point, it'll be in the press.'

The blog published by *Scent* jostled into Jesse's mind along with memories of the protest and the anonymous email. Was it true that there was a problem with the company? Were their parents about to share a secret they didn't feel secure discussing at the office? His stomach pitched. Jacqueline pushed on. 'It maddens me that something so personal could ever be considered news, but there it is. That's the world we now live in.'

Jesse knew it would be news if anything were wrong with

the company, and if there were any hint of a scandal, it wouldn't just be news but the premise for a Netflix mini-series.

It took a moment for what she'd said to sink in. *Something so personal.* The words hit Jesse in the gut first, and then his throat tightened.

'Mum?' It came out as a croak.

Jacqueline, however, sounded in control. 'A couple of months ago, I had my annual medical, and the doctor identified something she wanted to investigate.' Jesse glanced at Chloé and could tell she was thinking the same thing as him. Their mother was dying. 'This morning, I received the results of those tests. I have cancer.'

Jesse tried to wrap his mind around the news. Their mother. Cancer. The juxtaposition made no sense. Those things didn't belong together. Nothing could stop Jacqui M; she was a force of nature.

'The advice from the doctor is to start a combined course of chemo and radiotherapy,' Jacqueline said.

'How bad is it?' Chloé asked.

'It's stage one, lung cancer. It's not too late, but they want to move fast before it spreads.'

'Mum, Dad, I don't know what to say.' Jesse was true to his words, talking without knowing what he planned to say. Always dangerous. 'Mum, I'm so sorry. I can't—'

'Why are you saying sorry, Jesse?' A crinkle formed across his mother's brow. 'Are you responsible for my cancer?' she asked.

'Um, well, no. I guess not.' Thinking, of course not.

'You don't sound sure.' There was a subtle shake of her head. 'Jesse, how many times have we told you not to apologise? Especially for things that aren't your fault.' Her hands were folded on her lap.

He caught his instinctive 'I'm sorry' before it slipped from his mouth and instead said nothing. Christ, couldn't he even tell his mother that he was upset that she was dying? This was so screwed up.

'What are the odds?' Chloé asked. Nobody needed to clarify which odds she was asking about.

'Fifty, fifty,' Jacqueline said. 'I've got access to the leading doctors, and we can afford the best treatment. I'm backing myself.' Which would come as no surprise to anyone who knew her or even those who'd had a cursory glance at her Wikipedia page.

Jesse sensed what was coming next just before his parents said it. This meeting wasn't about the family pulling together to support their mother. It wasn't a chance to share emotions and comfort each other. No, their mother may have been diagnosed with cancer, but the meeting was solely about the business.

'As you both know, we were hoping to announce one of you as the new CEO,' Jacqueline looked unruffled. 'The problem with plans is that real life gets in the way.' Her eyes flicked towards Jesse. 'So, we've had to adapt.'

Jesse held his breath and stared at the floor because it was the judges more than the judgment he couldn't face.

'Real life? You mean your cancer?' Chloé asked.

'Yes and no. We have some other issues to deal with,' Jacqueline said, glancing at her husband.

'Okay.' Chloé dragged the word out for a full two seconds. 'So, what's the new plan?'

'We are a family business, and we will stay that way,' Jacqueline said. 'We have many talented leaders within our business, both family and non-family, but we want our family to lead this business for many generations to come.'

'You sound like a press release,' Chloé snapped. 'Just tell us who's going to be the CEO.'

'Very well.' Jacqueline leant forward and put her glass on the table. 'Your father will step aside, and I will assume the role of CEO.'

'You?' Chloé was staring at her mother.

'Do you think you would be a better appointment?' Jacqueline said coolly but didn't wait for her children to respond. 'It's no longer the right time for inexperience. The landscape has changed. Our firm is under attack, and we need a wartime leader.'

Jesse tried to digest to pivot in strategy. 'But why switch to you? Shouldn't you focus on your health?'

'We can't risk me being seen to be stepping back. The focus has to be on the company and its future. People will think there's a reason if I scale back my duties. And if there's one thing that I'm not going to allow to happen, it's the media rumourmongering about my health.'

Or, to put it another way, Jesse thought, reporting the truth. But it wasn't his place to say that; it never had been. He glanced at his sister.

'The interviews, everything we've both worked on,' Chloé said, 'were for nothing?'

'No,' Richard said. 'We've decided to create a new role, Deputy CEO, to work closely with your mother during the transition to CEO.' Jesse chewed his lip. It sounded like they'd made the decision. Whoever they announced as deputy would become CEO in a year or two. The drumbeat was getting loud now. Richard glanced at his children before carrying on. 'We want to ensure that the selection of the next

CEO leaves the future of House of Marcham in the best possible hands.' A bead of sweat prickled between Jesse's shoulder blades. 'We are therefore appointing three deputy CEOs.'

Jesse looked sideways to see his sister's eyes stretch wide as their father continued speaking.

'Three?' Chloé echoed.

'Obviously, the two of you,' Richard said. Jesse's mind was scrambling. Who else could it be? His heart thumped against his chest as he thought about his conversation with Kath. Their father cleared his throat. 'The third deputy CEO will be our niece, Isabelle.'

―――――

ISABELLE LOWE WAS one small step on the family tree but a giant leap in terms of the future CEO of the family firm— Isabelle was family on a technical basis only.

The contest between Jesse and Chloé had been painful enough, but a three-way promotion battle between Jesse, Chloé, and Belle was ... Jesse searched for the words.

'You've got to be fucking kidding me?' Chloé skewered the bullseye.

Jesse picked up his glass of water, his eyes prickling with heat. He hadn't been awarded the top job. When it came down to it, his pitch hadn't convinced. *He* hadn't convinced. He blinked to clear his vision and tried to calm his mind. His mother was critically ill, and now his parents tossed in the second grenade of Belle being in the race for CEO.

'I don't understand,' Chloé said. 'I mean, me and Jesse, sure. I get that. But Belle? She doesn't work in the business.

Hell, she's practically working at a competitor. You'd be better off including Cameron.'

Richard took a deep breath before speaking. 'I met with Rosie recently. We had a lot to talk about.' He pursed his lips. 'There were some things, things from the past, we needed to discuss. I'm not going into the details, but I promised her I'd do what I could for Isabelle. Her life hasn't been easy.'

Jesse's knowledge of Isabelle's life was sketchy. Her parents had divorced. Her father was a hedge fund manager, and the separation had been toxic. Aunt Rosie had spent years battling her ex-husband through the courts. Perhaps Jesse should feel sympathy for his cousin, but any previous family discussions around Isabelle—not that there had been many—were clinical, almost devoid of emotion.

'Doing what you can doesn't mean making her CEO.' Chloé wasn't pulling any punches.

'*Deputy* CEO,' Richard said. 'Whether she becomes CEO is entirely in your hands.'

'You can't seriously want her to lead our firm?' Chloé pivoted between her parents. 'Instead of me? Or Jesse? Really?'

'We don't think it will come to that.' It was their mother's turn again in the parental tag team. 'But we promised Rosie we'd give Isabelle a fair chance, and that's what we're doing. She's young and has time to develop.'

Chloé scoffed. 'She's only ten days younger than me.'

'She has a business studies degree and works in the industry,' Jacquline said. 'She might end up being better than you think.'

'Have you told her yet?' Chloé asked.

'Not yet, no.' Richard flicked a glance to Jacqueline, and something unspoken passed between them.

'Then don't,' Chloé said, waving her hands. 'Just make us the deputy CEOs. Give her a job if you must, but a different one, preferably in our most remote foreign office.'

A wave of heat shuddered through Jesse's body. He'd known he might not get what he wanted. He'd tried to understand how he would feel—imagined accepting Chloé's victory, but he hadn't anticipated a year-long contest with Chloé, let alone Belle.

'We've made our decision,' Jacqueline said. 'That's all we can share right now. Let's meet again in a few days to go over everything. We'll invite Isabelle and Daniel.'

Jesse frowned. Daniel was the firm's non-executive director, in addition to his day job as a lawyer.

'Why do we need Daniel there? Are you worried we'll sue you?' Chloé asked.

Jacqueline half-smiled at her daughter's quip. 'We've made some changes to the company shareholding.'

'What?' Chloé's tone seemed to foreshadow the coming of winter.

'We want to ensure the company's ownership better reflects our ongoing wishes,' Richard said. 'We'll discuss it when we meet.'

'With Isabelle there? Okay, well, that doesn't sound at all disconcerting.' Chloé was staring at her father, chin raised. 'Why can't you tell us now?'

'Because your mother and I haven't finished our discussions about it,' Richard said, his delivery very matter-of-fact.

'Well, I suggest you finish it whilst we're all here.' Chloé crossed her legs to demonstrate that she wasn't about to move.

Their father countered by standing up. It was like human chess. 'We will most certainly not discuss it now. It's time for you both to leave. Thank you for coming to see us. We'll be in touch about the next meeting.'

Chloé rose slowly, not wanting to cede ground. To anyone. 'Fine. If that's how you want to do it.'

'It is.' It was like watching a verbal snowball fight. The colder and icier, the better.

'Don't get up, Mum.' Jesse just wanted to leave now. 'We'll see ourselves out. I'm very, ah, upset to hear your news. Keep us posted on the treatment, and if there's anything I can do to help, then—'

'There's nothing you can do to help, Jesse. Unless you've discovered a cure for cancer.'

There were no hugs goodbye. No calls of 'love you.' As if nothing, absolutely nothing at all, had changed.

———

CHLOÉ AND JESSE walked out of the front door.

'I asked Ron to park near the High Street. Let's walk,' Chloé said. 'Jesus Christ. Isabelle. I can't believe it.'

Halfway down the driveway, Jesse's phone chimed with a text from Cameron.

> You around? Be good to catch up.

He pushed his phone back into his pocket. Cameron could wait.

'Poor Mum. Cancer, it doesn't seem possible,' he said.

Chloé rolled her eyes. 'Oh, she'll be fine, you watch. She'll enjoy judging us all over the next twelve months. She won't let herself die and miss out on that. Oh, don't look at me like that. I *am* upset about Mum. Of course I am. But it just doesn't feel real. I think they only told us because they wanted to put the company announcement into context.' The gates swung closed behind them, and Chloé let out a strangled cry. 'There's no way anyone is taking over my company.' She caught his look. '*Our* company.' But she saved her true conviction for her next statement. 'No way in hell.'

A thought had been nagging at Jesse.

'They didn't mention the protest. I get that it's not important, given Mum's news, but if their focus is on the company, don't you think it's odd they didn't mention it? Do you think that's what they meant when Mum said they have other issues to deal with?' His sister was staring ahead as if trying to see the future. 'Chlo?'

She shrugged. 'Maybe. I think it's more likely Mum decided she couldn't let go.'

'It's odd, though. The protest. The article in *Scent*. It feels as though...' he trailed off. He considered mentioning the anonymous email but decided against it.

She tilted her head and looked at him. 'It feels as though, what?'

'It feels like there's a link.' He couldn't make immediate sense of events, but maybe there was a connection between everything that had happened over the last few days.

'Mum might be right about needing a war-time CEO,' Chloé said. 'But if anyone's coming for us, we will destroy them together.' She squeezed his arm with all the strength of a newly appointed four-star General. 'Me and you, without bloody Belle.'

They crossed over the road. Jesse recalled his conversation with Grace about feeling like the odd one out with his parents and sister. While he was sure Chloé hadn't known about his parents' announcement, he couldn't shake the feeling that the three of them weren't sharing something with him.

'Is there something you're not telling me?' he asked.

'What? Of course not,' Chloé replied. She glanced at her watch. 'At least I'll have plenty of time to get to Core for dinner with Larry.'

Jesse knew his sister well enough to spot when she was lying and also when she was pulling the shutters down.

'There's our car,' she said, pointing to the Mercedes. 'Come on.' Then she linked arms with her brother and led him down the road.

The driver opened the door and waited for Chloé to climb in. Jesse walked around to the other side of the car and stood for a moment. 'Come on, Jesse.' Chloé patted the seat next to her.

He counted silently to three before stepping into the car. The door clicked shut, and he relaxed back into the seat. His nose twitched at the acidic waft of the air freshener as the driver pulled away from the curb and merged into the traffic.

'I didn't know Belle was working in the industry,' he said, remembering also that Chloé had referred to her working for a competitor. 'Where does she work?'

'Global Fragrances, in their London office,' she said. Jesse flinched but said nothing. 'She started her job about the same time I started mine. She's in marketing.'

'Have you spoken to her since she started?' he asked.

She glanced at him. 'No. Have you?' she asked with a hint of accusation. 'Why would I speak to Belle? I don't like her.'

'I didn't even know she was working there,' he said. Could that be the Global Fragrances connection? He shook his head to push the thought away. It didn't make sense. Belle was too junior.

Chloé sighed. 'I can't believe any of this. We were meant to know today,' she said, shaking her head. 'I really thought...' Jesse wondered whether she caught herself before saying she'd expected to be appointed. 'This issue with Belle is serious. I might have to do a Patrizia Reggiani.'

'Do a what?' he said, frowning.

'She hired a hitman to kill Maurizio Gucci. Paying someone to kill Isabelle is almost worth doing the jail time.' She nudged him in the ribs with her elbow. 'I'm kidding.' Then she added, 'It would *definitely* be worth the jail time.'

———

4:15 pm

JACQUELINE SAT IN THE CHAIR, watching her husband pacing the room. She wanted a cigarette, and her hand had moved involuntarily towards the chest of drawers more than once, but smoking was now a thing of the past.

Richard walked over to the drinks cabinet to pour them each a whisky, and Jacqueline reached out and accepted the glass. There was a splash as her husband dropped ice into his drink. On the rocks—now, there was a metaphor, she thought.

'We're lucky they didn't ask too many questions,' she said.

She had watched the children walk down the driveway. Chloé was a ball of anger, whereas Jesse seemed dazed. It had been interesting to see their reactions, and her intuition had been spot on. It wasn't a test, but if it had been, neither of them would have passed—one was too active, the other too passive. She pushed away the feeling of guilt she felt over delaying the CEO appointment. She'd meant what she'd said, the firm and the family were under attack, and she was best placed to lead —with or without cancer.

'I still don't think you did the right thing with the Trust,' Richard said.

Jacqueline took a sip of her drink. At least he was consistent. He had made the same point when she told him about her conversation with Martin Baxter. He hadn't liked her agreeing to his concessions, but she had no time for his protestations. He'd made the mess; she was the one who had to clean it up.

'You didn't leave me any choice,' she replied. 'You should have told me then how you'd dealt with Harold Baxter. Better still, you should have let me deal with it.' She took another sip of whisky and looked at him over her glass. 'If the truth comes out, you'd be forced to resign. You might even be facing jail,' she said.

'Well, you've fixed the first problem by firing me.'

Jacqueline let that one go. He was still angry, but she couldn't risk him staying on as CEO, not if the public might learn the truth.

Richard paced across the room. 'Martin didn't tell you how he knew?'

'No.' She thought about it for a moment. Harold Baxter had been dead for six years, and they had heard nothing. 'It's possible his father told him, and Martin waited until his mother died before broaching it. That would explain the timing.'

'He wanted to save his mother the embarrassment?'

'Yes, exactly,' she replied, but she was less interested in the past than the future. 'I think we've got off lightly,' she said.

'What do you mean?'

'Martin could have asked for money. The *Scent* article wasn't wrong—a well-argued case could cost us millions.'

Jacqueline had braced herself for a monetary demand from Martin Baxter. His banner had said that the Marchams must pay, and she'd taken it literally, yet he had been interested in justice, not money. People were a constant surprise to her. Neither of his demands was easy to accept, but even together, they were considerably more manageable than paying millions of pounds.

Everyone knew the House of Marcham story. Jacqueline and Richard created their vision and wrote the business plan that mapped out how to build a modern-day perfume company from the ground up, brick by brick, drop by drop. But it all started with the one thing essential to every perfume company.

Perfume.

The secret ingredient for the sweet smell of success.

With a stroke of good fortune and a touch of genius, Jacqueline resurrected *Evocation*, a long-forgotten perfume last seen in the 1800s, from the depths of her family history. A move which helped launch House of Marcham from a start-up into an iconic brand.

Everyone knew the story, but only a few people knew the truth.

'He'll come back for money,' he said.

'It's possible,' Jacqueline said, 'but the legal agreement Daniel drafted should prevent that.'

Richard massaged his shoulder. 'I wish you hadn't set up the trust—we don't need it. It reduces our control over the company,' he said.

That's the whole point, Jacqueline thought, but she kept

that to herself. It would only antagonise him if she pointed it out.

'When you owned it, you made all the decisions. It's not an issue provided we're both still...' He caught himself too late.

'...alive?' Jacqueline said.

Richard bowed his head and didn't reply for a few seconds. Eventually, he said, 'You'll beat cancer, Jacqui. I have no doubt about that.'

She nodded. She might, but if she didn't, Richard would be in sole control, and he'd demonstrated precisely why that wouldn't be a good idea. The trust solved that problem.

'We know Martin was the protestor, and he admitted he was behind the *Scent* column,' she said, 'but my real worry is that someone else knows.'

'He told you he was working alone,' Richard said.

'That doesn't mean I believed him. And, even if it's true, someone else could still know.'

His lips thinned. 'Only the two of us know the truth. I can't see how anyone else could know.'

'Three of us,' she corrected.

He frowned. 'You think Daniel's read the sealed letter?'

'No. He wouldn't do that,' Jacqueline said. 'I didn't mean Daniel.'

Richard blinked. 'Oh yes, Chloé. But she only knows what we told her a couple of weeks ago. She doesn't know any details. She doesn't even know about Martin. Besides, she's no more likely to tell anyone than we are.' He shook his head. 'You didn't let anything slip to Elaine when you met with her?' he asked.

'No, of course not.' She glared at him. 'Did you *acciden-*

tally tell Rosie?' She saw him wince, perhaps recognising he had been unfair.

'No. She doesn't know.' He rubbed his chin. 'I think I should visit Martin Baxter and ask him how he knows. It feels like a loose end. I'll go and see him after the meeting with Daniel and the kids.'

Jacqueline said nothing for a moment, simply absorbing his stare. There was nothing Richard could do. The arrangements she'd made were set in stone. If he felt the need to speak with Martin, she wouldn't try to stop him. It might make him feel better.

Her thoughts turned to the broader family. She couldn't deny that the prospect of battling a terminal illness had given her a fresh perspective. 'Perhaps some good will come out of my cancer,' she said.

'What do you mean?'

'It prompted us to bring the wider family together. We're at the beginning of a new chapter. If the family unites, we're strong enough to withstand anything.'

'What about Cameron?' Richard asked. 'It was only a few weeks ago that he came begging for help, and you sent him away with nothing.'

Jacqueline brushed a strand of hair behind her ear and smiled. 'What can I say? I'm a new woman.' She threw it out as a light-hearted comment, but she knew that, to some extent, it was the truth. She pushed herself up out of the chair.

Richard drained his glass. 'The announcement about the trust will be one hell of a surprise,' he said. He walked over and wrapped his arms around her, pulling her tight against his chest.

She rested her head on his shoulder. What he'd said was

true; she knew that. The family would be surprised, probably even shocked, but she'd had to react quickly to the Baxter family re-entering their lives. She'd devised the best plan she could think of and was confident it was a good one, but she couldn't ignore the quote echoing in her head.

No plan survives first contact with the enemy.

TUESDAY 9 JULY 2024

9

STRAND, LONDON

10 AM

JESSE TURNED OFF FLEET STREET AND HEADED NORTH. HE WAS wearing dark jeans, brown shoes, and a grey shirt—block colour and no labels. He preferred fragrances to do the talking, and that morning, he had opted for the lavender-based formulation of their own masculine, *Reduction*. He caught its scent as he ran his hand through his hair. He liked it, which wasn't an easy bar to clear, but he had a plan for a new masculine, and he wasn't thinking of a flanker, a derivative of *Reduction*; he wanted to move in a new direction.

The pavements were busy even though it was nearly ten in the morning. He stepped aside to avoid a barrister wheeling a pilot case along the pavement and then merged back into the pedestrian traffic.

He should have been in the lab at least an hour ago, but the news from his parents hadn't encouraged him to make an early appearance at the office. Jesse glanced at the coffee shop and hesitated. He had just resigned himself to deferring his double espresso until lunchtime when a hand grabbed his shoulder. He spun around, his heart rate spiking for the second it took for the features of the man opposite him to settle into the familiar face of his cousin, Cameron.

'Hey, Jesse. Good to see you, man.' Cameron slapped him on the back. He was wearing casual clothes—three stripes and a green crocodile—and had the attitude to match.

'Jesus, Cam. You made me jump.' Jesse relaxed and then pointed towards up the street. 'You heading this way?'

Cameron nodded, moving beside Jesse, his stride long and languid, as if Attenborough was filming him for an urban jungle documentary. 'Always be alert, Jesse. Particularly in a busy place like this.' He was grinning, enjoying spreading his street-smart philosophy—aping the walk and rabbiting the talk.

'I'm surprised to see you here,' Jesse said. Cameron lived and worked a few miles away and was straying away from his usual habitat. 'Not that it isn't good to see you.'

'I wanted to have a little chat with you.'

Cameron carried on walking, but something about the way he said, 'little chat,' and the slight hesitation before he selected those words caught Jesse's attention. Always be alert, as the man said.

Cameron steered Jesse off the main street and down a narrow passageway that opened into a square courtyard. The manicured grass was fenced in with black steel posts, shutting it off from the passing public. Cameron pointed at an empty bench just a few yards down the path and waited for Jesse to sit.

Jesse folded himself onto the seat and glanced at his watch, although he already knew the time. 'You'd better be quick, Cam. I'm late enough as it is.' Jesse stretched his legs out in front of him, his hands resting on his lap, with his thumbs tapping against each other.

'I think you'll be forgiven,' Cameron said, lowering himself beside Jesse, 'but don't worry, I won't take up much of your time.' He paused whilst a woman walked past. She was immersed in an argument with whoever was on the other end of her phone call, not so much as glancing at either of them, but Cameron's eyes lingered on her until she had turned the corner.

Jesse gave up waiting. 'What do you want to talk about?'

He'd always liked Cameron and still did, but he'd been guilty of not making enough effort to stay in touch over recent years. They'd both been busy working, and the last time they'd spent much real time together was when Jesse had agreed to lend him the money to launch his business. Cameron repaid the loan within a year and had never since approached Jesse about money. By all accounts, business was doing well. He'd started with a couple of gyms near his house, but now he was nearing twenty, spread across London, with the ambition for more.

'I want to talk business,' Cameron said. He glanced both ways along the path before speaking again. 'I want to talk about the *family* business.'

Which got Jesse's attention. The family business, what it meant and how it defined them both didn't need explicit comment. It was always in the background, but he wasn't sure what Cameron was building up to. It wasn't a topic they'd discussed recently, yet it seemed to be the only topic anyone wanted to discuss right now.

'To be precise, I want to talk about you selling the company to me.' Jesse shook his head. Had he heard him correctly? He tried to speak but couldn't find the words. Any words. 'I want to buy House of Marcham.' Cameron leaned back and stretched his arms along the top of the bench.

He waited for his cousin to laugh, but Cameron only offered a smile. Jesse frowned. His cousin was a successful businessman in his own right, but gyms and perfume weren't an obvious synergistic play. House of Marcham was also of a size and scale way beyond any business ambition Cameron might have—at least, so Jesse thought.

'Are you winding me up?' He asked.

'Absolutely not. I want you and Chloé to sit down with me and hear my offer before I take it to your parents,' Cameron said. Jesse caught the slight jutting of the jaw and the narrowing of the eyes. He was earnest, but a second later, his cousin looked like he did when he was a ten-year-old cheeky chancer, and it was as if they were both young boys again with their first steps into adulthood still ahead of them. 'I know it's come out of the blue, but the thing is, Jesse, I think it'll be good for you.'

Something opened inside Jesse, and Cameron's words echoed around the void. What would he do if the company was no longer in family ownership, if he wasn't the CEO and an outsider was running the show? Would he stay, working with Kath, continuing to learn his craft? He realised he hadn't ever considered it because he'd never thought it would happen.

Cameron started tapping on his phone. 'At least come and hear the proposal. I'm sending you the address—it's not far from here. I'll be there tomorrow. Bring Chloé with you.' He paused and gazed off into the distance with a thousand-yard stare, and Jesse imagined that his cousin was seeing each of those thousand yards paved with money. 'Me, you, and Chloé. Just like old times.' And then he was standing up and ready to go. He nodded at Jesse, flicked down his shades as befitted a man facing such a bright future, and strolled away down the path.

10

SOUTH BANK, LONDON
12:30 PM

JESSE SIPPED HIS COFFEE AND LOOKED AROUND THE BAR. HE had deliberately chosen a venue away from the office and somewhere 'normal.' Chloé gravitated to the exclusive and the expensive. She was a walking encyclopaedia of the powerhouses of the global luxury market, and not just perfume. She strayed well out of her lane into clothing, footwear, jewellery, watches, bags, and skincare; anything, provided it was an exclusive brand. She'd given Jesse a running commentary on LVMH's acquisition of Tiffany with as much enthusiasm as if it were the latest Netflix show to drop. Jesse didn't have an issue with that, but he thought occasional exposure to regular life helped to keep her grounded.

Chloé was late, which might be a statement of intent. They would start and continue on her terms, not his. He could tell that his sister had arrived without seeing her. All he needed to go on was the reaction of the guy behind the bar. Jesse watched the barman tracking Chloé as she walked across the room. The young Romeo scanned ahead to check her destination and met Jesse's gaze. The barman's head jerked down as he remembered that he had something urgent to do with the till, but Chloé had stopped on her way over to Jesse and was leaning towards him, elbows on the bar, giving him both blue-eyed barrels. Barman nodded and moved confidently to the coffee machine. No doubt, Chloé would get a bespoke pattern in her latte microfoam. She was smiling as she strode towards Jesse. People used to tell their parents that Chloé had a 'girl-next-door' charm, and Jesse knew what they meant; it just so happened that she lived next door to Louis Vuitton.

'Hey, bro.' She stood, waiting for him to do something. He opted for giving her a hug.

'Hi.' She looked great. A royal blue Alexander McQueen oblique wool-crepe jacket matched with a front-slit skirt, heels which Jesse knew would be Louboutin's, glossy blonde hair, and Cartier glasses—talking the talk and walking the catwalk of a luxury-brand future CEO. Jesse's nose twitched involuntarily. Bluebell, violet leaf, and ground ivy. Blue Belle by House of Marcham—one of Kath's early creations. Was it a coincidence his sister had chosen a house fragrance entirely free of her brother's influence?

Chloé waited and smiled at the bartender, who lovingly placed her cup of coffee on the table. The milk froth pattern was a disappointingly uneven spiral. As he moved away, Jesse shuffled forward on his chair.

'Hey, have you heard from Cam at all recently?' He tried to keep his tone light.

Chloé frowned. 'Cameron? No. Nothing. I spoke with him briefly at my twenty-first, but not since then.' She paused. 'And not much before then either, to be honest. Why?'

'He hijacked me on my way into work this morning.'

She sipped her drink. 'What did he want?'

Part of him wanted to lead with the shock announcement—he wants our company—but he knew that would put Chloé offside. She valued the company as much as he did. She'd spent the last year settling into House of Marcham and wasn't planning to move out any time soon.

Jesse chose his words with care. 'He wanted to talk about the company.'

'The company?' Chloé sounded puzzled.

'Yeah. The family company.'

Frost crawled across the table. '*Our* family company. Not *the* family company.'

Had Jesse's tone given it away, or was she naturally uber-protective? Perhaps she was still on edge from their parents' shock announcements.

'Yes.' He strung the word out as if not sure how to finish it. 'That's pretty much what he wanted to talk about.'

Chloé frowned. 'I have nothing against Cam, but what's our company got to do with him? It's called House of Marcham for a reason.'

'Well, he is a Marcham,' Jesse said.

'Barely,' she said, rolling her eyes. 'Does he want another job?'

'No.' Jesse was conscious that he was delaying the moment when he had to tell her. He balled his hand, released it, and balled it again.

'What, then?'

'He wants to buy the company,' he said.

Chloé looked at Jesse in a way that suggested she wasn't seeing him at all, and then her jaw tightened as if she had her brother back in focus. 'What did you say to him?' She took another sip of coffee.

'I'm not sure I said anything. I thought he was joking,' he said.

'He wasn't?' She glanced at her phone.

'No, I don't think so. He wants to meet with us tonight to explain the terms of his deal,' Jesse said, studying his sister.

'Okay.'

He blinked. 'You think we should meet him?'

'Yes. What harm could it do?'

He shook his head. 'I don't really see the point, Chlo. It's not as if Mum and Dad would ever sell the company to him. Or to anyone, for that matter.'

He wasn't sure what was behind Cameron's proposal. It felt like a sideshow, yet Chloé wanted to meet with Cameron. Jesse could rarely tell which way she would go. The heady days of *lil sis* blindly following *big bro* had ended when Chloé learnt to speak, and she hadn't looked back, or up, since.

'I'm happy to meet him,' Chloé said.

Jesse certainly didn't want her to meet Cameron without him being there. 'Okay. Let's meet him.' He shrugged. 'I'll send you the details.'

'Great.' She stared into the distance. 'Jesse, do you...' She trailed off.

'Do I what?'

She blinked. 'Nothing. It doesn't matter.' She stood up. 'I've got another meeting. I'll see you back at the office.'

Whatever she'd been about to say had evaporated like a top note, which was typical Chloé. Everything was done on her terms. She reached over for a cursory hug, and then she was off.

Jesse watched her leave the café, and the world seemed to

fall out of focus. He wondered whether that was how it would always be. He didn't necessarily enjoy Chloé's company, but there was no denying that he felt diminished whenever she left. It was as if he stole some of her energy when they were together—covalent rather than sibling bonding—and when she left, he handed it back.

11

THE CITY OF LONDON
6 PM

JESSE HAD NEVER BEEN INSIDE A BOXING CLUB BEFORE, AND neither, to the best of his knowledge, had Chloé. As a choice of venue for a business meeting, it was unusual. The mean, lean greeting machine behind the reception desk didn't appear to care why they were there and wasn't much interested in whether they wanted to go in. What was Cameron's reason for meeting there? Did he like the literal backdrop of bringing them to a fight, or was it to give a Fight Club vibe to their discussions?

Venue aside, there was one other problem. Cameron wasn't there.

Jesse dragged a couple of metal chairs away from the boxing ring, where Blue Hat and Red Hat feinted, bobbed and weaved, with the occasional jab thrown in. They seemed oblivious to the noise of the chair legs scraping on the concrete floor, and Jesse returned the courtesy by sitting with his back to them, his feet tapping on the ground. Five metres away, people were working hard, punishing punch bags of various designs and colours, some a blur of arms, others spicing things up with spinning roundhouse kicks. Jesse saw Chloé wrinkle her nose as she glanced around the gym, no doubt smelling the mix of sweat, plastic and antiseptic. Hardly the delicate perfumes that either of them were used to.

He wondered whether Cameron had been joking about the meeting. Perhaps the whole thing was merely a laugh at his expense. Just then, Blue Hat jumped out of the ring and walked towards them. When he pulled off his protective headwear, Jesse did a double take.

'Sorry, guys. Had to finish my training.' Cameron had always spoken as if he had to get all his words out in one go, and being short of breath exaggerated the effect.

'Cameron,' Chloé said, encasing his name in ice, 'please tell me that in addition to holding your meeting in a boxing club, you don't also plan to attend straight from your workout?'

He shrugged. He was toned, and his eyes were bright. Jesse was naturally slim, but he realised that he hadn't exercised properly for weeks, and he made a mental note to look into boxing clubs near home.

'Thank you both for coming,' Cameron said. He picked up a bottle of water and took a long drink, holding the pose for a fraction too long.

'Small sips, Cameron. Small sips are better for you,' Chloé said.

Cameron paused before continuing to guzzle water. If you want to make a point, make it twice - the first and second rules of Fight Club. The plastic bottle cracked loudly as he stopped drinking. He turned a chair to face the wrong way before he straddled it, staring at the two of them. 'I'm glad that Jesse persuaded you to come,' he said, looking directly at

Chloé before scratching his chin and staring at Jesse. It was as if he was getting them both in focus.

'Well, the main thing is we're all here,' Jesse said. Classic leadership advice. Take control of the agenda. He dropped into gear. 'Why don't we start—'

'Why don't *I* start,' Chloé said. Jesse stayed fixed in his position, wondering whether Cameron had noticed how easily Chloé had taken control from him. She was straight into full flow. 'I understand from Jesse that you have some misguided idea that we will sell you *our* family company. Let me be clear, Cameron, that's *never* going to happen.'

Cameron didn't say anything. He took another swig from his water bottle before placing it beside him.

'Why are you smiling?' Chloé asked, but Jesse wouldn't have described Cameron's expression as a smile. There was zero joy behind it.

'Because it's funny,' he said.

'What's funny?' Chloé's lips narrowed.

'You.' Cameron pointed at her. 'The way you act. A golden egg hatched in your mother's lap, and you act like you have some divine right to everything that followed.'

Jesse had expected Cameron to be nervous and hesitant in front of Chloé, but he wasn't holding back. He folded his arms across the top of the seat back.

'There's some chatter about the family notebook,' Cameron said.

Jesse blinked. He was getting sick of rumours and speculation. Now, he had to deal with chatter. The notebook in question was a battered leather-bound tome with a metal clasp to help hide its secrets. It didn't look much, but then notebooks could be surprising—DaVinci's science diary had sold for thirty million dollars. What was the value of the business built on the contents of the notebook handwritten by Jesse's great, great, great grandfather? The current best guess was close to three hundred million.

'Anything you want to tell me?' Cameron asked, studying both of them.

Jesse coughed before speaking. 'You already know everything. Mum found Alfred Marcham's perfume recipes and realised they had potential. She and Dad developed a business plan for launching, re-launching if you like, the perfumes.' Why had he said re-launching? He risked a glance at Chloé to see a darkness had fallen over her face. He pushed on, hoping to make up lost ground. 'Over more than twenty years, Mum and Dad built the company from nothing to the business House of Marcham is today.' At least he'd finished strong.

Cameron tilted his head, which showed that he was listening whilst evidencing scepticism. He looked at Chloé. 'Anything to add?'

'No.' Jesse could see the tightness in her jaw and the tension in her shoulders.

Cameron pushed himself up and grabbed a towel from the pile on a nearby shelf. He said nothing as he wiped his face and then his upper arms. Jesse was sure his cousin wasn't deciding what to say; he was just taking his sweet time. After he had finished his perfunctory wipe down, he said, 'I hear that there's more to it than that.'

'Do tell.' Chloé's words burned through the air.

Cameron tossed the towel into the laundry basket, which wobbled slightly from the impact.

'Something happened. I don't know exactly what, but it was something that your parents have kept very quiet,' Cameron said.

Jesse's head was scrolling through all the recent insinuations.

The Marchams must pay.

Our spies tell us there's a damages claim about to be filed against House of Marcham.

When you know what I know, you will do the right thing.

And their mother's admission. *Our firm is under attack, and we need a wartime leader.*

'Some people think it will end up being a very expensive secret,' Cameron said.

'Wow, you've read *Scent*. Congratulations,' Chloé said. 'Next, you'll tell us the earth is flat. Do you believe everything you read, Cam?'

'I didn't hear about it from *Scent*.'

Jesse shuffled on his seat. 'I don't understand,' he said. 'What do you mean—an expensive secret?'

Cameron shrugged his shoulders. 'I haven't been told the details.'

'How convenient,' Chloé shot back.

'Don't you think it's strange how Marchams of London just vanished?' Cameron said. 'It went from being a leading British perfumery to nothing, all in a generation.'

There was no historical record of Marchams of London's demise. Perhaps Albert Marcham's son had crushed the business into the ground. Whatever the truth, the history books had recorded no verdict. What was clear was that the French perfume houses had moved back in, untroubled, and carried on as if Marchams of London had never existed. In some ways, it was hard to believe that it had. Nothing remained, or so everyone had thought, until the day when Jacqueline Marcham relaunched *Evocation* as the debut scent from House of Marcham.

'What does any of this have to do with you? It's *our* family business.' Chloé spat the words out through gritted teeth. 'It's ours. Mum and Dad's. Mine and Jesse's. Not yours. Not anyone else's. I don't care about the damn notebook. You're full of bullshit.' A couple of boxers turned away from their punchbags to look at the site of this verbal sparring. Chloé was standing now. 'Why are you doing this? Is there something else going on? Are you trying to get back at our parents for firing you from our company?'

Cameron stood still, and Jesse held his breath. Cameron had been on an upward trajectory when he'd started at House of Marcham. He was smart, savvy, and good at building rapport. His approach was intuitive rather than polished—he should've been a success, possibly even a future executive, and yet, within the year, he'd gone. Jesse had never been told what happened; the truth had remained bottled up. Now Chloé was pulling out the stopper. Cameron frowned and started to speak.

'That's...' He trailed off, blinked, and started again. 'I can't deny that I don't have the best relationship with your parents, but that has nothing to do with this.' He swallowed. 'I'm telling you all this so you'll listen to the offer. If these rumours are true, this deal might be your best option.'

'You don't know the truth,' Chloé stared at her cousin. 'You don't know anything.'

With that, she walked out of the gym without so much as a glance at her brother. Jesse knew she wanted to know more; she wanted to know everything, but she wanted him to do the dirty work.

'Chloé doesn't change,' Cameron said.

'Do any of us?' Jesse shrugged. 'Can we go outside?' He looked around. 'I feel out of place in here.'

Cameron laughed. 'Sure. Give me ten minutes to shower and change, and I'll see you outside.'

His cousin headed towards the changing rooms, leaving Jesse alone with his thoughts. After a moment, he stood up and headed out of the gym. It was cold outside, the sun had gone missing, and it looked like rain was coming.

What should he do? He had no way of knowing the truth of Cameron's claims. All he could do now was try to extract whatever details he had.

―――――

JUST OVER TEN MINUTES LATER, the doors to the gym swung open, and Cameron strode out, wearing a white T-shirt, faded jeans, and desert boots and clutching a duffel bag and a red hoodie. His choice of sunglasses on a day when the sun had clocked off for the day was either a misjudgement, a fashion statement, or both. He walked over to Jesse. 'Where do you want to go?' he asked.

Something in the way Cameron spoke pulled Jesse back to those days when they spent all their time together until Jesse's parents decided they needed to move to a bigger house and a better area, and he'd left Cameron behind.

'Can we just walk for a while?' he asked.

'Sure. Let's head to the park down the road.'

Cameron's hair was still damp from the shower. He was a towel-the-hair-after-a-soak bloke rather than a blow-dry guy, cultivating the hard man more than the pretty boy image. He'd started on that path in his late teenage years, and his mid-twenties clearly wasn't the time for him to look for a new direction.

Jesse trailed silently along behind his cousin. After

walking for a few minutes, they turned into the park. The drizzle had pushed people away; the wet benches and the slippery coating of leaves were not hard-selling the environment. Just half an hour earlier, everything would have looked so different.

'What's this all about, Cam?' Jesse tried to reach the Cameron of their youth, striving to connect with his cousin. 'Why are you even involved in a bid for our company?'

Cameron reached into his pocket and pulled out a packet of cigarettes, drawing one out and placing it in his mouth. Jesse was forced to wait for him to light it and take the first drag before he answered. He blew out a cloud of smoke which lingered between them. Cameron took another long drag on his cigarette. 'I haven't got much, Jesse. My father's dead. He left my mum close to nothing. My stepdad...' His expression grew distant for a moment.

Jesse frowned. 'I'm sorry, but I don't know what you're getting at.'

Cameron dropped his cigarette and crushed it into the path with his heel. Jesse was relaxed with Cameron, but the casual violence in his movement triggered a tingle at the base of his neck. His cousin rubbed his hand over his mouth as if checking out his stubble before he spoke.

'I was approached by a man representing a group of investors.' Jesse absorbed the words as Cameron continued. 'They've been looking at the company. They think there needs to be a change. They have ambitious plans and think the current leadership would resist the new direction. They want to install a new leader, but they want to keep a family connection. A bloodline Marcham.' His foot tapped on the ground as he shot-gunned out the words. He kicked the cigarette butt onto the grass, and Jesse flinched as if he had been booted on the backside. 'These are serious people, Jesse, and they are prepared to finance a takeover.' His face was deadpan. 'And they want me to be the new CEO.' A chill worked down Jesse's spine whilst Cameron's words jostled in his brain. The company had been approached by outside investors before but never by a consortium led by his cousin. 'They've made it very attractive.'

'What about loyalty?' Jesse was shaking his head. 'Why would you do this to us?'

'I honestly believe it might be a better deal for you than holding on. Everyone will get good money. I don't need to feel sorry for your parents. Or Chloé.'

'How about me?' The words caught in his throat. 'I thought we were friends.'

'We are friends.' Cameron inhaled long and hard before continuing. 'It's a decent deal, Jesse. You get some money, actual cash rather than shares you can't do anything with.' He pointed his finger at Jesse's chest. 'And, you're free.' A prod punctuated all three words, hammering it home. 'What's more, if you want to stay on, you can stay. For as long as you like.'

The words spun between them, and for a moment, Jesse allowed himself to latch on to them and hear the siren call, but even as part of his brain rationally evaluated what Cameron had just said, his emotions were already pushing back. He couldn't give up everything his parents had worked so hard for—the business central to his immediate family. His instinct was to fight to protect them. Then he was hearing the explosions, smelling the acrid smoke, and reading the protest banner. He blew out a breath and shook his head.

'It doesn't matter whether I think it makes sense.' Jesse knew Cameron believed him, the silence that followed proved that. After a few seconds, Jesse started to walk again. 'So, what happens next?' he asked.

Cameron strode beside him, his bounce contrasting with Jesse's shuffle. 'We want the company, all of it. Speak to Chloé, although you might want to wait until she calms down. Speak to your parents. Then wait for them to calm down too.' His laugh was hollow. 'And if you're smart, you'll convince them to sell.'

'How much is the offer?' Jesse asked. It didn't matter. There wasn't an answer that Cameron could give that would make any impression on Jesse's family—no matter how high it was.

'Two hundred million pounds,' Cameron said.

'Two hundred?' Jesse could hear the confusion in his voice. 'It's valued at significantly more than that. It's not even worth mentioning it to my parents at that price.'

'Oh, come on. Have some faith in yourself.' Cameron was on his toes as if he was practising walking on water.

'No chance.' Jesse had meant to reinforce his point, only belatedly realising that he'd unwittingly psychoanalysed himself. 'The whole idea is ridiculous, but it's a non-starter at that price.'

Cameron was nodding, but he wasn't smiling. 'This is serious.' He emphasised the last word. 'I imagine you'd walk away with tens of millions, and if this rumour turns out to be real, you'll regret not taking the deal.' He dropped his voice to a whisper. 'Look, you're not like me. You're not cut out for the corporate world. You might think you are, but as your friend, I have to say, I'm not sure. Think about what's on offer here. Tens of millions of pounds, and you're free. You could do whatever you like. Create perfumes just for the fun of it. It's a good deal for you, Jesse.'

Jesse shook his head. Cameron's offer would persuade no one that mattered. He decided to throw in a grenade of his own. 'Tell me what the protest was for.'

'What?' Confusion clouded Cameron's face.

'A protestor stormed the stage at our 25th anniversary celebration last Thursday night and waved a banner. *The Marchams must pay.* That's what it said. Is that something to do with you and this offer?'

Cameron frowned. 'Not that I know of,' he said.

There was a hesitancy that hadn't been noticeable before. The news of the protest had spooked him.

Cameron glanced at his watch. 'I have to go,' he said.

Jesse flinched as his cousin lurched towards him and feinted a couple of punches.

'Let me know, Jesse,' he called over his shoulder as he walked away, floating like a butterfly, stinging like a bee.

12

HOUSE OF MARCHAM OFFICES, SHOE LANE, LONDON

7:30 PM

JESSE CLOSED THE OFFICE DOOR BEHIND HIM AND WAITED FOR Chloé to finish her telephone call. He'd opted against an office, preferring to sit out on the lab floor, but it was no surprise that his sister had gone the other way. He watched her pace around the room as she talked. It was as if she had choreographed her steps: stride, turn, and repeat. She never liked it when things slipped out of her control.

Her office was immaculate, carefully curated, and a dust-free zone. Her tastes were modern and minimalist. The square, wooden coffee table looked like the Egyptians had dropped a pyramid headfirst into the centre of a cream rug with unerring accuracy and perfect balance. Jesse sat in one of the bright orange chairs that contrasted strongly with the pale grey walls. There was a hint of lavender, with a smoky edge in the air. It was an unfamiliar scent for Chloé's room.

After a few minutes, he reached over and picked up a paper from her desk. Its title was *Funding our expansion into AsiaPac.* He started to flick through it. Jesse had never been comfortable with financial numbers. Unlike the measurements in a perfume recipe, they didn't represent something more significant. Just money. It left him cold. And so did the prose. What the hell even was 'a rare, inverted yield curve?' Chloé ended the call, and he threw the paper back onto her desk.

'Enjoy the read?' she asked.

Jesse shrugged. 'You had me at sushi bond but lost me at suicide pill,' He tried to keep his tone light.

'That call was about the opening weekend numbers for *Distraction*,' Chloé said.

'And?'

'We're fifteen percent down on where we wanted to be.'

Jesse didn't say anything. His gut reaction was to feel guilty and accept responsibility for the financial underperformance, but at the same time, he knew *Distraction* was a strong perfume. It was a depressing truth that remarkable perfumes didn't always translate into remarkable sales. There were many other factors: the bottle, the design, and the name. Then, you had to factor in the success or otherwise of the launch, product placement strategy, marketing decisions, advertising spend and pricing, and changing, or unchanging, consumer taste. Too many perfumes, such as *Chanel's Égoïste, Chopard's Madness* and *Yves Saint Laurent's M7,* had been put on commercial life support due, not to the scent, but other factors.

Many, if not most, of the larger perfumers tried to secure the commercial appeal of the product by using focus groups, and Jesse and Kath had historically battled the in-house marketing team's desire to tread that path. Eventually, Kath had taken the issue to Jacqueline. She'd never told Jesse whether she'd threatened to quit, but he could still remember the quote she'd given to him—*They can focus-group my ass as*

I walk out the building.' He shared her view that focus groups had no place in producing great perfumes. The issue was, as Chloé would endlessly remind him, not all great perfumes were cash cows. If anything, the link the other way was even weaker. Few of the best-selling perfumes were anywhere close to being great scents.

'We should've gone with another *Evocation* flanker,' Chloé said.

Jesse didn't want this fight. Partly because he didn't like arguing but mainly because they'd already had this debate and Chloé had lost. They had tried a flanker five years ago. *Evocation Floral* was the first perfume launched after he arrived at the company. He'd understood the logic of leveraging the name recognition of their star perfume and even the desire to twist it with a more modern note, but he hadn't liked the idea of making a new version of an existing fragrance. He didn't think he ever would, but it had been even worse than a philosophical difference. *Evocation Floral* had been marketed as a flanker, an echo of the original perfume, but the final fragrance had little in common with its predecessor. It was a pure trade on the name.

Chloé didn't care, provided it made money. He could still hear her argument. 'Do you think Dior is bothered their *Poison* perfumes have nothing in common? No, of course not. They're too busy counting a huge pile of cash.'

Evocation Floral had done well financially, but for Jesse, it was an example of a waning coherence in the family of perfumes released by House of Marcham. *Distraction* was the first step in fixing that, and he believed *Legacy* would be the scent to cement the new direction.

Chloé walked over to Jesse and sat in the chair next to him. 'So, what did you find out from Cam?' she asked.

'Two hundred million offer and Cameron to be appointed CEO as part of a strategy refresh,' he said.

She snorted. 'Wrong price. Wrong CEO. Wrong ownership. Apart from that, it sounds appealing.' He waited. Chloé seemed to be weighing something up.

'What is it?' he asked.

'Did he say anything more about the rumour?' she asked.

'Only that he thought we'd do better to accept the deal rather than waiting for any claim against the company.' He sighed. 'He said there's a group of investors.' Chloé was staring at him. 'Cam described them as serious people.

'That's all? Nothing about who the investors are? Trade or financial?'

'No. That's all he told me.' Jesse chewed his lip. 'You're more interested than I thought you'd be, Chlo.'

She shrugged. 'You know I'm always interested in the finances. Even though this deal has no chance of going ahead, it's helpful to know what the industry thinks about us.'

'They think our company is worth a third less than we think it's worth. I told Cam it's a non-starter.'

'This rumour is swirling around,' Chloé said. 'Mum and Dad are hiring Belle as a deputy CEO, and tomorrow, they want to discuss shareholdings. Maybe this offer is an opportunity.'

'What?'

'Don't you see?' She shook her head, too impatient to wait for enlightenment. 'We need to take control. The way Mum and Dad have been acting, it wouldn't surprise me if they were prepared to sell out.'

Jesse leant forward. 'You want to try and hijack Cameron's offer?'

'I don't think it will come to that, but we need options. If the company were to be sold, we should be the ones to buy it —not Cam, not anyone else. We could meet these investors. We don't need to be explicit, but we say just enough so they realise Cam is the wrong Marcham to back.'

Jesse relaxed back into the seat. Instinctively, he wanted to go in the opposite direction. To move as far away from deal talks as possible, yet standing in Chloé's way was like bracing for the impact of a wave. If the wall of water didn't smash you off your feet, the drag back would cut you off at the ankles. Add onto that the fact that she had a point and Jesse could see the merit in having a discussion at least.

'Should we tell Mum and Dad about Cam's offer?'

Chloé shook her head. 'Not yet. They're keeping things from us; we should do the same—at least until we find out what they're proposing with the shareholdings.' Just then, her phone started to ring. 'Hi Larry. Yes, I'm coming down now.'

Jesse eased himself out of the chair. 'Just over twenty-four hours ago, we thought one of us would be appointed CEO. Now, there's a possibility we might sell the firm. Too many things are happening at once, and we're reacting. We're not in control.'

'I agree. Let's not do anything until we've heard what Mum and Dad have to say,' she said, reapplying a dab of Marcham's latest scent. 'Tomorrow's going to be an interesting day,' she said.

'Yeah, great. Another one,' Jesse replied, following his sister out of the room.

WEDNESDAY 10 JULY 2024

13

HOUSE OF MARCHAM OFFICES, SHOE LANE, LONDON

5 PM

THE BOARDROOM ON THE TOP FLOOR OF THE OFFICE BUILDING had been chosen as the venue for the family meeting. The dual-aspect room had sweeping views over London, a pair of modern ceiling lights, and a rectangular glass table in the centre. A display cabinet against the wall opposite the door showed off the famous family notebook, which was framed with modern-day text explaining its history and some old family photos.

Jesse's stomach gurgled despite having eaten breakfast and lunch. Sweat prickled at his temples when the door opened, and Isabelle walked in. It was the first time Jesse had seen Belle for over a year, but there was no subtle re-introduction. Her choice of perfume, instantly recognisable from the burning maple leaves, fired her opening salvo - a message which, unlike the scent, was subtle. Most people wouldn't know that the name of the house that produced the fragrance was *CB I Hate Perfume*, but she'd have counted on Jesse instantly making the connection.

'When are Jacqueline and Richard coming?' Her voice

swung around the room, sweeping Chloé and Jesse in its path, but Belle's eyes were locked on Daniel Kane.

'Feel free to wait in another room,' Chloé said. She'd changed since lunchtime, and Jesse was sure the statement look was chosen primarily with their cousin in mind. A racing red, V-neck, silk-crepe jumpsuit with chunky, gold, hooped earrings to match the chain across her neck. It contrasted with Belle's low-key navy suit jacket and grey skinny jeans.

Daniel looked relaxed, and he had the charm button fully depressed.

'Jacqueline and Richard will be here any minute. If we could perhaps stay as we are for a short while, we'll be able to get straight into it when they arrive. And the sooner we start...' He let the promise of the end of the meeting hang in the air. Daniel walked across the room and swung the door open expansively, beckoning his clients inside. 'Hello, Jacqueline, Richard. Everyone else is here.'

Jesse watched as Belle walked over to greet his parents. Was there any warmth either way in the exchanges? Maybe not, but it wasn't as awkward as he might've wished it to be. The siblings hung back, greeting their parents with a seated wave.

'Do sit down, everyone.' Jacqueline fixed her gaze on her children for long enough to let them know that she had registered that they hadn't stood to greet their parents. Jesse's legs tensed, but he forced himself to stay seated. Jacqueline continued to speak as she settled into a chair. 'We've spoken with you individually about our plans regarding the CEO process, but we wanted to use this meeting for Daniel to take you through our specific plans regarding the company shareholding. The briefing will take twenty minutes, and then we will have time to answer any questions you might have.' No one spoke as she scanned the room. Jesse fought hard to stop his legs from bouncing up and down. 'Now, let me be clear. This is not the occasion for emotion. This is the time for duty and to remember your obligation to the wider family.'

Richard took over. 'We've reached an inflexion point in our business, and we will be stronger if we face the future together as a family.' He looked at them all, but Jesse couldn't help but feel that his gaze lingered on his children. The meeting had barely started, yet the scales had already tipped as if their parents favoured Belle over them. 'We need to put things right to address errors made in the past. And our actions will make us collectively stronger. So today, we are starting the process of moving the shares into the hands of the next generation.' Richard glanced at the lawyer. 'Daniel, can you take us through this please?'

Address errors made in the past. The phrase had an uneasy echo of *The Marchams must pay* protest. Jesse ran his hand over his face. What was going on?

Daniel stood as he started to speak, handing round copies of a bound document. 'This should help explain the changes.'

Jesse was tempted to flip through the document, but he wanted to show his composure, so he ignored it completely, earning a glare from his father.

'As I think you all know,' Daniel continued, 'when House of Marcham was created, Jacqueline owned all the company shares. In the last week, Jacqueline transferred her shareholding to a newly created trust, the Evocation Trust. The current trustee responsible for making decisions on behalf of the trust is Jacqueline.'

A chill worked down Jesse's spine as Daniel carried on speaking. 'The Evocation Trust was established to benefit a

defined class of beneficiaries, essentially the wider family.'
Jesse frowned. Had there been a stress on the word wider? He
shot his sister a glance whilst Daniel continued his explanation. 'The Trustee has total discretion to allocate absolute
interests in the shares to anyone who is a beneficiary.'

'What does wider family mean?' Chloé asked.

'The beneficiaries are from three families.' Daniel took a
sip of water.

Chloé's attention was locked on him, like an Exocet
missile.

Three families. Jesse pushed himself up to stand, clasped
his hands together, and held his breath.

————

DANIEL CLEARED HIS THROAT. 'The individual beneficiaries
are: Jesse Richard Marcham, Chloé Jacqueline Marcham.'
There was a slight hesitation. He hadn't said Jesse *and* Chloé,
which was enough to tell Jesse this was a list and that there
were more names to come. 'Isabelle Diana Lowe,' Daniel's
voice was impressively even, 'and Cameron Johnson Duncan
Marcham.'

Jesse's knees gave way, and he stepped forward to catch
himself.

Chloé threw her arms up in the air. 'What?' She made no
attempt to contain her rage as surprise spread across Belle's
face.

Daniel held out a hand to keep the questions at bay. 'Let
me finish, then we can discuss everything.' His voice kicked
up a level. 'The level of shareholding will be determined by
the Trustee later, but the four beneficiaries will own the
entire company shareholding.'

Jesse's head was spinning.

Chloé was pale, her hand over her mouth. 'Mum. Dad.' She stood up and waved vaguely towards Daniel. 'This is what you want?' Without waiting for an answer, she began to laugh. 'This has to be a joke, right?' She spun to face Jesse. 'You're giving each of us, your kids, the same as you're giving to...' Her mouth continued to move, but she couldn't bring herself to say Isabelle's name.

'It's very generous of you to include me,' Belle said.

'This is a starting point.' Jacqueline's lips were thin. 'We believe all of you should have some allocation, but that doesn't mean it will necessarily be split equally. We need to give careful consideration to the actual allocation.'

'Jesus Christ, I don't believe this.' Chloé tilted her head to the ceiling. But talking to the Man wasn't giving her any answers either.

Jesse didn't know what to say. His thoughts had turned to Cameron's offer, which would translate to fifty million pounds if each were allocated a quarter of the company. But the deal was probably also the death knell for Jesse's career at the firm. He brought his attention back to the room and caught Chloé shooting him a quizzical look.

Daniel looked to be choosing his words carefully. 'None of you have voting rights. Even if you had an allocation, the trustee decides what happens. You can't vote to sell the company or declare a dividend to be paid on the shares. The company documents also prevent you from selling or disposing of your shares without consent.'

Jesse was trying hard to process everything that he'd heard. He turned to face his mother. 'Are you going to tell us what's going on?'

'I don't know what you mean,' Jacqueline replied.

'Oh, come on, Mother. How can you even say that with a straight face?' Chloé said. 'For years, you've let Jesse and me believe the company will be passed down to us. There hasn't been the slightest suggestion that you would spread the ownership beyond the family.'

'Cameron and I *are* family,' Belle said, a frown flicking across her face.

'Did I hear something?' Chloé looked around, feigning puzzlement. She shrugged. 'There's never been any hint that you'd give part of our family company to outsiders. What the hell's going on, Mum? Dad? What is this?'

'There isn't any more to be said,' Jacqueline said.

'You said there'd be time for questions and answers. Well, I've heard questions. But no answers. Not one.' Chloé's speech was slowing, heading towards staccato.

Richard waved his hand towards his children and his niece. 'You, all of you, need to accept that we know what we're doing,' Chloé snorted. 'We want to protect the family and safeguard the company. You don't know everything that's going on, and it's best it stays that way.'

You don't know everything that is going on.

The words were chilling, but there was no prospect of any explanation for starting the thaw.

Belle hadn't said anything for a few minutes and chose that moment to break her silence. 'Are we done then?' She posed it as a question but was already walking over to say goodbye to her aunt and uncle. 'Thank you, Aunt Jacqueline and Uncle Richard. You've been very kind.' Then she turned, and her gaze swept over both Jesse and Chloé. 'I'll see you both in the boardroom.'

'Save yourself the effort, and count yourself out now,' Chloé said.

Belle took one step back into the centre of the room. 'I've heard a lot about you, Chloé. I look forward to discovering how much of it's true.' With that, she turned and left the room.

'I really can't believe that you're giving any shares in our company to...' Jesse watched as Chloé struggled to find a word. Eventually, she waved her hand towards the door and gave up.

Jacqueline turned to face Daniel. 'Could you please give us a few minutes alone with the children?'

'Of course.' Daniel nodded at Jesse and Chloé before leaving the room.

Jacqueline's face was, unusually for her, strained. 'Now listen very closely, you two. You have no idea, no idea at all, what is going on. I urge you to remember that your father and I love you both very much—more than the company, our niece, and our nephew. But what we are doing is necessary. And it is just.' Jesse's throat tightened. He had seen his mother in business mode many times, but never had she spoken to them as she was doing now. 'There are some decisions which it's not right to ask you to make alone. What we have done is as much for your protection as anything else. Try to remember that the Trust is your guardian.'

Jesse's mother pulled both him and Chloé into an embrace. He couldn't remember the last time that she'd done that. A perfunctory hug, yes, but this was different. Her arm pulled him tight, and she kissed the top of his head before doing the same to his sister.

'Jesus, Mum? What?' Jesse's words were mumbled, but Jacqueline was already drawing herself up to her normal posture.

'All the documentation has been signed,' Richard glanced

at his wife. 'Your mother and I are leaving for the Lake District this evening for a short vacation. When we return, we will formally announce the boardroom changes, and your period as deputy CEO will start. We know that you'll both do what needs to be done.' Richard nodded before taking his wife's arm, and together, they walked out of the room, leaving Jesse staring at his sister.

14

LUDGATE HILL, LONDON
7 PM

JESSE STOOD OUTSIDE THE WINE BAR AND TEXTED GRACE. THEN he walked through the doorway, slipped onto a stool, and waited for the barman to catch his eye. He recoiled from the overpowering display of chrome and glass, and his nostrils twitched at the aroma of flowery and fruity wines awkwardly twinned with the charcoal scent of the overcooked burger being devoured by a hungry customer further along the bar.

He watched his serving of Shiraz being poured. He'd known he wanted a drink, but only when his nose registered the plum, blackberry and underlying twist of pepper did he realise it wasn't want; it was need. He swirled the wine in his glass and then took a sip, holding it briefly in his mouth before swallowing. He allowed the drink to ease its warmth into his tight neck. He took a second mouthful just as Grace's voice snapped him back into the wine bar.

'Emergency assistance for Jesse?' she asked before sitting beside him and kissing him on the cheek. Her perfume, citrus with lily-of-the-valley, orange blossom and white musk, suited her. Energetic, with a sense of the open air.

'You're sleeping with the enemy,' he said.

'I like to try out the competition. Don't worry, I didn't buy it; it was a free sample.'

He smiled. 'In that case, I forgive you,' he said. 'Thanks for coming.'

'I've been running a seminar at your offices all day,' she said, reaching for his glass and taking a sip. 'Hmm. That'll do.' She flagged down the barman. She glanced at Jesse's glass and then back at him. 'I think you'll need another glass.' He caught her gaze. There was a question in her eyes, but also something else. Something uncertain. 'Do you want to tell me what's got you so worked up?'

Which was a great question. The half-whispered final monologue from their mother had been even more bizarre than the announcement about the shareholdings. She'd made it sound as though the family was preparing for war. But with whom and why hadn't been explained. Chloé had all but stumbled out of the boardroom. She'd messaged Jesse later to say she was back home and wanted to catch up with him the next day, but he couldn't wait that long without talking through the issue. Grace was still looking at him, and he realised he hadn't answered her question.

'I had the strangest meeting with Chlo and our parents this afternoon.'

'Okay.'

'The thing is, nearly all of it is confidential.'

'I understand,' Grace said. She nodded her thanks to the barman as he placed two more glasses of the Shiraz on the bar.

'Something is going on.' He shuffled on his stool. 'I don't know how to summarise it. Some changes are happening, and I'm having difficulty understanding them.' Grace reached for his hand and squeezed it, waiting for him to continue. 'I'm sorry. I'm not meant to talk to anyone about it.'

'Anyone outside of the family?'

'Yes.' He cleared his throat. 'Okay. Let me ask you this. If I had the chance to walk away from the company, with money, with good money,' he dropped his voice, 'with incredible money, should I take it?'

She frowned. 'Well, I would say, forget the money.'

'That's quite hard to do in the circumstances.'

'I'm sure, but I think you should try to decide without thinking about the money.'

He tried. Maybe he would be happy to leave all the expectations and pressure behind, but a sale would take away his core, hollowing him out. He wouldn't need to work, but the truth was that he wanted to. He wanted to create perfumes and build his career—no, not his career. He wanted to pursue his art and build a legacy, and keeping the family company and becoming CEO would give him the maximum freedom and support to do that.

Grace was still talking. 'I would also think about not just what you are leaving behind but what you're walking towards. It's easier to lose something than it is to replace it.' Her lips had left a smudge of lipstick on her glass.

What would he do if he wasn't tied to the company? He could start over and launch his own perfumery. But he could see that his own venture wouldn't be enough if simultaneously he had to witness House of Marcham's heritage being reduced to a profit-and-loss account. He'd want to recreate the company all over again. And why do that when they could hold on to the one they already had?

'Focussing on the future seems like a good plan,' Jesse said. 'How about we go back to your place?'

She swallowed a mouthful of wine. 'Well, that wasn't exactly what I was shooting for, but yes, okay. I need to pop back to the office to get my stuff. Are you happy for us to walk back together?'

She pressed him occasionally, but he was still sensitive to their relationship becoming public, but not for his own benefit. He knew that people at the firm would treat her differently.

'We're just two colleagues chatting outside the office. I think it's perfectly believable that we can bump into each other every now and then.'

'Is that what we're calling it now?' Grace smiled.

Jesse laughed. 'Why don't you head home when you've collected your stuff? I need to check on a few things in the lab. I'll get a taxi over to yours when I'm done. I shouldn't be long.'

His phone buzzed, and he checked the text. It was from Cameron.

> You need to convince your parents to sell. I'm
> not messing around.

Jesse's body tensed. He knew Daniel had been due to brief Cameron on the changes to the company shareholdings. Still, the text message made no reference to the fact that Cameron's new net worth could potentially put him within sparring distance of the top ten wealthiest boxers of all time. Jesse tapped his fingers on the bar. Then he put the phone away, glancing across the wine bar as he did so. A man was looking at him. He had a slight squint in his left eye. The man took a sip of his drink and turned his gaze away. The hair on the back of Jesse's neck stood up. What was it? The guy didn't look out of place; he was wearing a suit, and his tie was still done up, but it was pulled away from his neck, with the top button of his blue shirt undone. He seemed to be drinking alone, but he didn't have his phone, a newspaper, or a book in front of him. His eyes swung back toward Jesse, loitered for a long second and then pivoted away.

'Let's go,' he said to Grace.

Maybe the guy had nothing to do with Cameron or the protestor, but Jesse wasn't going to risk it. He threw one last glance at the solitary drinker and then walked out of the bar. A few minutes later, they were outside the office.

'I'll head to yours as soon as I'm finished here,' Jesse said. 'I should only be an hour.'

'Now we're back here, I officially don't care about you.' Grace winked at him. 'You're nothing to me.'

Jesse smiled and followed her laughter into the office, more acutely aware than usual of the family name hanging over him.

———

JESSE EXITED the lift with his imagination fast-forwarding to the rest of his evening. He waved goodnight to the security guard stationed at the reception desk and pushed through the rotating door. The perfume-scented air conditioning gave way to the smell of cigarette smoke. Plenty of mid-week revellers were standing outside the bar that adjoined the office, but Jesse turned the other way and headed toward Strand, weaving through the alleyways. Workers loitered outside the bars, and Jesse tried to give the cigarette smoke a wide birth. He scanned the road for an orange taxi light, aware of a man dressed in a dark suit, close behind him, also looking around. But Jesse had been there first.

A black van pulled over towards the stretch of pavement where Jesse was waiting. He rolled his eyes and started to walk further along the pavement when he felt a sharp sting in the back of his right leg. Jesse waved his hand, trying to swat the bug, and his hand caught the arm of the man behind him. Then everything went black.

15

ST MARY CRAY

8 PM

MARTIN BAXTER SLID HIS GLASS ONTO THE TABLE, NOT releasing his grip until he was sure that he had pushed it far enough that it wouldn't fall.

The Broker still hadn't called. Every time his phone rang, he hoped he'd hear that weird robotic voice. He couldn't believe what he heard the first time, but the cash envelope had been pushed through his door. He was told he'd get his next payment if he created a scene at that fancy dinner. He had been left all the stuff he needed in a box on his doorstep. They'd even arranged for his quick getaway. The truth was, he had enjoyed it—seeing Jackie Marcham's terrified face.

Martin had expected a call from the Broker after he had door-stopped Jacqui Marcham a few days ago. Perhaps that had been a mistake. Direct contact probably wasn't part of the grand plan but screw them. Martin Baxter was no one's fool.

He leaned forward and grabbed his drink. He gulped down the last of the vodka and shook his head as the alcohol burnt his throat.

The Broker would pay him more money than he'd ever dreamed of. It should have been enough to buy his silence, but what Richard Ford did to Martin's father—Martin still couldn't stomach it. What a bastard. They needed to pay for that.

His head turned towards the door. What was that? Was it a knock? He struggled to his feet, his mind racing. Hell, why had he drunk so much? He was sure he'd heard a knock on the door. He swallowed, his heart pounding. His eyes swivelled, hoping to find something to defend himself with. The Broker may have offered him a life-changing amount of money, but he didn't trust anyone.

Whoever it was, they were standing on his porch. A figure, their features obscured, stood there. He could see their fuzzy shape through the patterned glass but nothing more.

'Who's there?' he said. The words caught in his throat.

Martin listened intently but could only hear his heart thumping and the blood pumping in his ears. He blinked hard and opened the door.

16

LONDON
10 PM

A SHARP SLAP STUNG JESSE'S CHEEK. HE BLINKED HIS EYES open. He tried to get his brain into gear, but his nose kicked in first, picking up a snatch of a woody, aromatic grapefruit scent—possibly *Bleu de Chanel.*

It took Jesse a second or two longer to realise he was blindfolded. He heard footsteps walking away from him. He was sitting on a chair, but he wasn't in the firm's lab. There was an industrial smell of vinegar, which was almost greasy. Wherever he was, his shoulders were tight, and his hands were behind his back, tied together.

He shook his head to try to clear the mental fog. What was his last memory? He'd left the office and headed to get a taxi, but he couldn't remember getting in a cab. Something had surprised him. That was it—a jab, like an insect bite on his hamstring.

Jesse returned his focus to his current state. He was in discomfort rather than pain. And his body was sluggish. He couldn't move because he was restrained, but he wasn't sure his arms and legs would function normally in any event.

Someone had slapped him, trying to wake him, but he couldn't hear anyone now, and the scent of aftershave had faded.

'Hello?' His voice was croaky. Silence. 'Hey.' He said it louder this time. 'Who are you?' Jesse screamed. 'What are you doing?' His questions died in the still air.

He shivered and then flexed his hands, wondering whether there was enough slack in the rope to slip free, but there was no chance of that—the bindings dug into his wrists.

A voice made Jesse start. It was deep, almost mechanical in tone, and although distorted, it sounded male.

'Jesse Marcham. Welcome,' he said, as if Jesse had accepted an invitation. 'I am the Broker.' Jesse craned his neck. The voice seemed to be coming from above, perhaps from speakers in the ceiling. 'I am going to explain what you are going to do for me.'

The Broker.

Jesse had never heard that name before. His mouth was dry, but he forced himself to speak. 'What?'

'You will ensure the offer for your company is accepted.'

Jesus, this was connected to the offer. 'Cam?' he said. 'Is that you?'

A robotic laugh penetrated down to Jesse's bones. He sucked in a deep breath. Jesse couldn't imagine his cousin going along with an abduction plan, no matter how much he might want the sale to go ahead. There was a burst of static before he could make out the Broker's words.

'No. Cameron knows nothing about this. But you will speak with him and make the deal happen. Reparations will be paid.'

Jesse's head was thumping. He tried to keep up with what

he was hearing. 'I can't.' The words came out as a croak. He tried to clear his head. 'It's not up to me.'

There was a pause before the Broker spoke again. 'With the right circumstances and the right encouragement, you will do precisely what I want.'

There was a sudden pressure on Jesse's bladder. Please, no. Not that.

'I can't.' His legs were shaking now, and the tremors were spreading to his torso. His emotions started to slip away from him and pick up momentum. Was the Broker going to kill him? Either now or later. His knees knocked together, and tears pooled in his eyes. He dug his nails into his palms to fight the need to urinate and tried to pull himself back. He forced himself to breathe.

'Who are you?' he asked, throwing his voice towards the roof.

He struggled with renewed energy to try and free the ropes around his wrists, but his movement toppled the chair over. In desperation, he twisted sideways to try and save his face from the impact, and his arm and shoulder smacked against the floor. Pain shot down his back. The floor was polished concrete, and its touch was almost cold on Jesse's face.

The Broker didn't speak for at least a minute, during which Jesse tried to think, his breath now coming in big gulps.

'I'm going to release you,' the Broker said. 'If you try to remove your blindfold before I tell you to, I will kill you.' Jesse closed his eyes. He needed to stay calm, and he'd be free. He could worry about everything else later. His only objective was to get out alive. 'One final thing. I know about

Grace. If you want her to stay alive, don't go to the police or tell anyone about me.'

Before he could catch himself, Jesse was yelling.

'Leave her alone.' His heart was thumping in his chest. How did they know about her? His whole body was thrashing around on the floor. 'She has nothing to do with this,' he shouted. He was aware of how pathetic it must sound. He was yelling whilst lying on the floor, tied to a chair, but he didn't care.

He heard a click. A door opening or a gun being cocked? He tried to slow his breathing and listened to the rapid footsteps. Then, someone grabbed his hands and cut the bindings. Jesse picked up the same waft of scent. Whoever it was didn't speak, and Jesse stayed still until he heard the door close. Even then, he didn't move. After perhaps another minute, the Broker spoke.

'You're free to leave now.'

Jesse slid the blindfold off and pushed himself up from the floor. He blinked as his eyes adjusted to the light. He was in an industrial warehouse, although God only knew where. The high ceiling was held up with metal struts fixed on top of a three-foot-high brick wall. He saw his mobile phone lying on the floor a few yards away. He bent down to pick it up and unlocked the screen.

He stumbled towards the door. His abductor must be only metres away, but given that they'd freed him, it seemed likely they'd planned to stay out of his way. He yanked the door open and stepped outside, the chill in the air stinging his face in an echo of the slap. He was surrounded by buildings similar to the one he had been held in, but there was a road leading towards what must have been the exit of the industrial park.

He glanced at his phone. The time had clicked past eleven o'clock, several hours after he was due to arrive at Grace's flat. There were three messages and multiple missed calls from Grace. The most recent message, still visible on the screen, was from Chloé asking to meet for breakfast tomorrow. He read the texts from Grace.

> Where are you? xx
>
> Have you changed your mind? xx
>
> Okay, I assume you're not coming. You're going to have to explain that to me. xx

He called her number as he started to walk, but the call was diverted to voicemail. As he listened to her recorded message, a sense of dread wrapped itself around his body. Had the Broker got to her already? He hung up. Seconds later, his phone rang. It was Grace.

'So, you're alive then?' Her voice was surprisingly neutral, but it was clear her question was loaded with no knowledge of what had happened to Jesse.

He let out a slow breath, trying to conceal the deep sense of relief flooding his body. He didn't want to tell her over the phone what had happened, and he wasn't sure he should tell her at all.

'I'm really sorry. Look, can I come over? I can explain everything when I get there.'

He wasn't sure how he would have reacted in the circumstances Grace had found herself in. He braced himself for a curt response and the end of the call.

'Okay. I'll wait up.'

Jesse ended the call just before a full-body convulsion. Seconds later, he was doubled over, retching on the ground.

THURSDAY 11 JULY 2024

17

GRACE'S FLAT, GROVE PARK
5:20 AM

JESSE COULDN'T SLEEP. THE EVENTS OF THE PREVIOUS NIGHT kept replaying in his head. He rolled over to avoid disturbing Grace and picked up his phone from the bedside table. There were no new messages. He couldn't risk going to the police. Not yet. He was meeting Chloé for breakfast at eight o'clock but wasn't sure what to say to her either. Then there was the fact that the Broker knew about Grace. How did anyone know about their relationship? His throat was tight.

He opened the last text from Cameron.

> You need to convince your parents to sell. I'm not messing around.

He typed his reply.

> I need to meet you. Today.

Then he locked his phone's screen and turned over onto his back. Grace was snoring quietly. He rested his head on the pillow and sighed. If someone had asked him what he'd do to keep her safe, he'd have answered without hesitation. *Anything.* That was still his answer, but if the Broker were true to his word, that resolve would be pushed to the limit.

His phone buzzed. Cameron had replied.

My house. 10 am.

18

BILLINGSGATE, LONDON

8 AM

JESSE HAD LEFT GRACE STILL SLEEPING, UNAWARE OF HIS abduction and the threat that had been made against her. As the taxi pulled away from the traffic lights, Jesse's mind turned again to going to the police. The Broker had warned him not to, but how would they know? He closed his eyes, muttering under his breath, as conflicting options tore at him. His thoughts traced around the same circle until the taxi turned into Billingsgate Market. The window was cracked open, and the smell of fish swarmed into the car.

The Broker wanted him to force the sale through, but how would he do it even if he could be persuaded to try? It wasn't like a public company where a potential purchaser could buy a toehold shareholding before launching an offer or manoeuvre a director onto the board. A purchaser could only buy shares in a private company if they found a willing seller and agreed on terms. There wasn't a mechanism for a hostile takeover of a private company—unless you counted the Godfather route and made an offer that couldn't be refused.

A purchaser could offer the shareholders more money than the company was worth. Sometimes, a healthy premium would be enough because money talked loudly—and a personal fortune practically screamed. But family companies were strangely resistant to the siren cash call. His father was fond of telling him that almost a third of business owners had no plan to retire—ever—although Jesse was sure that most owners also believed they were immortal.

What made the Broker think Jesse could get the deal done when the votes remained with his mother? It was her decision, not his. The trust hadn't changed that. Would she sell if Jesse begged her to, he wondered? It wasn't impossible, but it was close to it.

What would the Broker do if the offer was rejected? Jesse tapped his fingers against the palms of his hands, and his foot bounced on the taxi floor. It wasn't a comfortable question to answer.

'Here we are, mate,' the taxi driver said.

Jesse paid his fare and walked over to the café. Chloé was already sitting under a canvas awning at one of the outside tables. The café itself was packed, with customers favouring the warmth of indoors. A walkway separated the two areas with a steady stream of commuters staring at their phones or sipping their takeaway coffees as they moved past. The stress of the previous night had woken Jesse's appetite, and the smell of sizzling eggs and bacon and strong coffee jacked it higher. Chloé stood to hug him, looking like she had come straight from the gym. She wore a jet-black zip-up Stella McCartney tracksuit top, leggings, and bright orange trainers.

'I've ordered us both the usual,' she said. The café had a special status—the only non-upmarket restaurant Chloé liked.

'Great, thanks.' He sat down in the seat opposite. It was a cold morning, but he knew she'd chosen that table because no one was around to overhear their discussion.

'Are you okay, Jesse? You look terrible.'

'Thanks,' he said. 'I didn't sleep well.'

Chloé nodded. 'Tell me about it. I still can't believe what Mum and Dad have done.'

He smoothed his hands over his thighs. 'I know. Have you heard anything from Cam about the offer?' He tried to keep the tension from his voice.

'No, but he seems to have chosen you as his point man.' She held his gaze, but he couldn't read her. 'I've been thinking about his offer.' Chloé dug into her handbag and pulled out a folder. 'These are the accounts for his company —Mad Cow Holdings Limited.' She started to flick through the pages, her eyes scanning, her lips pursed. 'They tell an interesting story.' She passed him the folder. 'Take a look for yourself.'

Jesse wasn't experienced in reviewing accounts but knew enough to determine that the company didn't look financially healthy. There had been increasing losses in the last few years, and some chunky bank loans. 'You tell me, Chloé, but it doesn't look like his business is doing well.'

She took the folder back from her brother, tossed it onto the table and snorted. 'Not very well is an understatement.' She never missed the chance to score a point, and finance was her domain. 'It's on life support. He gambled hard on expansion just before the pandemic. He's taken some furlough money, but the business has struggled. The last accounts are nearly a year old, but my guess is the company is close to breaching their banking covenants.'

Jesse frowned. 'Really?'

'Yeah. Worst-case scenario, they pull the funding, and he's insolvent.'

Jesse digested the information. He clasped his hands together, his thumbs tapping against each other. 'He hasn't said anything to me.'

'He hasn't asked you for money?'

Jesse shook his head. 'No. He hasn't even hinted at it recently. Maybe he's fixed his debt issues some other way.'

'I hope so, for his sake because otherwise, he's going bust.' She frowned. 'He told you that his offer is backed by serious people with deep pockets.'

'That's what he said. What are you thinking?'

'Do you know which luxury goods company had the highest compound annual growth rate for financial years pre-pandemic?' She must have known he couldn't answer the question. Why couldn't she have just told him? He gave a slight shake of the head. 'Farfetch. And most of that growth came from its acquisition of New Guards Group. Luxury streetwear.' She leaned towards him. 'Three of the other top five growth companies were in the luxury sneakers or sports-wear sector.'

'Where are you going with this?' he asked, glancing at his sister's gym attire.

'Maybe we've been underestimating Cam and his back-ers. What if the new direction is to expand into luxury sportswear? They offer Cam a deal to come on board. He has business experience, and he could credibly help launch a sportswear range. They keep the family heritage for perfume and get his gym brand. Added to that, his surname...'

'...is Marcham,' Jesse said before falling silent momentar-ily. 'I don't know, it feels like a stretch.'

'Well, they've got him on board somehow, and he's clearly motivated to try and make it happen,' Chloé said.

The Broker's voice echoed in Jesse's head, but he had decided not to tell Chloé until he had a better idea of how serious the risk was. 'I mean, maybe. But if he was desperate to keep his own business afloat, and he's struck some deal, maybe he doesn't need it now that he's one of four beneficiaries of the new trust,' Jesse said.

'He doesn't know how much he might be allocated—it could be nothing.' She paused. 'It *should* be nothing. Even if he had, you heard what Daniel said: Cam can't sell. He can't even borrow against the shares. The shares are useless to him in helping fund his business.'

'Unless the company is sold.' Jesse's guts twinged as he said the words.

Chloé didn't say anything, but she grimaced.

The waiter brought over their plates of poached eggs, chorizo, tomatoes, and mushrooms, the smell of the fat teasing Jesse's nostrils. Jesse waited until the waiter returned with the mugs of steaming coffee before he tucked into the food, which, as ever, was heaven on a plate. He took a mouthful of the coffee, which was good but still very much grounded on Earth.

'Given everything you've just said, do you think Cam's deal might be worth looking at?' he asked.

Chloé pushed her chair back, the metal legs scraping against the concrete. 'Not Cam's deal, no. If we can make it *our* deal, then maybe.' She pushed a strand of hair away from her face. 'Jesus, Jesse. Surely you don't think we should sell to outsiders. It's bad enough that Mum and Dad might give Belle and Cam shares.'

He shrugged and met Chloé's expectant gaze. 'I don't

know.' He shuffled forward in his seat, the Broker's words echoing in his ears. 'Maybe...' His words faded away with his nerve.

'Maybe, what? Come on, Jesse.' It wasn't unusual for his younger sister to hassle him. 'Out with it.'

'Maybe we...' He blew out a breath. 'Maybe we should sell if there's a genuine offer.'

'Only if we are part of the deal. The key part.'

Jesse said nothing. Any chance he had of convincing his parents to sell was remote, but without Chloé's support, it disappeared entirely. He took another mouthful of breakfast. He was leaning towards the Broker simply being a scare tactic, an illegal one for sure, but he didn't know whether they would follow up on their threats. They'd targeted him to try to make the deal happen when his mother had all the power - when it would make more sense for the Broker to do something to apply pressure to Jacqueline.

'Why are you looking at me like that?' Chloé asked.

He smiled to hide the truth. 'Just glad you're on my side.'

They left cash on the table to settle the bill and walked to the office. Jesse was listening to the sound of Chloé's trainers pounding on the pavement—like a drumroll—when his phone buzzed. It was a text from Grace.

Can we talk? Something odd is happening.

Jesse felt the ground tilt. He glanced up from his phone to see Chloé looking at him. 'Are you okay?' she asked.

'I don't know. I need to deal with something. I'll see you back at the office.'

Chloé frowned, nodded, and continued walking, leaving Jesse behind, staring at his phone.

19

HOUSE OF MARCHAM OFFICES, SHOE LANE, LONDON

8:50 AM

Jesse waited down a side lane, around the corner from the office.

Five minutes later, Grace was heading towards him. She smiled briefly. He thought for a moment that she would link arms with him, but she held back, walking next to him, her handbag over her shoulder. To all the world, it looked as though they had arranged to go to a meeting. There was no outward sign of distress, and she looked as great as always.

'What's happening?' he asked.

They were a few blocks from the office, walking through one of the squares, past the statue of a dog. Grace still hadn't said anything. Had the Broker approached her? Jesse balled his hands.

She reached into her handbag. 'This was posted through my letterbox this morning,' she said, holding out an envelope. His stomach pitched. It had to be the Broker. His hand trembled as he took the envelope from her. It was small and white, with GRACE NELSON typed on the front.

'Open it,' she said.

Jesse pulled up the flap and then slipped the paper from inside. It was doubled over, and with a sense of unease, he unfolded it. The message, like the name on the envelope, was typed.

Why don't you ask your boyfriend about his family secret?

He heard the words in his head as he read them, delivered in the distorted voice of the Broker.

'Okay,' he said. Except things were anything but okay.

'I'm sorry, Jesse. I don't know what to do. I wasn't going to say anything to you; I was going to ignore it, but I'm slightly freaked out.'

Neither spoke as they crossed Fleet Street and headed towards the Thames. Jesse tried to organise his thoughts.

'Who even knows about us?' Grace reached out and squeezed his hand. 'Perhaps your mum and dad—'

'I haven't told them about us,' Jesse said.

Grace nodded. 'They might still know. Someone could have seen us together and told them.'

He chewed his lip. It was possible his parents did know. He'd told Chloé, but she wouldn't have said anything to them. But if someone had followed Jesse over the last week, they'd have quickly run into Grace. It was the Broker. It had to be, but he couldn't say anything to Grace.

He thought once again of going to the police, but if the Broker found out, that would make things worse—much worse. Jesse respected the police, but they weren't a personal security detail. He blinked. *That* is what he needed. Grace could move in with him, but it wasn't as if he could really protect her. They needed a professional.

'How about moving in with me for a week or so and I'll hire some personal protection. I can use the firm that the company uses. We have people who travel with Mum and

Dad sometimes. They're professionals.' They carried on walking, and Grace seemed to be lost in thought. 'What do you think?' he asked.

Grace stopped and turned to face him. 'What's going on, Jesse? I assumed the note was someone trying to get to you or the company, but you're acting like I'm in danger.'

Jesse swallowed. 'Look, there's an issue with the company. I don't know what. There've been suggestions of a family secret—just like this letter.' He waved the envelope. 'I swear, I don't know what it is, but there was the article in *Scent,* the protestor at the party, and now this. Someone is trying to buy the company, and my parents are circling the wagons. It's as if we are under attack.'

Grace glanced skyward. 'Look, Jesse, I like you. I really like you, and I knew this would be complicated with you being a Marcham.' She sighed and looked down at the ground. 'I just didn't have any idea it might be dangerous.'

Guilt twisted in his gut. He had no right to expect her to stay with him. 'I'm sorry. I never wanted to drag you into anything like this.'

'I still feel as though there's something you're not telling me.'

Jesse nodded. 'You're right, there is, but I can't tell you.' His voice cracked. 'I wish I could.' He handed back the envelope.

Grace rubbed the back of her neck and didn't answer immediately. 'I'm not sure I can cope with this.' She reached out to retake his hand. 'Perhaps, when this is all over, what-ever this is, we could try again?' she said. He didn't trust himself to speak, so he nodded. 'Say something, Jesse?' Her voice was barely a whisper.

He tried to compose himself. 'I'd like that.' He squeezed

her hand. 'I'd like that very much.' He blinked away a few tears. 'I'm sorry, Grace.'

'I'm sorry too, Jesse.'

She kissed him on the cheek and then turned and walked away. Jesse watched as she glanced back and waved her fingers. The Broker had issued him an ultimatum—selling the company was the only way to guarantee Grace's safety. A line of the hymn seeped into his mind.

It was Grace that taught my heart to fear.

He watched her turn the corner, and then she was gone.

Jesse stood still for a moment. He needed to fix things, yet he had no earthly idea how. But he did know where to start— he was going to confront Cameron.

20

CAMERON'S HOUSE, CLAPHAM

10 AM

JESSE SAT AT THE BREAKFAST BAR WHILE HIS COUSIN STARTED gathering equipment on the kitchen worktop. Jesse studied him, trying to work out what he was doing.

'You grind your own coffee?' he asked.

'I've got a jar of instant hidden away, but yeah, normally. I enjoy the ritual.'

'And the coffee?'

'That, too.'

Jesse blinked as the grinder kicked into action, picking up subtle hints of almond and chocolate. Cameron worked methodically through the steps, but he was missing his usual bounce. His weight was back on his heels rather than his toes. There was an unusual strain in his features, and his movements were laboured as if he'd done a full-body workout without a cool-down.

'You okay?' Jesse asked.

Cameron sighed. 'I didn't sleep well last night. I haven't slept well for days.'

Jesse's throat tightened. 'I came here to talk to you about the offer for the company,' Jesse said.

'I figured as much.'

Jesse had decided not to lead with his ordeal at the hands of the Broker. They had claimed that Cameron knew nothing about his abduction, but it was time to find out precisely what Cameron did know.

'You've told me the offer price. What are the other terms?'

Cameron lifted his head. 'You sound as though there might be some interest?'

Jesse shrugged. 'You know it's not up to me. Even if there was agreement on the price, all we've had so far is a discussion with you. We need to know the details.'

Cameron nodded. 'You'll have it soon.' The enthusiasm had drained from his voice.

Jesse decided to change tack. 'I take it you've heard about Mum and Dad's changes to the shareholding.'

'Yeah, their lawyer called me.' He blew out a deep breath. 'That was quite the surprise.'

'Does it make any difference to your bid to buy the company?' Jesse kept his tone neutral and studied his cousin carefully.

Cameron sighed. He looked deflated. Defeated. 'God. You'll never know how much I wish I'd just walked away.'

Jesse blinked. It was a dramatic shift from the confidence his cousin had exuded in all previous discussions. 'What do you mean?'

The water percolated through the coffee. Each drip sounded like a finger click, marking time. 'I mean, I wish none of this was happening.' He sighed. 'This guy called me out of the blue to sound me out about the deal.'

'Who?' A burst of adrenaline shot through Jesse. 'Have you met him?'

Cameron shook his head. 'No. Never. We've just spoken on the phone. He said we'd meet when we need to.'

'What does he sound like?'

Cameron shrugged. 'I don't know. Normal, I guess. No real accent. Not posh, either.' He frowned. 'What does it matter?'

Jesse let his cousin's question slip away unanswered. Cameron groaned and turned towards Jesse. It was only then that Jesse noticed that his cousin's eyes were bloodshot.

'I should have just come to you first, but he made it sound easy. He offered me a loan for half a million to join the bid. He wanted me to have a couple of chats with you. A bit of negotiation. He wants me to be visibly connected with the company but not to have to do anything much. I couldn't believe it.'

At least Jesse now knew Cameron's price. 'What it would do to me, to Chloé, to Mum and Dad, none of that mattered?' The accusation hung in the air between them.

'I was angry.'

'Angry with whom?' Jesse asked.

'Your parents.' He rubbed his forehead and shook his head. 'I'm not proud of this, but I asked them for help a few months ago. I needed a loan, and they turned me down.'

'You were angry with them for that?' It was news to Jesse, but it didn't sound like a basis to kick-start a commercial war.

'It sounds stupid, but it was how they did it.' He wiped his hand over his face. 'When I worked at the company, I was doing well, really well. I was good at my job, Jesse. But I was drinking. Other stuff, too.' Jesse swallowed as his cousin continued. 'I made some mistakes.' He shook his head as if trying to erase his errors from history. 'Nothing I did impacted the company, but then I asked some questions. I'd been working on promotional material for a launch, and I wanted to use extracts of the original notebook and build it into a campaign. I had only started my research; your parents heard about it and fired me. They didn't do anything more. I guess I should be grateful about that, but there was something, something in their manner when they fired me. It was as if it was personal. Like they'd always known I'd let them down.' He sniffed.

'I'm surprised you asked them, given what you've just told me.'

'I was desperate. All the banks were pressuring me and I didn't want to ask you again. You were so generous in supporting me when I started.' He hung his head. 'I didn't want you to know I was a failure.'

Jesse swallowed hard. 'What did they say?' He tapped his fingers against his leg.'

'The way they looked at me when they let me into their house—I'm sure they'd be more welcoming to a dog covered in fox crap. I was irritated from the get-go, and from then on, there were little glances between them and the phrases they used. *It wouldn't be very prudent. We're not sure it would be for the best.* And my personal favourite, *none of us would want to end up there again, would we.*' He wiped his hand over his mouth. 'I'm sorry, Jesse. It was all I could do to keep my cool. I didn't say anything, I just walked out.'

'And then what?'

'This guy called and offered me the deal. I jumped at it.' He paused, pain flickering across his face. 'I'm not an idiot, Jesse. I know your parents will never sell, no matter how good the offer is, but my deal isn't conditional on the sale happening.' There was tension in his jaw. 'The strange thing is this guy is confident the deal will go through.' Cameron stared at the ground. 'It doesn't make any sense.'

'I agree,' Jesse said. 'My parents aren't likely to sell.'

Cameron met Jesse's gaze. 'I don't know who I'm dealing with, but his confidence unsettles me.' He closed his eyes for a few seconds. 'There's something else.' He dropped his gaze to the floor. 'They're going to drop the offer price.'

Jesse flinched. 'The offer price will be less than two hundred?'

'Much less.'

'Jesus.' Jesse tried to process what he was hearing.

'I told him, even at two hundred million, it was almost impossible to imagine a deal. At a lower price, there's no way.' Jesse waited, sensing there was more to come. 'He said the deal is certain to happen. When I asked how that was possible, he said, *That's not your concern. Just do as I tell you.*' Cameron groaned. 'Jesus Christ. What have I got into? This guy's played me like a PlayStation pro. I'm so sorry, Jesse.' He hung his head.

'Why not walk away?' Jesse asked, but if this guy was the Broker, he knew the answer.

'I can't.' Cameron was blinking now. 'I needed the loan. My business was going under. I was desperate. That's why I approached your parents in the first place.'

Jesse was silent for a moment. It all hung together. Cameron had chosen to protect his business, just as Jesse and his family would fight to protect theirs. 'Have you spoken to anyone other than this guy?' he asked.

Cameron shook his head. 'No. Just him.'

'You've got his number?'

'Yeah. He never answers, though. Always calls me back.'

Jesse's fingers were tapping against his leg. The coffee machine beeped, and he stood up to pour them each a cup, handing one to Cameron. His parents wouldn't sell at a full price. A reduced offer? He was with Cameron; there was no way that deal was happening.

'Remember when we used to build dens in the woods?' Cameron asked. Jesse struggled to shift himself back in time. 'I've been thinking about those times over the last week. I think it was possibly the last time I was truly happy.'

Jesse reeled with the emotional sucker punch. It was a very different side of Cameron from the one he'd experienced since moving away to the big house in the countryside. But had Jesse grown used to him or away from him? He knew the move wasn't the seismic shift that broke their world apart. Cameron's parents had divorced shortly after the move. Jesse had never spoken to Cameron about it; he'd seen very little of him after the move. He could have done something about it, but he'd allowed himself to drift apart, carried on emotional plate tectonics, moving them inexorably in different directions.

A flood of memories hit him. When they were young, the two of them had been close. Very close. Laughing, playing football, watching films, listening to music, and living the good life. And now nothing remained of that. Fifteen years of life had overwritten their shared history to create what they had now. A fading sketch of their early friendship. He glanced at his cousin, wondering whether the sadness was showing on his face, but Cameron wasn't looking at him. His expression was unfocused, as if he was trying to see back in time. And somewhere deep inside Jesse, something cracked. How did it happen? The inno-cence of youth. Uncomplicated friendship. Easy-going camaraderie. And then what? It was washed away by adult cynicism—the harsh realities of life.

And whose fault was that? Someone else's, or was it all on them? It was too easy for Jesse to blame the business. What would his life have been like if those notebooks had never been discovered? Would he have discovered perfume through some other route? Perhaps he would have stayed close to Cameron, and they would be in business together now, happy, like they were when they were ten years old and digging holes in the back garden, flooring the freshly excavated den with old carpet, and improvising a roof with old planks.

'This isn't how I thought things would work out,' Cameron said.

'Me neither, Cam.' Jesse finished the last mouthful of his coffee. He hesitated whilst he shuffled his thoughts. 'Good brew,' he said, walking over to put the mug next to the kitchen sink. 'Right, I'm going to go.'

For a moment, it was the old Cameron and Jesse—ten years old and ready to take on the world—and then the real world shuddered back into focus. He walked towards the front door.

'Jesse?'

He turned back to face his cousin.

Cameron, usually bouncing with energy, looked drained and broken. 'I'm sorry,' he said. 'For everything.'

———

JESSE NEEDED some time to think before he travelled back to the office. At least he was now clear on Cameron's motivation. There'd been a renewed connection with his cousin, and he believed Cameron's regret was genuine. He hadn't wanted to ask Jesse for money. More than that, he didn't want Jesse to think less of him. He'd been desperate enough for funding to approach Jesse's parents. After their rejection, the anonymous offer to refinance his business had been too hard to resist. And the chance to poke Jesse's parents had been the emotional icing on the cake.

Jesse's phone rang. He snatched it from his pocket and looked at the screen—an unrecognised number. 'Hello?' he said.

'Jesse Marcham?' There was no electronic echo.

'Yes, speaking.' He swallowed.

'Mr Marcham, this is Constable Rowbotham. I'm a Family Liaison Officer with the police.' Jesse's heart rate jacked up. 'I've called your home and your office. I was hoping to speak with you in person.'

'I'm in Clapham. I'm on my way back to the office right now. What's this about, Constable?'

There was a hesitation, and Jesse's fear grew into the space.

'I'd prefer to speak to you in person if possible.'

Had something happened to Grace? His heart was pounding. 'Just tell me, please.'

'Is there someone with you?'

He could return to Cameron's house, but he didn't want to wait for the news. 'No. Please go ahead.'

There was a brief hesitation before the office replied, 'I'm so sorry, but your parents have been involved in a road traffic accident.'

Jesse's mind ran ahead of the conversation. 'Oh my God. Are they okay?'

'No. I'm very sorry, Mr Marcham. Your father died at the

scene, and your mother has a head injury and is in a critical condition. She's in intensive care at the Royal Preston Hospital in Lancashire.'

The words spun in his mind, and he heard himself speaking. 'Lancaster?'

'Yes, sir. It's the closest trauma centre to the accident.'

Jesse blinked. 'I'll let my sister know. We'll come straight there.' He swallowed. 'What happened?'

'It appears that your father lost control of the vehicle. There's no sign of any other vehicle being involved. I'm so sorry.'

The conversation was over, almost impossibly quickly, with only a few further grim details.

Jesse stared at his phone, blinking, trying to process what he'd just heard. After a minute or two, he took a deep breath and called Chloé.

'Hi, Jesse.' He didn't reply immediately; he was struggling for breath. 'What's wrong?'

'I...'

'Jesse, are you alright? Where are you?'

'I've just left Cam's house.' He pushed the words out. 'I have some bad news.' His breathing was ragged. 'It's Mum and Dad. They...' he trailed off. 'They were in a car crash.'

'Oh no,' she said.

'They were ... in an accident. The police just called me.' He sucked in another breath. 'Dad's dead. Mum's in intensive care. They want us to get to the hospital.'

'Oh my God, I...' Chloé couldn't finish the sentence.

Jesse's throat tightened, and he blinked away the tears pooling in his eyes. 'I'll arrange a helicopter. I'll come to the office, and we can travel together.' Jesse ran his hand over his face. 'I need to stop off at home to grab some clothes. I'll be as quick as I can.' Clean clothes? On some level, he disliked himself for having the presence of mind to think of such practicalities.

'I can't believe it.' There was a long silence, and Jesse had no words to fill it. 'What did ...' He heard his sister swallow. 'What did they say about Mum?'

'She's in critical condition.' Jesse was hollow. Nothing felt real. 'She's got a head injury.' The whole world was out of focus. 'I'll be there as soon as I can.'

21

HOUSE OF MARCHAM OFFICES, SHOE LANE, LONDON

12 PM

THE JOURNEY TO THE OFFICE HAD TAKEN TOO LONG, TOO MANY minutes for Jesse to be alone with his thoughts. His visible distress had unsettled the taxi driver. After a few seconds, the radio had been switched on to smother any chance of conversation, which had suited Jesse just fine. He no longer knew the rules. At least their mother was alive, but until they got to the hospital, they wouldn't know any more. Jesse exited the car and walked toward the office, focusing on putting one foot in front of the other.

'Jesse.' Chloé appeared on the road that ran around the side of the building. She'd changed from her gym gear to a dark green trouser suit, and sunglasses shielded her eyes. He put his arms around her and held her close. Their hug was different from any they'd shared before. Chloé constantly buzzed with energy, but not then. It was all that Jesse could do to keep her upright. 'I can't believe it,' Chloé said, her face pressed into Jesse's shoulder.

'Let's get in the car. Come on,' Jesse said.

Chloé nodded and rubbed her hands over her face. He

guided her towards the Mercedes, which was waiting for them. The driver opened the boot and loaded the overnight bag Jesse had grabbed from home and Chloé's small suitcase.

The accident dominated Jesse's thinking, but another thought was scratching around in his head, fighting to be heard. With everything happening right now, was it possible that the crash wasn't an accident? A cold shiver crept down his spine.

With their parents holding the votes, a sale was highly unlikely, but what about now? He had no idea how it worked, but if the votes were now exercisable by the beneficiaries, Isabelle and Cameron had half of the vote between them. If that was correct, the ability to sanction the sale was potentially in his hands. A vote to sell only needed a 75% majority to pass. The Broker's words echoed in his mind.

The right encouragement.

Jesse's body shook.

The right circumstance.

Was it a coincidence? Or had the people behind this offer for the company attempted to murder both of his parents?

Chloé pushed her sunglasses up and stared at her phone. 'Larry's in New York with work. He's not due back until next week.' Her delivery was stilted as if unsure of what she was saying.

'Have you told him?'

She shook her head. 'Not yet.' She blew out a deep breath. 'I'll call him once we're at the hospital. I'm sure he'll come back early if I ask him.' She sniffed.

'Good.' They climbed into the back seat, and Jesse confirmed the heliport address with the driver. 'Have you spoken with Daniel?' he asked.

'No,' she replied.

'Okay. I'll call him. I think we need to talk to him.'

'Why?' Chloé was pulling her hair in front of her face.

'We need his advice,' Jesse said, taking a deep breath. 'I think we need to consider that all of this might be linked.' He saw her frown. 'The protest. Cameron's offer. There's other stuff, too.' He swallowed. 'I think all of it could be connected with Mum and Dad's accident.'

'What?' Her hand covered her mouth as she made the connection. 'No.' His sister's voice was strangled, and the colour drained from her face. 'No. It can't be. Have the police said anything?' she asked.

Jesse shook his head. 'They said it was an accident, but I didn't speak to them for long. We'll find out more when we get to the hospital,' he said.

'Oh my God, Jesse.' The tightness in her voice made his eyes tear up. 'What are we going to do?'

'Mum will be getting the best care.' He said it as much for his benefit as for Chloé's. 'All we can do is hope for the best.'

He saw Chloé bite her lip. She was struggling. He was, too. Even travelling by helicopter, it would take maybe two or three hours to get to the hospital, which was nowhere near enough time to get his head around the fact that their father was dead and their mother was on life support. That was unfathomable. The possibility that someone had targeted them deliberately...

Jesse closed his eyes and tried to block out the world.

22

ROYAL PRESTON HOSPITAL, PRESTON

3 PM

THE SENIOR NURSE MET THEM AT THE INTENSIVE CARE UNIT reception. He was shorter than Jesse, with thick black hair and brown eyes. He introduced himself and offered to take them through to the ward. They waited as he swiped his pass to release the double doors. He followed him down the corridor, turning left into the ICU ward.

'I'll go and get the consultant,' the nurse said. 'I shouldn't be long.'

Jesse's phone started ringing.

'Hello, this is Constable Rowbotham. I'm just checking in.'

'Oh, yes, hello. We've just arrived at the hospital.' Jesse was conscious of Chloé watching him. 'We're about to meet with the consultant.'

'I'll leave you to talk to the doctor, but I'd like to come and see you at an appropriate time.'

Jesse swallowed. 'I think we'll be here for a few days at least.'

'Okay. I'll be in touch. I hope your mother improves.'

'Thank you, Constable.'

It wasn't long before the nurse returned, accompanied by a colleague. The doctor looked exhausted. Her white hair was held in place by a transparent blue plastic hairnet, and she wore a white surgical mask and latex gloves. She pulled the mask down from her mouth as she approached them. Jesse caught a whiff of disinfectant and antiseptic.

'Hello, I'm Doctor Hathaway, the lead intensive care consultant. I'm so sorry for your loss.' She paused for a moment before pushing on. 'Your mother has suffered a brain injury, and we may need to operate to remove part of the skull to accommodate the swelling. Unfortunately, it's unclear whether the procedure will make enough of a difference.'

Jesse reached for his sister's hand and squeezed it tight.

'Can we see her?' Chloé asked.

'Yes, of course. Follow me.' The doctor turned and led the way through the ward to the beds at the far end. The doctor continued walking and led them to a separate room. 'We've put her in here.'

Jesse had had hours to prepare himself for the sight of his mother in the hospital, but no amount of time would have been enough. His breath caught in his throat. The relative calm of the whole ward had surprised him. The doctors and nurses attended to the patients with an air of efficiency and control. The machines standing by each bed beeped with a reassuring regularity.

Their mother was linked up to tubes and drips, lying motionless. She was covered with a dark green sheet, folded back from her chest, and her head rested on a matching pillow. A computer screen next to the bed displayed a blizzard of vital statistics. The collection of tubes and supports around her neck and head left her eyes and forehead as the only visible part of her face. Her arm was similarly loaded with pipes, and a blue plastic clip was slipped over one of her fingers.

Jesse rested his hand on his mother's arm, blinking rapidly. There was no reaction. He gently rubbed her skin and muttered a silent prayer. He could smell her perfume, recognising it without thinking. *Distraction.* Jesse brushed away the tears rolling down his face as Chloé pulled him into a hug. After a few seconds, Jesse let her go.

'What happens next?' he asked the doctor, his voice thick.

'We'll continue to monitor your mother. The neuro-surgery team is making its decision now. I'll let you know as soon as we've concluded on the best way forward.'

'Shouldn't we consult with the family doctor?' Chloé asked Jesse.

The doctor answered. 'We'd be happy to liaise with anyone the family wants.'

Chloé sniffed. 'I want to ensure that she has the best possible treatment.' She glanced around the room.

'I'm sure she's in the best place here, Chlo,' Jesse said.

The doctor cleared her throat. 'This hospital is one of twenty-seven major trauma centres in England and one of only a dozen that deal exclusively with adult trauma patients. I can assure you your mother is in the best possible place.'

'What about private hospitals? Surely—'

'I'm sorry to be blunt, Miss Marcham. No private hospital is set up to deal with a patient in your mother's condition. This is what we do, all day, every day.' She started to move out of the room. 'Now, if you'll excuse me, I must get to theatre.'

Chloé nodded, her whispered apology floating after the doctor.

A nurse was hovering at the doorway. 'Excuse me, there's a visitor here to see your mother. They're asking for you.'

Jesse frowned. 'Who is it?' he asked. He'd tried to contact Rosie and Elaine but had to leave messages for both.

'Rosie Ford. She's waiting in the family conference room.'

'I'll stay with Mum,' Chloé shuffled closer to the bed.

Jesse nodded and followed the senior nurse out of the ward and along the corridor. He indicated a room on the right. 'She's in there.'

'Thank you,' Jesse said. He took a deep breath before pushing open the door. 'Aunt Rosie?'

She was wearing black leggings, a baggy jumper, and the lightest touch of makeup, which had been smudged by her tears. 'Oh, Jesse.' She walked over and wrapped him in a hug. 'I can't believe it.' He caught a hint of orange, jasmine, and hibiscus over the base notes of rich coffee, vanilla, and cedarwood. Yves Saint Laurent's *Black Opium*. Her jet-black hair was held in a clip, but some strands had escaped and dropped in front of her ear. Jesse pulled away.

Rosie's face was pale. 'I'm so sorry to hear about your mother. I got here as soon as I could. What have the doctors said?' she asked.

'Mum's...' Jesse cleared his throat and tried again. 'She's in a coma, with suspected brain damage.' He swallowed. 'Chlo's with her, now.'

To his surprise, Rosie reached out and rubbed his arm. 'Jacqueline's tough, Jesse.'

He was glad she hadn't told him his mother would be okay, but he wondered whether she was talking to herself as much as to him. She exhibited a natural warmth in the CEO panel, differentiating her from his father. His stomach twisted.

'I can't believe Richard's gone,' Rosie said. Jesse swallowed. His aunt was crying, and she reached for his hand. 'I'm so sorry.'

He sniffed. He didn't know what to say.

'Do you think I could see her?' Rosie asked.

'Yes, of course.' He bit his lip. 'I don't know the visitor policy, let me check.' He walked back out into the corridor and approached a nurse who was standing nearby checking her notes on a clipboard. 'Excuse me, would it be okay if my aunt joined me and my sister to visit my mother, Jacqueline Marcham?'

The nurse tilted her head. 'Technically, we're only meant to allow two visitors, but given the circumstances, I think that'll be fine.'

'Thank you,' he said. He collected Rosie and led his aunt through the corridors to the wardroom. Chloé was sitting on one of the chairs beside their mother's bed. She stood up as Jesse and Aunt Rosie approached, and the two women embraced before Rosie moved to Jacqueline's bedside.

Jesse saw Doctor Hathaway striding towards them. She slowed as she approached and introduced herself to Rosie before addressing Jesse and Chloé.

'I wanted to update you. We've decided that we should go ahead with the craniotomy. That operation will involve removing a part of her skull. We'd like you to sign a consent form, but in situations like this, we can decide on purely medical grounds.'

'Of course,' Jesse said. 'We'll sign whatever you need.'

'Thank you. We're going to move your mother to theatre now. You're welcome to wait in the family conference room.'

Jesse swallowed. 'How long will the surgery take?'

'Anywhere between three and five hours.'

Which sounded like a lifetime. Jesse nodded. His aunt's hand rested on his back. 'Come on, let's go. Thank you, Doctor.'

Jesse's thoughts drifted as he walked. His aunt was a reassuring presence, but he didn't know her well. Everything was crowding in on him. He'd become the senior family member, at least until their mother recovered—if she recovered.

Days ago, he'd been planning his bid for CEO of the company—but not like this. He'd never wanted anything like this.

———

'Hi, Daniel. I'm sorry; I know it's late, but I needed to talk to you.' Jesse took a deep breath. He'd come outside the hospital, hoping the air would help to clear his head.

'Is everything okay?' the lawyer asked.

Jesse ran through what had happened, his voice almost robotic.

'I'm sorry. I can't believe it. What have they said about Jacqueline?' Daniel asked.

Jesse swallowed the lump in his throat. 'She'll be lucky to make a full recovery.' His chest tightened. 'We'll find out more once she's out of surgery.' He looked around the car park. A lorry was trying to edge past some parked cars, and its warning alert was blaring. Jesse turned away from the noise and the belch of petrol from the exhaust. 'Chloé's here too. We're staying at the Royal Crown Hotel, just down the road from the hospital. Mum and Dad were on their way to the Lake District.'

'Do you know what happened?' Daniel asked.

Jesse sucked in another breath. 'The headlines, yes. Their

car was found upside down in a ditch by the side of a country road. They think Dad must have lost control. Another driver called 999 when he spotted their car while driving past. The police have appealed for witnesses, but no one has come forward.'

'I'm so sorry,' Daniel said again. 'Thank you for letting me know. I'll speak with the wider leadership team and handle things with the company.'

'Thanks.' Jesse said it without thinking. He cleared his throat. 'What happens to the votes?'

'Don't worry about the company, Jesse. You need to focus on your mum and Chloé.'

'I know, but I want to understand. It's important.'

There was a hesitation. Daniel was no doubt trying to understand why Jesse would care about the votes, now of all times. 'Well, I'd need to reread the trust deed, but from memory, because the current trustee can perform her duties, the four of you would become the trustees.'

'The four of us would have equal votes?'

'Yes, that's correct. But now isn't the time to be making any decisions.'

Jesse agreed, but he wasn't sure they would have that luxury. 'Daniel, I need you to promise me that you won't tell anyone what I'm about to tell you.'

The silence down the phone stretched. 'I'm afraid I can't promise you that.'

Jesse chewed his lip. He kept the phone against his ear whilst his other hand tapped against his leg. He wasn't surprised by what Daniel had said, but it made it harder for him to decide what to do.

'I need you to trust me, Daniel.'

'I do trust you,' he said, 'but I can't guarantee to keep a secret when I don't know what it is.'

'I understand,' Jesse said. He ran his thumb over his fingers. Over and over. 'Let me think about it. I should go back into the hospital.'

Jesse slipped his phone into his pocket. The police seemed convinced Richard had lost concentration, or perhaps some wildlife had startled him, and he'd veered off the road. But Jesse wasn't so sure. Even without the spectre of the Broker, he wouldn't have been convinced that it was an accident. He'd never known his father to lose concentration when driving. But given the Broker's threats, he had to believe there was a connection. And that meant he couldn't risk Daniel deciding to involve the police. Who knew what the Broker would do next?

He sighed and pulled his phone back out of his pocket. He'd chosen WhatsApp because he would be able to see not only whether his message to Grace had been delivered but also whether she'd read it. And he'd tried to keep it light.

Just wanted to check you were okay. Would be good to speak.

But he knew he was treading a fine line. He also knew before he'd sent it that he'd obsess over getting a response. Or, more accurately, not getting a response. He clicked on WhatsApp and swiped at the message he'd sent Grace.

Delivered 18:51

Read...

His message was unread. He sighed and went to put his phone away when it started to ring. He didn't recognise the number, and he hesitated before answering.

'Oh, Jesse, I'm so glad you answered. It's Elaine. I'm still at work and had my phone switched off.' It took him a second to connect the name with his aunt. 'I've only just picked up your message.' Her words were tumbling over one another. 'I can't believe Richard's gone. Such awful news. How's Jacqui doing?'

'She's in surgery. She was badly injured.' He almost choked on his words. It wasn't getting any easier with the retelling.

'So terrible. You must be so shocked. Is Chloé with you at the hospital?'

'Yes. Aunt Rosie is here, too.'

'Good, yes, that's good. I'd like to come up tomorrow.'

'Of course. We'll be here.'

'Okay. Well, I'm thinking of you all. Give my love to Chloé.'

'I will. Thanks, Elaine.'

He turned off his phone and walked back into the hospital.

———

THE SURGERY HAD GONE WELL. Jacqueline's brain would continue to swell for a few days, but removing the section of the skull should help her recover. Chloé had finally fallen asleep in a chair in the wardroom, and Rosie was sitting next to her, reading a book. Jesse stood beside his mother's bed. He wasn't sure precisely which tube was for which function - the ventilator, IV, and nutrition, but Jacqueline looked peaceful. The doctor had warned them that even if she made it through, she was unlikely to return to being the person she was before. And the road to recovery would be daunting. She may never walk or talk again, and the expected damage to her frontal lobe might result in her being moody and easily aggravated. Because half her skull was missing, she would have to be careful not to fall until her skull was patched up. The next few days would be critical. There was a risk of Jacqueline developing pneumonia, a common complication the longer she stayed on a ventilator. All they could do now was wait and hope for the best.

Jesse sat beside his aunt, who offered him a half smile. His phone buzzed, and he pulled it out of his trouser pocket. The message was from Grace.

I'm fine.

A little of the tension unwound from his shoulders. Grace was okay. Perhaps his parents' accident had been bad luck. Perhaps the Broker just wanted to shock and awe, counting on the abduction alone to coerce Jesse to do what they wanted. Jesse's eyes closed, and he blinked to keep himself awake. He reached over and gently shook his sister.

———

THE HOTEL WAS ONLY a short walk from the hospital. Jesse shut the door behind him and sat down on the bed. His body was ready for sleep. He lowered his head toward the covers and sniffed. The synthetic, clean molecules of Galaxolide filled his nostrils. He scrunched his nose. Even at the best of times, he'd not be able to sleep with his head resting on that pillow. He dug into his bag and pulled out a t-shirt, washed with a detergent on his approved list. He pulled off the hotel cover and slipped the pillow inside his t-shirt. Still dressed, he lay down on the bed and started at the ceiling, waiting for sleep to come.

FRIDAY 12 JULY 2024

23

MOOR PARK, PRESTON
3 PM

JESSE ARRIVED AT THE PARK. THE SUN WAS SHINING, AND THE air shimmered with the smell of freshly cut grass. He was skirting along the edge of a football field when he saw Aunt Rosie walking along the other side. He waved and started heading in her direction.

Rosie had wanted to talk and suggested meeting at Moor Park, just a few kilometres from the hotel. She was wearing a red summer dress dotted with white flowers to match her white trainers and sunglasses nestled on top of her head.

'It feels wrong,' she said as he approached her, 'being able to walk in the sunshine.' She didn't need to finish the sentence.

'I know.' The silence stretched into awkwardness. Jesse cleared his throat. 'Dad told me that you spoke recently.' He glanced at his aunt.

Rosie nodded as they started to walk together along the path. 'It was long overdue, really.'

'He didn't say much about it, but he seemed, I don't know, satisfied, I guess. It's like it gave him some clarity about the future.' Jesse hesitated, not sure whether to go into any detail. Rosie nodded but didn't immediately respond. 'Just before the accident, Mum and Dad made some decisions about the company.' He paused. 'House of Marcham.'

Rosie smiled. 'I know what you mean by the company, Jesse.'

'Yes, of course.'

'I found your pitch fascinating. It convinced me to vote for you.' She scratched her nose.

Jesse absorbed the words. His aunt, Isabelle's mother, had voted for him. He hadn't been able to call it that day. 'I don't know what to say.' He could feel her studying him. 'Thank you.'

Rosie shrugged. 'You have such a passion for the business, for perfume.'

'Well, I'm afraid it wasn't enough to get me over the line.'

'What?' Rosie frowned.

Jesse hesitated. 'You don't know?' He scratched his nose. 'Mum and Dad didn't appoint me. They decided to run a three-way process.'

'Three-way? Who's the third candidate?'

Jesse stopped walking. 'I'm sorry, I just assumed you knew.' He started walking again, keeping an eye on his aunt. 'The third candidate is Isabelle.'

Rosie blinked rapidly. 'Isabelle? Really?'

'Yes. They said they'd made a commitment to you, and they wanted to give her a chance.'

'Richard did mention helping where he could, but he wasn't specific. I had no idea he was thinking of something like that.'

Jesse tried to process what he'd just heard. Isabelle hadn't told her mother about being appointed as one of the company's deputy CEOs, and it sounded as though Richard hadn't told Rosie either.

'They also decided to put the company's shareholding in a trust for the next generation: Me, Chlo, Cam, and Belle.' He left the sentence hanging.

Rosie narrowed her lips. 'I'm stunned. I thought Richard might speak with someone in the industry to help Belle get her next job. I never expected him to do anything with the company.' She shook her head.

Jesse cleared his throat. 'The proportions haven't been agreed.' As he spoke, he wondered how it would work following the accident. Daniel had confirmed that the four of them would vote on any proposal to sell the company. Was it the same for any decision on the allocation?

'Even so, it's incredibly generous of your parents to include Belle.' Jesse forced himself not to agree and counted slowly to ten in his head. Rosie brushed her finger across her lips, her gaze on Jesse. 'Do you think they've done the wrong thing?' she asked.

Jesse shook his head. 'No.' He paused. 'Well, I don't know.'

'You don't sound very sure, Jesse.' There was a hint of a tease. 'Look, I'm sure your parents had their reasons. They built that company from nothing. Your father told me he was keen to try and rebuild the wider family. The shareholding must have been one of the ways he decided to go about it.'

Jesse shrugged. 'I just thought you might have a perspective. A different way of looking at things. People keep talking about the family notebook.' He didn't have to wait long for her reaction.

'Ah, the famous notebook,' Rosie said, half smiling. 'There's nothing contentious about that. If anything, it's a heart-warming story.' Rosie's blue eyes locked on to him.

Could she tell he was trying to evaluate what she knew about the notebook? 'I'm only guessing, Jesse, but I don't think their decision has anything to do with any notebook.'

'What makes you think that?'

She was quiet again momentarily as if she was weighing things up. 'When your father and I met recently, we discussed our relationship, what happened between us, not the business.' Jesse waited, sensing that his aunt would continue. She sighed before carrying on. 'I'm not sure this is the best time to be raking over the past.'

'It would help me. I can't ask my parents.' The words caught in his throat.

Rosie looked at him for a few seconds. 'Fair enough. Your father and I fell out over his marriage.'

Jesse blinked. 'His marriage?'

'I'm afraid so, yes. I had nothing against your mother as a person, but she was a Marcham.'

'And that was a problem?' Jesse didn't know where this was going.

'It's silly, really. I was only sixteen, and my parents still had a certain influence over me.' Jesse shook his head. He had no idea what his aunt was talking about. 'Our father hated the Marchams.' Rosie placed her sunglasses on her nose as they turned directly into the sun. A shirtless teenage lad walking the other way gave Rosie an appreciative glance up and down.

'Why?' Jesse asked.

'I don't know. I asked years ago. My parents simply told me that the Marchams were a nasty bunch.'

'And then Dad married a Marcham.' Jesse knew that his parents were third cousins, but he'd been blissfully unaware of the tension their marriage had provoked.

'Yes. It caused quite a stir. My parents didn't speak to Richard ever again.' She scratched her nose. 'I guess their reaction rubbed off on me. Even on his deathbed, my father was obsessed about it.'

'And you held it against my mum?'

'Oh no, not really.' Rosie brushed her cheek. 'I'm sorry, Jesse. I *really* think this isn't the best time.'

'I'd like you to continue,' he said. 'Please.'

Rosie paused for a moment before continuing. 'It was Richard I was angry with. For a long time, I felt he'd betrayed us.'

Jesse knew that his mother hadn't taken the Ford name from his father when she married, and perhaps that now made some sort of sense. Richard had gained a wife but lost a family.

'But you've come to terms with it now?' he asked.

Aunt Rosie didn't flinch. 'Yes, I have. It took a while. Stephen was quite hostile to Richard too, which didn't help.' She must have caught his frown. 'Stephen Lowe. My ex-husband.'

'Ah, yes, sorry.' He was quiet for a moment. 'Did Dad approach you?'

'Yes. He'd tried repeatedly over the years—when I got married and again after Isabelle was born. He sends her a card and a gift every year, you know, like clockwork.' Jesse twinged at his aunt's grimace. 'He tried again when I got divorced. Thankfully, despite me stonewalling him repeat-edly, he didn't stop trying, and finally, I thought it was time.'

A black spaniel came bounding towards them, and Rosie flinched. The dog circled them and then sped back towards its owner, and Jesse saw his aunt relax. She shook her head.

'I can't bear the thought that Richard's gone. I only just

got him back in my life.' She flicked a glance at him. 'I'm sorry, Jesse. That was thoughtless of me.'

'It's okay,' Jesse said.

It was strange to hear the family history from his aunt. His father was a private man, and he hadn't heard any of this before. There was perhaps a hint, here and there, that the relationship was strained, but certainly never any family manifesto. He glanced at his watch. 'I think I'm going to head back to the hospital,' he said.

Rosie nodded. 'Okay. I'm going to stay here a little longer, but I'll see you and Chloé later.'

She stepped forward, and they hugged. He'd lost so much, but perhaps it could at least be the springboard to a better relationship with his wider family.

Jesse cut across the football pitch, heading towards the park gates. The short stroll into the past had kept his mind off his parents' accident. He'd felt a sense of pride at hearing about his parents marrying despite the family pressure against them. He tried to imagine what that would have been like, not just in the moment but to live with the consequences. He'd been surprised to learn that his father had persisted with birthday presents for his niece, but the shock wasn't so much at his father's actions, more that Jesse had been totally unaware of it.

24

ROYAL PRESTON HOSPITAL, PRESTON

5 PM

Jesse was waiting for Aunt Elaine in the car park. The last time he'd seen her was on the CEO interview panel.

She didn't speak as she hugged him and rubbed his back, but she looked pale and drawn. After a few seconds, she released him and took a step back. He'd always liked Elaine but knew she'd had a difficult life—widowed and then divorced. She had experience in coping with shocks and living with the pain.

'It's so awful,' Elaine said, dark hollows under her eyes. 'I'm so sorry about your father.' He didn't have any answers, so he simply nodded. 'And Jacqueline...' She shook her head. 'How are you holding up?' she asked as they started to walk through the car park.

He shrugged. 'I'm not sure I am. I don't feel as though I've been able to grieve for Dad.' He stopped and took a deep breath. 'We've spent most of the time sitting with Mum.'

'That's understandable. Is there any change in her condition?'

Jesse led the way towards the hospital. 'Not really. Shall

we go to the family room? We can talk properly there.' Elaine walked with him in silence until they arrived at the room. Elaine exchanged hugs with Chloé and introduced herself to Rosie before sitting down.

'I'll get us all a cup of tea,' Rosie said, standing up and moving towards the door.

He looked at Elaine. 'I'll take you through to see Mum if you want.'

'Thank you.' She didn't move. 'Before I do, I wondered whether I could speak with you both in confidence?' Jesse and Chloé exchanged a glance and nodded. 'I feel terrible raising this at such a difficult time for you, but the truth is, I'm very worried about Cameron. He's not been himself these last few days, and I wondered whether you knew what might be going on.'

Jesse frowned. He hadn't been expecting that. 'I saw him yesterday morning. I was leaving his place when I got the call about Mum and Dad.' Elaine bowed her head. He was juggling the impossible. His emotions were scrambled, and he was attempting to smooth out Cameron's relationship with his mother. 'His company has some cashflow problems, but he's working them out. I think he'll be okay.'

Elaine clasped her hands together as she continued. 'I know he spoke with your parents. I saw him immediately afterwards, and he was upset—angry, even.' She was stumbling over her words. 'I'm sorry, this is inappropriate...'

'You're worried about him. That's understandable,' Chloé said. 'I'm sure he's okay. Did you know that Mum and Dad included him as one of the beneficiaries of their family trust?' Elaine stared at Chloé, her mouth opening and closing, but unable to speak.

'I don't believe it.' Elaine started to cry. 'Jacqueline said they had something in mind, but I'd no idea.' She sniffed and shook her head. 'I can't...' She gulped and tried again. 'I can't...' And then she gave up trying to speak.

Jesse glanced at Chloé, who shrugged. He walked over and put an arm around his aunt's shoulder. 'I think Cam's going to be okay, Aunt Elaine. He'll be fine.' It was odd. On some level, he'd expected his aunt to be there to comfort them. This was a total about-turn.

'Thanks.' She smiled at him through her tears. 'I'm sorry. Just give me a minute to compose myself. I really would like to see your mother.'

———

Rosie returned with the teas, but after one glance at Elaine, she said she was returning to the hotel, allowing the others more time together. Jesse led Elaine through the ward to the room where his mother was lying in bed. Her eyes were bloodshot, but she'd stopped crying.

'I think your parents would be very proud of you for taking over the company. You know that, don't you?'

He grimaced. He knew she was trying to say the right thing. 'They didn't appoint me as CEO.'

Elaine stared at him. She shook her head. 'I don't understand what you mean.'

He kept his gaze on his mother. 'They decided I wasn't ready.'

'Oh, gosh. I'm sorry. When we left the room, the vote was two to one in your favour. I just assumed ... I've put my foot in it. I'm sorry, Jesse.'

Jesse let that sink in. 'You and Rosie left the room?'

'And Kath. The three of us voted first.'

He nodded, as time seemed to stretch. Rosie had voted for him, and Kath was in his corner. He must have read Elaine totally wrong; he'd been sure he'd had her on side. His stomach twisted as he realised that notwithstanding the support of Kath and Rosie, his parents hadn't been able to back him. He blew out a breath.

'I guess my vote didn't count for much in the end, but perhaps that's as it should be.'

He stared at her. 'You voted for me?'

'Yes, of course I did.' Confusion clouded her eyes.

'But you said the vote was two to one?'

'That's right.' She held up her hand to cover her mouth. 'I've said something else wrong, haven't I? I'm sorry. I shouldn't have told you that.'

'No, it's fine.' He closed his eyes for a few seconds. 'It doesn't matter. It was Mum and Dad's decision ultimately.'

His mother's chest continued to rise and fall, but it was impossible to tell how much of the movement was due to her and how much was the machines. Jesse's breathing was synchronising with his mother. Thoughts crowded into his head, but he couldn't think clearly.

'Excuse me, I need to get some air,' he said. Then he walked out of the room, leaving his aunt beside his mother's bed.

SATURDAY 13 JULY 2024

25

HOTEL, PRESTON

7:45 AM

JESSE HAD SLEPT FITFULLY, THE HUM OF THE AIR CONDITIONING
the price to pay for the coolness of the room. Every time he'd
stirred, there'd been a period of no more than a few seconds
when his mind had forgotten the horrors of his parents' accident. And then it would kick in, like the sharp jab of a
migraine.

The hospital had promised to call him with any updates
on their mother, and so he'd left his phone on overnight.
There'd been no calls, which was good news. He pushed
himself up and tapped his feet on the carpeted floor. His face
was stretched, and he blinked several times to get his eyes to
focus.

He typed in the name of Aunt Rosie's ex-husband into the
search bar and spent the next few minutes reading about the
highs and lows of Stephen Lowe's life. He'd worked as an
investment banker. He left to set up a hedge fund and retired
when he was only thirty-four, which was when all the marital
trouble started. Too much time, too much money. Drinking.
Gambling. Everything in life became a trade. He played his

hand one too many times with Aunt Rosie, but she beat the odds and sent him packing. Their divorce crawled through the courts, with enough cash and bitterness to grab the attention of the media.

The sound of feet padding down the hallway outside his room snapped him away from his thoughts. There was a knock on the door.

'Jesse?'

He put his phone down and walked over to open the door. Chloé's eyes were red, and her hair was still damp from the shower. She hugged him, and Jesse kissed the top of her head. She shuffled into the room and rolled onto his bed.

'Are you ready to go back to the hospital?' she asked.

Jesse nodded. 'I think I might go home tomorrow, just for a day or two. Mum could be in a coma for weeks, and we need to start sorting things out. Dad's estate. The company.'

'I know.' Chloé brushed her hair away from her face. 'I don't like the idea of being so far away from Mum.'

'Me neither,' he said. 'You could stay. I'm planning to meet with Daniel at his office on Monday morning. You could call in from here.' He had baulked about going into the House of Marcham offices. He had no real idea how he would get through all of this. He didn't know what the hell he was meant to do. One step at a time was the usual advice. So, he just had to get to the meeting with Daniel, and after that, he would have to decide on the next step and work towards that.

'Maybe. Larry's coming over tomorrow afternoon. His flight gets in tomorrow morning.'

'Good,' he said. 'Is he coming here or to your flat?'

'Here.' She closed her eyes and let out a deep sigh. 'It's so hard to believe that just a few days ago, we were thinking about the CEO succession, and now this. I can't get my head around it. What are we going to do?'

Jesse lowered himself onto the stool next to the desk. He knew Chloé meant what should they do about everything, but it was easiest to focus on the company. 'I suggest we wait and see what Daniel says. It's going to take time to adjust to everything.'

'Do you think he'll appoint an interim CEO?'

He wondered about her motivation for asking that question. She'd always been ambitious, but this was different. He didn't think that she was seeking his validation. She was genuinely wondering what would happen.

'I imagine he'll have to.'

Chloé nodded, but her head barely moved. 'Will there be anyone else at the meeting with Daniel?' She didn't name anyone, but she didn't need to.

'No,' he replied. 'It will just be the two of us.'

Chloé sniffed. 'Good.'

26

ROYAL PRESTON HOSPITAL, PRESTON

12 PM

THE FOUR OF THEM WERE IN THE FAMILY CONFERENCE ROOM. The sandwiches and crisps from the hospital café remained untouched on the table in the middle.

'How are you doing, Jesse?' Aunt Rosie placed her book on the seat next to her.

'I feel so useless,' he said.

Chloé lifted her head. 'The doctors sounded more hopeful this morning.'

The prognosis had been better than Jesse had expected, but they'd also been told not to get ahead of themselves. It would still be a long haul. He turned to face his aunts.

'I'm going back to London for a couple of days. At least I can start to sort some things out,' he said.

Rosie tucked a strand of hair behind her ear. 'That might do you some good. It helps to stay busy,' she said.

'We'll keep you posted on your mother,' Elaine added.

Jesse walked over to examine the sandwich selection. There was a knock on the door, and a nurse popped her head into the room.

'Mr Marcham, the police are here. They'd like to talk to you.'

His heart rate spiked. 'The police?'

'Yes, Constable Rowbotham, the family liaison office.'

He nodded. 'Yes, thank you. I'll come now.' He followed the nurse down the corridor towards the reception area. The nurse indicated the middle-aged man standing at the desk, chatting to the receptionist.

'Mr Marcham?' The man had a Scottish accent. 'Constable Rowbotham.' He held out his hand.

'Yes, hello. Please, call me Jesse.' The handshake was firm and brief.

'Thank you. I wondered whether we could have a chat?' He looked at the nurse expectantly.

'There's a room just around the corner,' she pointed behind the reception desk. 'You're welcome to use that for a few minutes.'

'Perfect,' said the police officer. 'If that's okay with you, Jesse?'

'Sure.'

A few minutes later, Constable Rowbotham shut the door behind them.

'What's this about, Constable?'

'I wanted to update you on the investigation into the crash.' He flicked open a notebook and turned over a couple of pages.

'I didn't think there was much to say?' Jesse studied the man for some clue as to what was going on.

'We've had some new information.' He cleared his throat, and Jesse's heart rate kicked up. 'Another driver reported seeing a car being driven aggressively behind your parents' car. It was a few miles before the site of the accident, and it may not be connected, but we're trying to track down the second car's driver.'

'You haven't found them yet?'

'No, I'm afraid not. We're studying CCTV footage from nearby cameras to see if we can identify the second vehicle.' The police officer tapped his pencil on his notebook.

'What are you saying, Constable? It might not have been an accident?'

'Well, I don't want to get ahead of myself, but there might be more to it. I take it that your parents weren't travelling in convoy?'

'No. As far as I know, it was just the two of them. They normally have a driver for business, but Dad likes driving. And they wanted a few days' holiday in the Lake District.' He was about to explain his mother's cancer diagnosis, but something made him hold back.

The Constable must have picked up on his hesitation. 'Was there something else?'

'No.'

'You're sure?' He waited with his pencil poised above his notebook.

'Can I tell you something in confidence, Constable?' Jesse asked. He waited for a nod before continuing. 'My mum had just been diagnosed with cancer.'

'That day?' The police officer raised his eyebrows.

'On Monday. My parents told us the news on the same day. We met with them on Wednesday afternoon, and after that, they left for a short break. I assume they would've stopped somewhere overnight, but I'm sure they were alone.'

'Do you know where they stayed on Wednesday night?'

Jesse shook his head. 'No, sorry.'

'And, you said that you *met* with them on Wednesday. I'm

sorry if I've got the wrong end of the stick, but that sounds formal. Was there something in particular that you discussed?'

He shuffled on the spot, and his shoulders tightened. 'You may already know that my parents are the founders of a company. We had a meeting about the company.'

The police officer scribbled in his notebook. 'I just want to get the best understanding of your father's state of mind. Whether he was preoccupied or distracted.'

'I understand,' Jesse said. The meeting was just family business stuff. I don't think there was anything that would have affected his driving.' The officer nodded, but he frowned.

'I have one more question. CCTV shows that your parents headed south before heading up to the Lakes. We think they drove round the M25, coming off at junction four, to Orpington.' Jesse blinked. That made no sense to him. 'Do you have any idea where they would have been going?'

'No.' He shook his head. 'I've no idea at all.' He balled his hands.

'Maybe they said something? Mentioned a stop off?'

'No. They just said they were going to the Lakes.' His mind was spinning. Where could his parents have gone? He was as confused as the police officer.

'You're quite sure?'

Jesse sensed that Constable Rowbotham believed him, but he was persistent. As much for his benefit as the officer's, Jesse paused to think back to the meeting. Could there be a connection with his mother's cryptic sermon? What had she said? *The trust is your guardian.* But his mother was the trustee, and the only other person who knew about the trust was Daniel, who lived in central London. He had a sudden thought.

'Hold on. I'd forgotten. We have a factory near Orpington, but I've no idea why they would've visited it.' He frowned. 'If that is where they went, I should be able to find out.'

Constable Rowbotham flicked his notebook closed. 'Okay, then. Thanks for your time. I'll let you know if we track down the second vehicle.' He fixed Jesse with a stare. 'And you'll let me know if you find out where your parents went before the Lakes?'

Jesse nodded. 'I will.'

'Thanks. I hope your mother makes a full recovery.'

Jesse stayed in the room by himself for a few minutes. As far as he knew, neither of his parents had been to the factory for months, and he couldn't think of any reason they would travel there together. He emailed his dad's secretary, asking her to confirm whether a trip had been arranged for Wednesday evening. He'd ask Chloé and his aunts, too. Maybe there was some connection that he'd overlooked, but it had to be something important for them to drive to the opposite side of London before heading North on holiday.

His body felt heavy, and his mind was stuck in first gear. Whatever was going on made no sense to him. He sighed and closed his eyes.

SUNDAY 14 JULY 2024

27

HOTEL, PRESTON

8 AM

JESSE STEPPED OUT OF THE SHOWER, TOWELLED HIMSELF DRY, and quickly got dressed. He poured himself a glass of water, gulped it down, and refilled the glass. He paused, considering calling his sister before deciding against it. He'd let her sleep.

There was a buzz as his phone received a new message. He squinted at the screen. An unknown number. Holding his breath, he clicked to read the text.

> I have Grace.
>
> You will receive a formal offer for the company today.
>
> Make sure the offer is accepted if you want her back alive.

Adrenaline surged through him, and his hands started to shake. He dialled Grace's number and listened to the rings.

One. Two.

Then it stopped.

'Grace?' There was no answer, and Jesse strained to

listen for any sign that she might be on the other end of the line. 'Grace? Is that you?' He could hear the strain in his voice.

'It's not Grace.' Jesse's heart thumped against his chest. It was the Broker's distorted voice. 'She will be released once the sale completes.'

'Jesus. No, I can't do that. It's not possible. Just let her—'

There was a click, and the call disconnected. He hit the redial button and waited. This time, the phone rang seven times before diverting to an automated message service.

The person you have called is unavailable right now.

Jesse slammed his phone on the table. He closed his eyes, muttering under his breath. Conflicting options tore at him.

The Broker had Grace. He'd threatened he would, and now he'd made his move.

He massaged his forehead. 'Think. Come on, think,' he said to himself. It was possible the Broker only had Grace's phone. He typed a reply to the Broker's message.

> How do I know you don't only have her phone?

He hit send and scratched his head. Grace used an iPhone and a work-issued iPad. Maybe that could tell him where she was, or at least where her phone was. He called the hotel reception.

'This is Jesse Marcham, Room 219. I need a helicopter to London.'

'I'll see what I can do, sir.'

'It's urgent. Thank you.'

He picked up his phone and called the number for House of Marcham security. As soon as the line connected, he started speaking. 'This is Jesse Marcham. Who's this?'

'Hello, boss. It's Ben.' There was a pause. 'I'm really sorry to hear about your parents. How's Jacqueline doing?'

'Thanks, Ben. There's no real change, but the doctors are reasonably positive that she'll make some sort of recovery.' He took a deep breath and switched the subject. 'Look, I need your help with something.'

'Of course, boss. What is it?'

'Grace Nelson. I need access to her iPad.'

He could almost hear Ben frowning. 'I don't understand, boss.'

Jesse weighed up the risks. He wouldn't mention the Broker, but he needed to find Grace. 'I was due to meet her yesterday and had to postpone. She hasn't been in contact, which is unlike her. I know we can access company mobile phones in emergencies, and I'm worried about her.'

'You think she's missing?' Ben asked.

'Yes.'

'But, it's the weekend.' Ben was treading carefully, no doubt mindful of who he was speaking to and the stress Jesse was under. 'Isn't it more likely she saw your message and thought she'd wait to talk to you on Monday? Especially with everything that's going on?'

For a second, he thought Ben was referring to Grace's kidnap before the realisation sunk in that he was referring to his parents' accident. 'Look, I don't want to be indiscreet, but she finished with her boyfriend last week. He got violent with her.' He sighed. 'I just need to find her.'

'Have you contacted the police?'

'No.' He swallowed. 'I will, but I don't think they'll do anything until it's been over twenty-four hours. I was hoping that the iPad could show us the location of her phone.'

'I don't know if—'

'I'll authorise it. I'll sign whatever you need.' Jesse didn't like abusing his position, but he had no choice.

Ben cleared his throat. 'Okay, boss. Email me the authorisation and I'll get right on it.'

'Thanks, Ben.'

Jesse ended the call and immediately sent the email. Then he picked up his key and walked out of the room. He checked out and climbed into the back of the taxi that was waiting to take him to the heliport.

The car pulled out into the traffic, and Jesse thought of his mother lying in the hospital bed. Chloé, Rosie, and Elaine would be at the hospital most of the day. Their mother wouldn't be alone.

But he had to get back to London. He needed to find Grace.

28

FLIGHT TO LONDON

9 AM

JESSE SAW BEN'S NAME FLASH UP ON HIS PHONE. 'ANY LUCK?' HE asked.

'No. Sorry, boss, I couldn't get any location details from her iPad or the phone company.' Jesse slumped back into the seat. 'I've checked her emails, too. There's nothing that helps. Does she have family?'

'No,' Jesse replied, the last Nelson comment echoing in his head. 'I'm on my way back to London. I'll head to her flat. Maybe someone has seen her.'

'Okay, boss. Let me know if there's anything else I can do.'

The Broker hadn't replied to Jesse's text, and Jesse couldn't relax until he found Grace. It would be at least another three hours before he reached her flat.

He stared out the window, looking down on the flow of traffic beneath tem. He was tired, and his eyes started to close. His phone ringing woke him up. He blinked his eyes open and forced his jaw to work.

'Hi, Daniel,' he said.

'I'm sorry to bother you. How's Jacqueline?'

'No real change. I'm on my way home.'

'Really? We can do our meeting on the phone,' Daniel said.

'It's not just that,' Jesse replied. 'There are other things I need to sort out. I'll head back up in a few days.' He swallowed. 'What can I do for you?'

'I know this is terrible timing, but we received an unsolicited offer to buy the company this morning.'

Whoever was behind the offer had sensed an opportunity —or created one. He shivered; his body wanted to shut down, to close everything off.

Make sure the offer is accepted if you want her back alive.

What the hell was he supposed to do? He took a couple of quick breaths.

Daniel cleared his throat. 'The offer lapses at six o'clock tomorrow evening. We can ask for an extension. Given the circumstances, I'm sure they'll agree.' His assumption was based on standard reasoning, but he didn't know the Broker was forcing Jesse to play by different rules.

'What are our options?'

'We could ignore it because you're not going to sell anyway, but technically, the trust deed requires that the Trustees formally consider any offer.' Daniel spoke as if he was delivering an apology.

'What would that involve?' Jesse stared out at the clouds.

'I'd send the details of the offer to the four of you, and we'd arrange a meeting, or a call, to have a formal vote,' Daniel said.

'A vote?' His stomach flipped.

'Yes. The deal can be rejected if two or more of you vote against it.'

If Cameron and Belle voted in favour, Jesse could force the sale.

The right circumstances.

And the Broker had Grace.

The right encouragement.

There it was. The guillotine would drop at six o'clock tomorrow.

He ran through it a couple more times, but there was only one conclusion. He would have to sell the family company unless he could find Grace in time.

'Okay. Please arrange the meeting.'

There was a pause before Daniel responded. 'Are you sure that's what you want?'

'I'm sure.'

Another pause. 'Very well. I'll circulate the offer and let the others know about the vote. The offer price is very low.'

'How low?'

'One hundred million pounds.'

Jesse blinked. 'Jesus,' he said, more to himself than to Daniel. Cameron had told him to expect a reduced offer, but he hadn't anticipated the price being halved. One hundred million was only a third of the company's own internal valuation.

'There's something else.' Jesse could hear Daniel tapping on his keyboard as he spoke. He closed his eyes. He was already at his limit. 'They've alleged that House of Marcham has done something wrong. The suggestion is that it's something your parents did when they set up the company. Something criminal.' Jesse froze. 'That's why they've halved the price. They've included a one hundred-million-pound liability in their valuation of the company, in effect, a restitution payment.'

Jesse shook his head. *Reparations* was the term that the Broker had used. Competing thoughts jostled for space in his brain. What claim could be worth as much as one hundred million pounds? His palms were sweaty, and his mouth was dry.

'Okay. Send the offer through, and I'll have a look. Do we know what this is all about?'

'No,' Daniel said. 'That's all they've disclosed for now, but I'll ask them for more details and see what they're prepared to tell us.'

Daniel's email arrived a second later, and Jesse plugged in his headphones to speak to Daniel while reading the details. A company called Scent Holdco Limited was making the offer.

'Do we know who owns the company?' he asked.

'Yes. It's complicated because they've used a Channel Islands company.' Jesse couldn't help but hear an echo of his sister's voice, referring to Jersey and Guernsey, as she always did in a fake French accent as the *Chanel Islands.* Daniel was still talking. 'Whoever set this up isn't keen on transparency, but we know the ultimate beneficial owner. Hold on. Here it is. David Crosby owns it. He lives in Jersey.'

The name didn't mean anything to Jesse. 'What do you know about him?'

'Only the headlines. He made a fortune in the drinks industry by selling his company to Diageo. Now he's a financial investor.'

Jesse typed the name into Google, and seconds later, he was looking at a picture of the man trying to buy his family's company. He didn't recognise him. He scrolled through the hits. It didn't make any sense that this man was the Broker.

Why would a successful businessman risk everything by resorting to extortion?

'Okay, well, at least we know who we're dealing with. I assume you're in contact with his lawyers?'

'Yes. Winslow Associates is an M&A specialist law firm. They sent the offer through on behalf of their client.'

'Okay.' He tapped his fingers on the seat of the car. 'I need to read this. Find out everything you can about this claim. I'll call you later.'

———

JESSE WAS in a taxi from the heliport. He was less than ten minutes away from Grace's flat when his phone buzzed. He glanced at the screen. It was an unknown number. There was no message, just an audio file. Jesse plugged in his headphones and hit the play button.

Jesse, it's Grace.

His stomach pitched at the sound of her voice. He was sure it was her, and he could hear strain in her every word.

I don't know what they want you to do. Jesse, I'm scared.

And then it stopped. The entire clip was only eight seconds long.

Eight seconds was all it took to convince him beyond any doubt it was real. Grace had been taken.

He stared at the message as if it might tell him something more: some clue as to where Grace was or some inspiration to get her back. Guilt started to scratch his stomach. She'd been taken, and she was in danger because of her relationship with him. He no longer doubted the Broker would carry through on his threat. If he didn't do what had been asked of him, she could be killed.

The taxi pulled into Grace's road, but there was no longer any point calling at her flat. She wasn't there, and he had no clue where she was. He shuffled forward on his seat and asked the taxi driver to drive him home. Then he called his sister.

'I've just spoken to the doctors,' Chloé said as soon as she answered the phone. 'There's no real change, but they still sound positive. Where are you?'

'I'm nearly home,' he said. 'Look, I know this is the last thing any of us want to think about right now, but we've received a formal offer for the company.'

'Jesus. From Cameron? Surely he wouldn't do that?'

'I'm guessing this is out of Cameron's hands. The guy behind it is called David Crosby. He's—'

'I know who David Crosby is.' There was a pause. 'But I'm surprised he's interested in us.'

'Why?' Jesse's arms were tingling.

'He's a veteran of the drinks industry,' she said.

'He seems to know more about our company than we do.' He could not shake the feeling that a secret had wormed its way out into the world, like a post on a blog published in a dark corner of the internet, which was starting to trend.

'What do you mean?'

He cleared his throat. 'He's halved the price because of a potential liability against the company.'

'Halved the price from two hundred?' Chloé paused as if searching for the right words. 'They're valuing this liability at a hundred million?'

'I don't know any more than that, but Daniel's trying to find out.' He sighed. 'I know the timing's terrible, but maybe we should have a meeting. Technically, the trust deed requires us to have one. The offer expires at six o'clock tomorrow.'

'Screw the trust deed,' Chloé said. 'Why are you even suggesting it? Surely, you don't think we should consider selling?' He didn't immediately answer, allowing her to fill the gap. 'You're joking, right? You'd actually sell the company. With Dad not even buried and Mum in a coma. And for way, way less than its real value.' Her voice was stone cold.

'God, calm down. I didn't say I'd vote to sell.'

'You didn't say you wouldn't,' she said.

Jesse's head spun, but he couldn't risk telling her the truth. 'I think we need to consider the offer once we have the details. There's a lot to take in. We need to understand this alleged liability, whether we sell or not.'

'Who's we?' she asked.

'Sorry?'

'You keep saying we. Daniel told us Mum had the vote. She can't vote. So who is we?'

Jesse bit his lip. 'Daniel says that the four of us have an equal vote. You, me, Cam, and Belle.'

'Sweet Jesus,' Chloé whispered. 'And it needs three votes to sell?'

'Yes.' The word caught in his throat. 'That's right.'

'If we're having a vote, I need to come back down. I'll discuss it with Larry when he gets here.'

The call ended abruptly, and Jesse slumped back against the seat. He pressed his fingers against his forehead, then slipped them into his hair to massage the top of his head. What the hell was he going to do?

Grace's words echoed in his head.

Jesse, I'm scared.

She hadn't implored him to do what they asked, yet, to

borrow Chloé's argument, she hadn't told him not to, either. He closed his eyes and tried to think, but every option led him to a decision he didn't want to make.

The taxi driver was talking to him.

Jesse opened his eyes. 'Sorry?'

The car was parked, and the driver turned round to repeat what he'd said. 'This is it.' His eyes narrowed. 'You alright mate?'

Jesse nodded and looked at the fare on the display. He paid by card and climbed out of the taxi.

29

JESSE'S HOUSE, WAPPING
11:30 AM

JESSE LET HIMSELF INTO HIS HOUSE AND TAPPED IN THE ALARM code. He closed the door and bolted it shut, slipping on the security chain. He rubbed his hands over his face before turning on the kitchen tap and waiting for the water to run cold. He cupped together his hands and dipped his face into the pool of water. He swept the water from his face and ran his fingers through his hair.

He froze. The Broker was pressuring him, so it would make sense that he'd do the same to Chloé. He would try to find some leverage, yet Chloé had sounded set against any sale.

Could it be that there wasn't any leverage? What if the worst thing that could happen to Chloé was selling the company, the very thing the Broker wanted her to do? She loved it all—the business, the brand, the kudos—she wore the perfume like a birthmark. Chloé loved it. Their parents had even *named* her after a perfume. Had the Broker focused on Jesse and Jesse alone because Chloé was unbreakable?

He needed a coffee. He was so tired he couldn't think

clearly. He switched on the machine and selected his current default espresso flavour. A few seconds later, as the smell of thyme and rosemary hit his nostrils, he turned his mind to the veiled accusations that had been made against his family. He tried to run through the chronology.

First, the blog was published by *Scent*. His hunch was that the Broker was behind the hit piece. The anonymous email came next. *When you know what I know, you will do the right thing.* And that had been rapidly followed by the protestor and his banner. *The Marchams must pay.* Then Cameron challenged them about a potential claim. Jacqueline had responded by telling Jesse and Chloé that the two of them had no idea at all what was going on. As it turned out, that was one hundred percent true.

What hadn't she told them? Everything that had happened had to relate to that secret. The prospective purchaser claimed there was an issue connected to the launch of the business, and their parents' recent behaviour suggested there was at least some truth behind the rumours, but Jesse was unable to ask them. Then there was the weirdest quote of them all. *The Trust is your guardian.* What could that even mean? He had no idea. And the hits kept on coming with the anonymous note delivered to Grace. *Why don't you ask your boyfriend about his family secret?*

The Broker seemed less fixated on any secret than on forcing the deal through. The reference to reparations had been the only hint that their actions were tied back to something in the past. Perhaps the note to Grace had been sent by someone else entirely—but who? Jesse buried his head in his hands and let out a deep sigh.

Hearing the coffee machine beep, he picked up the white espresso cup, filled it, and drank the shot in one. Then, he placed the empty cup back on the coffee machine. His legs trembled, and he rested his hand on the kitchen worktop. He stood for a minute, concentrating on breathing, trying hard to release the tension. After a few seconds, he regained a little control. The shaking passed, and his breathing became shallower. He needed to act. He plugged in his headphones and dialled Daniel's number.

'Hi, Jesse.'

'Have you received any more details on the company's liability?'

'Nothing yet, I'm afraid. Their lawyer said she needed to discuss it with her client, and she couldn't speak to him until tomorrow morning.'

Jesse sighed. 'Really? Crosby's given us a deadline of tomorrow evening, but he can't be interrupted on a weekend?'

'I'm sorry. There's nothing I can do to force them to release the information,' Daniel said. 'I don't—' The lawyer cut himself short.

'What is it?'

Daniel sighed. 'Look, I know it's not my place to say anything, but I can't understand why you'd consider a sale.'

Jesse remained silent for a while. He didn't blame Daniel for raising the point, but he also couldn't give him a satisfactory answer.

'Can we try asking them to extend the deadline so they can give us more time?' he asked.

'I can try, but I'm not hopeful.'

Jesse tapped his fingers against his palm. 'Let's try. I spoke to Chlo. She thought it was odd that Crosby would want to buy us.'

'I agree. It's a departure from his usual industry. It's still luxury consumables, though, so maybe he thinks he can use his drinks industry knowledge to redefine the perfume business, or maybe it's a diversification play?' Daniel sounded like he was trying hard to stay professional. 'It's an attractive asset, especially at the price they're suggesting.'

'How does he know about a material liability we're unaware of?'

'Good question,' Daniel said. 'I have no idea.'

Jesse switched to Google, took a screenshot of a photo of David Crosby, and sent it to Cameron with a message. *Do you know this guy?* He could hear Daniel's breathing down the phone. 'Alright. Thanks. Call me if you hear anything.'

Jesse ended the call, pushing away the guilt itching in his stomach. He found the anonymous email in his deleted items folder and reread it.

WHEN YOU KNOW WHAT I KNOW, YOU WILL DO THE RIGHT THING.

He typed out a reply.

If you have something to say to me, why don't you say it to my face rather than hide behind an anonymous email?

He chewed his lip as he read it back. Then he hit send. His phone buzzed immediately. Cameron had replied to his photograph of David Crosby.

Sorry mate. No idea who that is.

He stared at Crosby's picture. Why would Crosby be so invisible? He'd disclosed his ultimate ownership of the bidding company to House of Marcham's lawyers, yet he seemed entirely peripheral to the whole thing. He was missing something, or more accurately, someone. Someone who was using Crosby, someone who'd stop at nothing to get control of the company. He scratched his head and hit the button for his second espresso.

————

JESSE HAD TRIED to get hold of Chloé, but she hadn't answered. Maybe she was still cross after their call. Jesse massaged his neck and dialled Rosie's number.

'Hi, Rosie. I was wondering whether there was any update on Mum, and I can't reach Chloé.'

'Oh, hi. She's with one of the doctors at the moment.'

He could hear a man's voice in the background. 'Are they there now? Perhaps I could listen in?'

'They're not here,' she sounded confused.

'I heard voices. I thought it might be Chlo and the doctor.'

'That's Larry Blackwood, Chloé's boyfriend,' Rosie said. 'Would you like to speak with him?'

'Oh no, that's okay.' He didn't want to sound rude. 'We've not met properly yet.'

'Really?' Jesse could hear the surprise in his aunt's voice. 'I think you'll like him.'

'I'm sure.' He was glad Larry was there. They could all do with as much help as possible. 'Do you know if Chlo's coming back to London tomorrow?'

'She hasn't mentioned it to me. Hold on.' He could hear a muffled conversation, and then Rosie started talking again. 'Larry said they're leaving tonight or possibly very early tomorrow morning. Chloé's keen to attend a meeting. Is that what you wanted to know?'

'Yes, thanks.' He wasn't surprised. 'Perhaps you could let her know I called?'

'Of course I will.'

Jesse rubbed his neck. 'Can I ask a favour? If Chlo and I are both in London—'

'Don't worry. Elaine and I plan to stay here for at least a few more days. We'll let you know if your mother's condition changes.'

The tension released from his shoulders. 'That's great. Thanks, Rosie.'

MONDAY 15 JULY 2024

30

DANIEL'S LAW FIRM OFFICES, NEW BRIDGE STREET, LONDON

11 AM

JESSE AND CHLOÉ SAT AT THE TABLE WHILE DANIEL POURED them coffee. Chloé had, as expected, made the trip back to London. Jesse hadn't managed to sleep much, and his sister looked more drawn than he could ever remember seeing her.

'I can't imagine how you both must be feeling. It's so awful,' Daniel said. He straightened the knot of his tie.

'Thank you, Daniel,' Chloé said. 'The doctors think there's a chance that they might be able to bring Mum out of her coma sometime in the next couple of weeks.'

Daniel was nodding. 'That's great news.'

Chloé straightened up on her chair. 'I think we should push on with the company stuff. It might be good to have something to concentrate on besides Mum and Dad.'

'Yes, of course,' Daniel said, picking up a small stack of paper from the desk. 'We need to make an announcement, both internally and to the press. I've drafted something for you both to review.'

Jesse was grateful they had Daniel in their corner. He was a consummate professional and a good man. Jesse also appreciated that he'd said the draft statement was for their review rather than simply giving them a copy, having already published it. Jesse and Chloé each took the sheet of paper the lawyer offered them. He started to read.

Daniel Kane, Non-Executive Director, gave the following statement: Following the terrible news of the accident involving Jacqueline and Richard, the company has decided to make some interim appointments. The company is a family business, and I know it would be the founders' wish for the company and everyone connected with it to continue thriving. Their son, Jesse Marcham, 26, will take on the CEO role, and their daughter, Chloé Marcham, 21, will be appointed to the board. Daniel Kane will act as the Chairman. These appointments will be for an interim period. All our thoughts at this time are with Jacqueline, Jesse, Chloé and their wider family and friends.

The floor pitched under Jesse's feet. Had he read that correctly? He was being appointed as the CEO. He looked up to see Daniel staring at him.

'It looks fine to me,' Chloé said, which was as much of a shock as the announcement itself.

Jesse finally managed to find his voice. 'Really?'

'It isn't necessarily permanent,' Daniel said. 'We need to create some stability, and you've been at the firm a number of years; you're well-liked and respected.'

'I'm not sure,' he said. It was all he was focused on just over a week ago, but everything was different now. He tried to organise his thoughts. This wasn't the role to launch a new direction for the firm—this was an interim role to steady the ship.

'I'll do everything I can to support you,' Daniel said. 'I know Chloé will too. We can run it as a team, but I think announcing you as the interim CEO is the best message to the outside world and internally.'

'What do you think, Chlo?' Jesse asked instinctively.

His sister was already nodding her head. 'It should be you. I'm not the right choice.'

He frowned. 'Isn't there someone else? Someone within the company. Kath?' Her name slipped out before his brain had fully considered the idea.

'I've given it a great deal of thought,' Daniel said, 'and, of course, I'm willing to consider any suggestions you have, but I don't think Kath would be the right choice. Ideally, it would be one of you. I'll understand, though, if you don't want to, in the circumstances. It won't be easy.'

Jesse didn't say anything for a few seconds. It had surprised him, but he could see that it made some sense. 'Okay, I'll do it. But just for an interim period.' He swallowed. 'Obviously, we're hoping that Mum will be able to return.'

'Thank you,' Daniel said. 'I'll get that statement issued.'

'What's next?' Chloé asked.

A flicker of frustration crossed the lawyer's face. 'We need to decide whether to hold a meeting today to consider the offer. My request for an extension was rejected.'

Jesse shook his head. The purchaser was exerting maximum leverage, and Grace was still missing. He tipped his head back and let out a deep sigh.

'Do we need to hold a meeting?' Chloé asked.

'No.' Daniel drew out the word, looking between the two siblings, 'The deed only requires everyone to be notified of the offer. If you both plan to reject it, even if Belle and Cameron vote in favour, there's no majority. There'd be no need for a meeting.'

Chloé was looking at him. 'My brother wants us to consider it. He's the acting CEO now, so...' she trailed off.

Jesse blinked. What did that mean? He said nothing, but Daniel knew that he wanted the meeting to go ahead, even if he had no idea why.

Daniel stared at him as if willing him to change his mind. Eventually, he spoke. 'Okay. If you're both sure, I'll let Belle and Cameron know.' Jesse managed to nod, and Daniel clicked a button on his keyboard. 'I've invited you all to a meeting at 3:30 p.m.' He looked at Jesse. 'And I've sent the announcement to the company.'

Jesse's stomach pitched. His course wasn't yet irreversible, but he'd just taken a step towards the Broker.

————

DANIEL STOOD and buttoned his jacket. 'Right. Are you sure you want to go to the company office?'

Jesse stood at the window of Daniel's office and looked down at the road. Chloé was heading home for a few hours before returning for the meeting. She'd promised to check in with the hospital. He watched her blonde hair bobbing as she walked. She was holding hands with Larry. He looked a few inches taller than her, perhaps touching six feet, and had dark hair. Chloé needed someone other than her brother—someone who could help carry the weight rather than merely sympathise with the heaviness of the burden—exactly as Grace was for Jesse. Grace. He nearly gagged. Then he swallowed hard and turned to face Daniel.

'Yes, I'm sure,' he said.

'I can come with you,' the lawyer said.

He shook his head. 'I appreciate the offer, but I think I'd better do this alone,' he said.

There was a knock on the door, and Daniel's secretary walked in. Her hair was dyed fashionably silver-grey, and she wore a navy trouser suit twinned with the scent of damask rose, leather, and patchouli. *Firedance*, one of Jesse's all-time favourite perfumes, was designed to evoke the experience of smelling a rose in the garden to the explosion of fireworks.

'Daniel, I have India Starling from Winslow Associates on the line for you.'

The lawyer glanced at Jesse, who nodded. 'Put her through, please, Nicola.' He indicated to the chair that Jesse had just vacated. 'I'm guessing you'll want to hear this.' He clicked the speakerphone button, and a woman's voice filled the room.

'Hello Daniel, this is India from Winslow. I've spoken with my client and been authorised to share certain additional information with you.'

'Thank you, India. I'm all ears,' Daniel replied, raising his eyebrows at Jesse.

The cool voice cut through the room. 'We became aware of a potential claim against House of Marcham a few weeks ago. We've been in discussions with the claimant and believe the claim has merit.' India sounded sure of each word as if she was reading a script. Jesse edged forward on his seat.

'What's the basis of the claim?' Daniel asked.

'It's complex, and I'm afraid I'm not authorised to release any more details at this stage.'

Daniel reached over his desk and poured himself a glass of water. 'You appreciate that we can't evaluate your offer without understanding the liability?'

'I can tell you that my client has signed a binding agreement with the claimant.' India had ignored Daniel's point. 'My client will make a series of payments to the claimant. I can send you a redacted copy of that document, but I'm not authorised to share any additional documents or details at this time.'

'I look forward to reading it,' Daniel said.

'Okay, I've just emailed you the Reparation Agreement,' India said. Jesse's head jerked up. *Reparation.* The exact word used by the Broker. He caught Daniel frowning at him and tried to neutralise his expression. 'I hope you find it useful. Let me know if I can be of any more assistance.'

'It doesn't sound as though you're authorised to give me any more assistance, India.' Daniel's delivery was dry but not unfriendly.

There was a pause. 'We look forward to hearing from you before six o'clock today.' The line went dead.

The document was already printing and Daniel handed a copy to Jesse, taking the second one himself. Jesse scanned the first page, with sections redacted with solid black lines. Neither the name nor a single word of what the claim was for had been shared.

Daniel flicked through the pages. 'If the sale goes ahead, this contract automatically completes, and the Claimant will receive their payment. The amount is redacted.'

'I still don't understand how we could owe anyone one hundred million.' Jesse tried to think. 'Perhaps one of our rivals is alleging that we copied their perfume.'

'It's notoriously hard to protect a perfume's intellectual property,' Daniel said, picking up his glass and taking a sip of water. 'We didn't copy or reverse-engineer anyone else's fragrances, but even if we had, it's virtually impossible for us to be successfully sued.'

Jesse had grown up understanding the tension: to establish a claim that a competitor had stolen a trade secret, the owner would have to share detailed information about the secret they wanted to protect. That information would be shared with both the court and the very people they were trying to keep it secret from. Moreover, if the information was voluntarily disclosed, it was no longer a protectable trade secret—a classic catch twenty-two.

To make things worse, perfumes couldn't be patented, other than in specific circumstances such as protecting captive molecules, because it would require demonstrating that the scent had a use, a concept so mundane that it was the last thing any firm would wish to attribute to a luxury product. Perfume was *fabulously useless*, as the House of Marcham marketing team liked to say. All of which meant that product protection was a constant challenge.

Some houses had even turned to the blockchain to allow customers to authenticate their purchases directly. While the idea that customers could be sure they were buying the original was encouraging, it wasn't enough to stop anyone who wanted to buy the cheaper knock-off.

'In any event, no single perfume accounts for anywhere near half of the company's value,' Daniel said. '*Evocation* only accounts for just under ten percent of sales.'

Jesse dropped the document on the table. His eyes settled on the document's title. It couldn't be a coincidence that the word reparation had been used. He frowned as all the allegations swirled in his head.

'Are you okay?' Daniel asked.

He snapped back into the room. 'Yeah. It's a good point. This claim is bigger than any one perfume. It must be something central to the company.' He massaged his forehead. He didn't know what his parents had done, but none of it mattered.

There was only one relevant fact: The Broker had Grace.

Jesse had to vote to sell the company and persuade Cameron and Belle to vote with him.

He needed to betray his parents, and he couldn't even tell anyone why.

31

SHOE LANE, LONDON

12 PM

IT WAS ONLY A TEN-MINUTE WALK FROM DANIEL'S OFFICE TO House of Marcham's building, but Jesse couldn't remember a single step. He felt a certain level of detachment as he approached his firm's headquarters. He reminded himself that he was going into the building, not for his own sake but for everyone else who worked there. They would all have heard the news about Richard and Jacqueline; by now, they would have read Daniel's announcement. Jesse took a deep breath and stepped inside.

Everyone was lovely, from reception through security to everyone at the coffee bar, those eating in the canteen, people waiting for the lifts, walking the floors or in their offices. Some couldn't stop talking, sharing stories and anecdotes as freely as condolences; others communicated with nods, supportive smiles, and tears in their eyes. Some were expressive and tactile, others more reserved. Jesse appreciated every variation.

Once he'd finished his tour, he parked himself in Chloé's office because he couldn't bring himself to set foot in either of his parents' rooms. Jesse had scheduled a conference call with the department heads at Daniel's suggestion. He felt somewhat ashamed not to know some of them very well, but again, they were nothing but supportive and evidenced plenty of ability in the broader management ranks. It would have been easy for them to score points, to show their disappointment at being overlooked for the top job or a promotion, and there was no question Jesse was predisposed to spot any of that, but there were no signs of it at all. As the call was winding up, Jesse caught sight of his father's secretary, Mandy, hovering outside the office. He waved for her to enter the room.

'Thanks, everyone. I appreciate you all making the call at short notice, and I know you'll continue doing a great job. We're fortunate to have this team. I understand it's hard for us all, but let's keep going. That's what my parents would want.'

He ended the call and stood up to hug Mandy. Her eyes were blood-shot, and her make-up was slightly smudged. Jesse smiled as he smelled her *Distraction* scent.

'I'm so sorry, Jesse. I can't believe it. It's so awful,'

'Thanks, Mandy. Mum's doing better. We're hoping for good news in the next couple of weeks.' He saw her nod, but she didn't speak. 'Did you have any luck with the Orpington factory appointment?' So far, no one had an answer that explained his parents' trip.

Mandy cleared her throat. 'I checked, Jesse. There's no record of any meeting in any diaries. I spoke with security at the factory, too. Neither of your parents visited on Wednesday. The last visit was your father, nearly six months ago.'

She looked uncertain as to whether her answers were good news, and the truth was that Jesse didn't know either.

He caught a movement from outside the office. Kath Newman was waiting to see him.

'Thanks, Mandy.' He smiled, and she turned and walked out of the room, exchanging a hello with Kath as they passed.

'Hey,' Kath said.

Jesse indicated to a chair, then closed the office door before sitting opposite her.

'That was a good conference call,' she said. 'I think you struck just the right tone.'

Jesse nodded. 'Thank you.'

His thoughts drifted to his conversation with Elaine about the CEO vote. It didn't matter any longer, and he knew it shouldn't bother him, but it did. His aunts had voted for him, which meant Kath voted against him.

'How can I help?' he asked.

'I wanted to let you know I spoke again with my friend at Global Fragrances,' she said. 'She found out who attended that meeting.' He swallowed. 'The thing is, I'm not sure it's appropriate given everything that's happened.' She looked at Jesse. 'You're the new CEO. It's probably academic.'

'Acting CEO,' Jesse corrected. 'I think I should know. It's important to know who thinks what on some of these key strategic questions.'

'Maybe,' Kath said. She shuffled in her seat.

'Who was it?' Jesse asked.

For a second, he thought she wasn't going to tell him, but after closing her eyes momentarily, she spoke.

'It was Chloé.'

Jesse kept his expression fixed before trying to force a laugh. 'Of course it was,' he said. It had been an unusual period when Jesse and Chloé worked separately to prepare their case for becoming the new CEO, because they had shared less than they would normally. Chloé was entitled to explore different strategic options. Jesse had planned out a whole new direction, too. It just so happened that his plan didn't eliminate his sibling's role in the firm. Kath was looking at him.

'Chlo's always on manoeuvres.' He smiled, suddenly aware of how unnatural it felt.

'Perhaps it's better to know the truth,' she said.

Jesse knew she was talking about Chloé, but it triggered the thought of which way she had voted for the new CEO.

'Kath, I'm not sure how to say this. So I'm just going to ask.'

'Okay.'

'Did you vote against me for the CEO role?' he asked.

She said nothing, but she touched her fingertips together. Jesse swallowed. Maybe her silence was all the answer he needed.

'Now, that would be telling, wouldn't it,' she said, smiling.

'Okay.' Jesse wasn't sure how to interpret that.

Kath pushed the chair back and stood up. 'I'm late for another meeting. See you later, boss.'

32

HOUSE OF MARCHAM OFFICES, SHOE LANE, LONDON

3 PM

JESSE WALKED INTO THE MEETING ROOM TO SEE CAMERON, Belle, and Chloé already there. All of them avoided eye contact, but he wasn't surprised. He could taste the bile in his mouth as he imagined his parents watching over the meeting, listening to the words he would utter that would allow their company to slip from the grasp of their family.

Daniel was standing at the far end of the room next to the window.

'Hello, Jesse. Thanks for coming.' He paused as Jesse pulled out a chair and sat down. 'Well, I'll get straight to it. We find ourselves in a very unusual situation. Richard and Jacqueline have grown House of Marcham into a highly successful company.' He kept his gaze level. 'Following Jacqueline's decision to transfer the company shareholding to the *Evocation Trust* and the recent tragic accident, the four of you are now the trustees and have the right to vote on whether or not to accept an offer for the company.'

Cameron was staring hard at the floor, and Belle was focused on Daniel, who was walking around the room.

'How are the shares allocated?' Chloé asked.

'There's no change,' Daniel replied. 'Until the four of you agree on any allocation.'

Ordinarily, that would have been enough to trigger open warfare, but Jesse didn't have the stomach for that fight. Chloé seemed to accept the position with not much more than a nod.

Daniel continued speaking. 'The company was recently valued internally at more than one-quarter of a billion pounds. Today, as you are all aware, we received a formal offer to buy the company for one hundred million pounds. The bidder has asked for binding, irrevocable commitments to sell from you all.'

'I've read the document you sent me, Daniel. I don't understand the basis for their offer,' Belle said. 'I know it's still a huge number, but can you explain why it's so much lower than the internal valuation?'

'I'm here today, in my capacity as Chairman of the company, not as a lawyer,' Daniel said, 'but perhaps I can offer some thoughts.'

Chloé looked like a ghost of her usual self and had barely moved since Jesse had joined the meeting, but she found her voice whilst staring at Belle. 'Thanks, Daniel. Please go ahead.'

He nodded. 'I've been told that the purchaser has been negotiating with someone who has a claim against the company. If they succeed in buying the company, they will pay this person to drop their claim. Unfortunately, we have no details of the potential claim, so we can't easily evaluate it. Still, my guess is that any damages awarded by a court would be materially less than the provision made by the potential purchaser.'

'Which would mean this offer significantly undervalues the company,' Chloé said.

'But the purchaser isn't offering more?' Belle asked. 'Nor is anyone else. This is the only offer we have?'

'That's correct,' Daniel said. 'They've also made it clear this will be their only offer, and it lapses at six o'clock tonight.'

'Let me get this straight,' Belle said. 'I either agree and receive my share of one hundred million, or I refuse, and I'm left holding an unknown minority stake, with the company likely facing a protracted legal dispute.' She had the tone of a barrister summing up for the jury. 'A dispute which will no doubt be enthusiastically covered by the papers. A story that will lack the nuance to distinguish between those who were part of the company,' her gaze swept over Jesse and Chloé, 'and those who have been pulled into it, purely by bloodline.' It was good, Jesse had to admit. It sounded as though her lawyer had scripted it. But it was still good. 'What are the other options?'

Daniel cleared his throat. 'You don't sell. We run the CEO process once we've steadied the ship, and we fight any claim. Yes, it could take years, incur significant legal fees, and generate unfavourable media coverage. Still, on the other hand, your shareholding could be worth double or triple the value put on it by this deal.'

'Is there any other choice?' Belle asked. Jesse watched her closely. Her style wasn't aggressive. It was as if she was hoovering up the facts to make a dispassionate decision.

'You could liquidate,' Daniel replied.

'Liquidate?' Belle repeated with a frown.

'Shut everything down. Sell everything off,' Daniel said.

'Make everyone redundant,' Jesse added, 'lock up shop and go home.'

'But we get our share of the cash?' Belle asked.

Daniel nodded. 'Eventually, yes.'

Chloé started talking, but she still wasn't looking at Belle. 'The liquidation value would be considerably less than the current value of the company because the goodwill value will drain away. Any cash payout could be much lower than even this offer.'

'Okay, then.' Belle looked at each one of them in turn. 'Liquidation doesn't sound attractive. I vote in favour of accepting the offer.'

It wasn't surprising after what she'd just said. Jesse wasn't even sure he could blame her. She'd gone from being worth nothing to twenty-five million pounds over only a few days. He glanced at Chloé and frowned. He'd expected her fuse to spark, but she looked pale and listless.

'You are, of course, all free to vote how you want,' Daniel said, his voice disapproving. 'It's also up to you whether you wish to consider what Jacqueline and Richard might want if they could express an opinion. Legally, you're unfettered.' Daniel shrugged. 'As you know, the sale requires three votes in favour. If two or more of you were to vote against the deal, it would be rejected.'

Cameron coughed before speaking but still wouldn't meet Jesse's gaze. 'I vote in favour.'

Jesse had expected that, too, purely on the deal's merits, but it made even more sense if you knew that Cameron's business was about to go bust.

Chloé was shaking her head. She muttered something under her breath that he didn't catch. If her anger was simmering at Cameron and Belle, Jesse knew she would save her most extreme reaction for him voting in favour. He swallowed as an image of Grace floated into his mind. He still couldn't believe he had to vote to sell the company. He looked at his sister, who was staring at him, blinking. He didn't want to let her down, didn't want to sell out his parents. Be he had no choice. He couldn't risk anything happening to Grace.

'Noted, Cameron. Thank you,' Daniel said. 'Chloé, Jesse, if either of you votes in favour, we have a qualifying majority.'

Chloé cleared her throat to speak next. Jesse railed at the theatre of it. The way things had unfolded, it would all come down to him. Maybe he should have voted first. But ultimately, it made no difference. He just had to hope that Chloé and their mother could forgive him someday.

'I vote in favour,' Chloé said.

Jesse gulped in air as if he'd been sucker punched, and Cameron spun to face her. Even Isabelle's head jerked in Chloé's direction. Jesse tried to say something, but he couldn't form any words.

Daniel didn't move for a moment, but then he composed himself. 'So noted,' he said. 'In which case there is a qualifying vote in favour, and I will record in the minutes that the trustees have accepted the offer. I will communicate the decision to the potential purchaser.' He handed around a one-page document. His voice was monotone, as if he couldn't quite believe what he was witnessing. 'The three of you must review and sign this commitment letter.'

Chloé had signed her page and was out the door before Daniel had finished speaking.

Jesse's mind was still spinning. He couldn't believe Chloé's decision, but his anger was muted by the expression on her face when she shot him a glance. It wasn't the look of someone getting their way. It was the haunted expression of someone who'd betrayed someone, or everyone, she loved.

———

No one spoke until Belle signed her page and handed it to Daniel.

'So, we're done here?' she asked, standing up.

'There are some details we should run through,' the lawyer said.

'I'm happy to leave you and Jesse to sort those out,' Belle said.

Daniel nodded, and with that, she walked out of the room. Jesse noted the similarity between Chloé and Belle, one that, ironically, he was sure they would both emphatically reject.

He stayed sitting down, not sure he could stand. He'd watched his sister, rather than ascend to the throne, melt it down and sell it off. Chloé, the heaven-scent perfume princess. He'd expected her fire to turn on him, not to torch her lifelong dream. He scratched his chin.

Cameron's head was hanging; he wasn't bobbing and weaving with the joy of a newly crowned heavyweight of the business world. He offered his signed page to Daniel. 'I'm not a detail guy,' he said, looking at Jesse. A glance which seemed to say *I'm sorry*. He held out his hand towards the Chairman.

'I'll be in touch,' Daniel said as they shook hands. The door clicked shut, leaving Daniel and Jesse alone in the room.

'Jesus Christ,' Jesse said. 'Did that just happen? A company that took my parents years to build—sold just like that.' Even though he'd prepared himself to vote for the sale, the fact that the offer had been accepted and the company would no longer belong to their family seemed unreal. Daniel unbuttoned his jacket, sat down, and ran his hands through his hair. Jesse couldn't ever remember seeing him cowed before. 'I can't believe Chloé voted to sell,' Jesse said.

Chloé's life was eat, dab, sleep, repeat. Jesse knew there was only one reason she'd give up on that.

The Broker had got to Chloé, too.

Jesse thought breaking Chloé would be as challenging as getting perfume back into the bottle, but the Broker had found something—something that had smashed her apart. Could she have been told about the threat against Grace? Or Jesse? Or had there been a threat against Larry? That was possible, too. Jesse shook his head.

'No,' Daniel said. 'It's all hard to believe. You didn't even get to vote.'

He said it as a statement, but Jesse knew there was an invitation to tell him how he would've voted. Jesse didn't want to answer that right then. 'If no one changes their mind, the deal happens, whether I like it or not.'

'No one can change their mind. The three of them have signed, whether *we* like it or not,' Daniel echoed. Which at least made it clear what Daniel thought of the decision. 'It doesn't matter how, or even if, you vote.'

'So that's it. It's over,' Jesse said.

Daniel was tapping on his laptop keyboard. He peered over the top of the screen. 'No, that's not quite true,' he said.

Jesse jolted upright on the chair. 'I'm listening.' Adrenaline surged through his body. He tried to analyse his physical reaction. Was it excitement that there could be a way out, or fear that the deal wasn't yet done? 'There's only one way that the deal can be stopped now, but it's still out of your hands.' Daniel must have seen Jesse frown. 'When your mother created the trust, she added a specific provision—a protection that she hoped would mean that the right thing would be done if there was ever a sale of the company.'

The hairs on the back of Jesse's neck stood up. He tried to keep his heart rate down. 'What did she do?' he asked.

'She appointed a protector.' When Jesse looked blank, Daniel explained. 'A protector is someone who has the power to veto certain actions of the trustees.'

'I'm sorry, I don't understand.'

'For any sale to be approved it also requires the protector not to block the deal.'

'The protector can stop the deal?' Jesse asked.

He could hear his mother's words. *There are some decisions which it's not right to ask you to make alone. Try to remember that the Trust is your guardian.*

'Yes,' Daniel said. 'Exactly that.'

Jesse nodded. There was only one next question. He looked at Daniel, who shrugged.

'I don't know. She didn't tell me who the protector is.'

The lawyer pushed his chair back and reached for his briefcase. He rested it on the desk and spun the dials on the locks. He moved his thumbs sideways on the catch, and the lid sprung open. 'When we created the trust deed, Jacqueline gave me an envelope to open only if a deal was approved without her knowledge. I retrieved it from my firm's safe before coming over here.' He reached into his case and produced a white A4 envelope. It was sealed, but Jesse recognised his mother's writing on the front.

Re: The Evocation Trust.
Strictly private and confidential.

FAO of Daniel Kane.

Jesse's mouth was dry. Daniel removed a letter opener from his briefcase and scored the blade across the top of the envelope. He replaced the knife in his case and slid a piece of paper from the envelope onto the table. His eyes flicked up at Jesse as he picked up the letter. He cleared his throat.

'The Protector for the Evocation Trust, as referenced in the Evocation Trust Deed, is the youngest living descendant of Arthur Baxter, who has attained the age of twenty-one.' Jesse blinked. The name Arthur Baxter meant nothing to him, but his mind spun with possibilities. 'As of the date of this letter, I believe the Protector is Martin Baxter, of 81 Mountfield Close, Orpington.'

Jesse's eyes widened. The protector lived in Orpington— the last place that his parents had visited before their crash. A last discussion before they were forced off the road. He cleared his throat.

'This guy, Martin Baxter, can stop the deal?' he asked, but he already knew the answer.

'Yes. The deal completes automatically within forty-eight hours from when I send over these acceptances unless the protector exercises his veto.'

Two whole days until it was done. It wasn't over yet.

'What's it all about, Daniel? Why has my mother given Martin Baxter this power? Who is he?'

He'd been given one answer but had so many new questions.

Daniel sighed. 'I don't know. Your mother didn't tell me. I've never heard the name until just now.'

A thought struck Jesse. 'Do you think he could be the person making the claim?'

'It's possible,' Daniel replied. 'If your parents believed that Baxter had a valid claim against the company, they might have wanted to deal with it by giving him the power to influence a company sale, to right-size his entitlement.'

Jesse nodded. It made some sort of sense. 'Do you think Mum would have agreed to this deal?' Jesse asked, holding up his one-page contract.

'Not in a million years,' Daniel said immediately. 'I don't know what she was thinking when she included the protector veto, but for what it's worth, I think your mother would have negotiated directly with Martin.' Daniel scratched his head. 'I think that's how she intended this to work. At the very least, she would have tried to.'

Jesse ran his fingers over his mouth. The deal wouldn't finalise until Wednesday night, which meant Grace wouldn't be safe until then. A thought struck him. Perhaps he could get the Broker to release Grace before stopping the deal. He felt tightness in his chest as he pulled out his phone and typed a text to the Broker.

> The offer has been accepted. I've done what you asked. Release Grace now, or I'll go to the police.

He hit send and then looked at Daniel.

'Mum and Dad stopped in Orpington before they drove up to the Lakes,' Jesse said. 'The police tracked them on CCTV.'

Daniel looked at Jesse and blinked.

Jesse had made up his mind. 'I'm going to visit Martin Baxter,' he said.

33

ST MARY CRAY, ORPINGTON

7 PM

JESSE TOOK A DEEP BREATH AND KNOCKED ON THE DOOR AGAIN —still nothing. Martin Baxter could be out or asleep. Jesse turned around and looked along the street. There was no one in sight. He walked towards the front window and peered inside.

The room was sparsely furnished. There was a solitary photograph on the mantelpiece and no pictures on the walls. The sofa looked like it was seldom used, and a well-worn armchair was opposite the TV. The only remarkable object in the room was a saxophone leaning against the wall, cradled in the far corner. Jesse frowned. He could see two feet in the doorway to the room. Someone was lying on the floor, half in and half out of the room. His heart rate spiked. Jesus, was Baxter dead? The thought swamped his mind. What should he do? Should he leave? But what if Baxter was injured but alive; what if Jesse could help him?

A shout caused him to turn around. A middle-aged woman was walking down the driveway. 'Hey. What are you doing?' she asked, staring at him over the top of her glasses.

Jesse started to raise his hands. 'I was just...' There was no way he could leave now. He swallowed. 'I came round to speak with Mr Baxter. There was no answer, and I...' He stopped. 'I think we need to call the police.'

'The police?' the woman said. 'Why?'

Jesse was already pulling out his phone. 'He's lying on the floor. In there.' He pointed to the window of the front room. 'It doesn't look like he's moving.' The woman's eyes narrowed, and she shuffled over to look for herself. 'Police, please.' Jesse's mind was racing. He gave the address, but the rest of the call was a blur. He reminded himself that he'd never even met Martin. He sucked in a deep breath.

The woman knocked on the window and shouted. 'Marty. Can you hear me?'

A siren echoed from a few streets away. Jesse paced around, uncomfortable under the gaze of the neighbour. He'd have to explain his presence at Baxter's house. What was he going to say? A police car turned into the road, drove in their direction, and pulled up to the side of the road outside the house. Jesse didn't have long to make up his mind. A young male policeman climbed out of the car and walked up the drive. He looked Jesse in the eye. 'I'm Constable Hussain. Are you the man who made the 999 call?'

Jesse nodded. 'Jesse Marcham.' He pointed into the house. 'He's in there.'

'He looks dead as a doornail.' The woman pushed her glasses up her nose. 'I'm Hattie. I live over the road.'

'Okay. Wait here, please.'

Jesse heard a crackle, and the constable picked up his radio but couldn't hear what the policeman was saying. He took a couple of paces down the drive and wiped his hands over his face. He shouldn't have come. He shook his head as tears pooled in his eyes. Christ. How had he ended up here?

Constable Hussain had finished on the radio. He knocked on the window and shouted. But there was no response. 'Stand back, please, both of you.' And then, in one swift movement, he smashed the window, knocking out the loose glass. He climbed into the room.

'Jesus Christ.' The constable's outburst was involuntary and carried clearly to where Jesse was standing outside.

'What's going on?' Hattie asked, edging toward the window to get a better view. Hussain was back on his radio, this time keeping his voice low. But one thing was clear: Martin Baxter was dead.

There was a click from the front door, and Constable Hussain appeared. 'Both of you need to move down to the pavement. This is now a crime scene. My colleagues will be here soon. In the meantime, I'd like to ask Mr Marcham a few questions.'

'Yes, of course.' Jesse sniffed.

'He was snooping around.' Hattie was pointing at Jesse. 'I only came over 'cos I saw him looking in the window. I've never seen him before. He's not local.'

'Please, you can give a formal statement in due course. Let me speak with Mr Marcham first, Miss...'

'Brown. Harriet Brown. Everyone calls me Hattie.'

'Okay. Thank you. After I speak with Mr Marcham, perhaps I could come and speak with you. Do you live over the road?'

'Yeah. Number twenty-seven. The one with the blue door.'

'Thank you, Ms Brown. I will be over shortly.'

'Hattie,' she said, sauntering off, crossing the road just as another police car arrived.

Constable Hussain turned to Jesse. 'Wait here, please.' The officer walked over to the second police car. A man and a woman stepped out and spoke briefly to Hussain. It was clear from their collective demeanour that the woman was in charge. The new arrivals walked over to Jesse.

'Jesse Marcham, my name is Detective Constable Mayfield, and this is Detective Sergeant.' Mayfield was over six foot tall, and his black hair was cut short. Roberts was nearly as tall, but her hair was auburn and in a ponytail.

'Hello,' Jesse said.

'Mr Marcham, can you tell me what happened?' Mayfield continued. 'Why were you here, and what's your relationship with Mr Baxter?'

Jesse tried to compose himself. Martin Baxter had been murdered. Where to start? 'I came because I wanted to speak with Mr Baxter about a business matter.'

'At eight o'clock in the evening?'

'Well, it's a family issue, too.'

'You're related?' Detective Sergeant Roberts had been silently studying Jesse, her nose twitching as if trying to make up her mind about him.

'No. That's not what I mean. Sorry. Let me try again.' Roberts raised her eyebrows but said nothing. 'I've never met Martin Baxter before. Earlier today, I was given his name. He's involved in a transaction.' He hesitated. 'A sale of my family company. I wanted to talk with him.'

'Okay. So what happened?' asked Mayfield.

'Well, nothing. I came here and knocked on the door. There was no answer, so I looked through the window.'

'Why did you do that?' Mayfield's expression was neutral.

'I wondered whether he was asleep on the sofa or something.'

'Or something?' Roberts repeated.

Jesse bit his lip. 'And then, the neighbour, Hattie Brown, she came over. And I called 999.'

'Did you see or hear anyone else or anything suspicious on your way to the house or whilst you were on the doorstep?' Mayfield asked.

Jesse tried to think back. He couldn't remember seeing anyone on foot on his walk to Baxter's house—only cars on the roads. 'No, nothing that I can think of.'

Detective Sergeant Roberts nodded slowly. She glanced at Mayfield and then walked back to the car.

'Am I free to go?' Jesse asked.

'We'll need to arrange for you to come to the station to make a statement,' Mayfield said, 'and we'd like you to stay in contact, but for now, yes.'

'Of course. Thank you, Constable.'

'Please leave your details with Constable Hussain.'

Jesse walked down the drive, where Roberts was giving Hussain his instructions. 'Find out who's been assigned as a family liaison, and get me an ETA for forensics.'

'Yes, Ma'am.'

Jesse coughed. 'Detective Constable Mayfield asked me to leave my details,' he said, looking hopefully at Hussain. The Constable nodded and dutifully recorded Jesse's name, address, and telephone numbers in his notebook.

Detective Sergeant Roberts was still looking at Jesse. 'Your family business is House of Marcham, right?'

'Yes, that's correct.'

'And Martin Baxter is involved in the sale of your company?'

'Yes.' This time, Jesse's voice cracked as he spoke. 'I only found out about his involvement myself earlier today.'

Roberts stroked her chin, absorbing his answer. 'We'll be in touch, Mr Marcham. We're going to have some more questions for you.'

34

JESSE'S HOUSE, WAPPING, LONDON
9:30 PM

JESSE HANDED DANIEL THE CUP OF COFFEE AND SAT OPPOSITE him at the kitchen table. Daniel had sat silently while Jesse made the coffee and told him about Martin Baxter's death. He sipped his coffee.

'Are the police sure that your father was at the house?' Daniel asked.

Jesse grimaced. 'They seemed pretty confident. They'll link up with the police investigation into the accident. They have CCTV showing my parents' car in Orpington.'

'I probably shouldn't say this...'

Jesse looked at the lawyer. 'You have to say it now.'

Daniel sighed. 'Your mother was worried about your father's reaction. She was the one who made the deal. She instructed me to draft the changes. She was the sole trustee. She hand-wrote the letter with the details of the protector. It was all your mother's plan. She told your father about it when he returned from China, but he didn't take it well.'

Jesse was incredulous. 'You think my father killed Martin Baxter?'

'No,' Daniel said. 'But your father was a tough negotiator. I never knew him to back away from a conflict.'

Jesse shook his head. 'What are you saying?'

Daniel was quiet for a long time. 'There's something else I wanted to tell you about the deal.'

'You didn't answer my question.'

'I don't know what to say. I didn't like that your mother didn't tell me what was going on. She asked me to prepare those documents in a vacuum. Now, a man's dead. None of it looks good.'

Jesse pushed his chair back and walked over to look out the window. It was pitch black outside.

'What did you want to tell me about the deal?'

He could see Daniel's reflection in the glass. It had been a long day, a long few days. Daniel was still immaculately dressed, his top button fastened with a Windsor knot in his tie.

'I found out today that Scent Holdco has a buyer lined up.'

'What?' He turned around and returned to the table.

'The purchaser, Scent Holdco, David Crosby—whatever you want to call them—is going to buy House of Marcham and immediately sell it to another buyer.'

'Why would they do that?' He rested his hands on the back of the chair before him.

'I imagine it was always their intention. They'll make a nice profit on the quick flip.'

Jesse let the thought settle. 'How do you know?' he asked.

'India Starling explained to me that the second buyer is insisting on certain conditions. Some of those conditions require Scent Holdco to take certain steps.'

'Such as?'

'She will only tell us immediately before completion,' Daniel said.

Jesse nodded. He hadn't expected anything else. 'Who's the second buyer?'

'She said their name by accident. I think it was SHLB. When I asked her to confirm the name, she refused. It doesn't change anything in some ways, but I thought you'd want to know.' Daniel stood up and checked his watch. 'I need to go. Unless there's anything else?'

'No. Thanks, Daniel,' Jesse said, following him to the front door. 'I'll speak to you tomorrow.'

———

JESSE WALKED to his study and pulled his laptop in front of him. He logged in to the Companies House website and searched SHLB. After a few minutes of scrolling through companies without finding anything helpful, he wondered whether Daniel had the order of the letters wrong. Perhaps the L stood for Limited. He tried searching on SHBL.

This time, the first company listed was SHBL Scent Limited. The registered office meant nothing to him. He clicked on the third tab and headed up to *People*.

1 officer:

Name: STYLES, Brandon

Correspondence address: 12 King Martin Road, Notting Hill, London, United Kingdom, W11 7AE

He didn't know anyone by that name. There was a sub-tab on the webpage.

Persons with significant control.

He selected it and waited for it to load. He read the information and then stared at the screen. The company that would ultimately own House of Marcham was controlled by one of the last people on earth he had anticipated being the owner.

1 active person with significant control: Isabelle Diane Lowe

Correspondence address: 12 King Martin Road, Notting Hill, London, United Kingdom, W11 7AE

Nature of control:

Ownership of shares – 75% or more

Ownership of voting rights - 75% or more

Right to appoint and remove directors

If it was correct, then Belle was buying House of Marcham, yet Belle hadn't so much as mentioned it.

He didn't think that Belle would recognise his mobile number, which meant she might at least answer his call; whether he would get beyond that was another matter entirely. He found her mobile number on the Global Fragrances website.

'Isabelle Lowe.'

'It's Jesse. Don't hang up, Belle. I have some questions for you.' He had decided on the direct approach.

There was a pause. 'I'm fine, thanks. How are you?'

He counted silently to five. Why couldn't she be more like her mother? 'You need to explain yourself?'

'Explain myself? What are you talking about?'

'You control a company that's planning to buy House of Marcham.' He said it as an accusation because that's what it was.

'What are you talking about?'

'Companies House shows you own more than seventy-five percent of a company called SHBL Scent Limited.' He stared at the screen as he said it. 'I'm looking at the statement now.'

'I've never heard of it,' she said. 'What's it got to do with House of Marcham.'

He wanted to believe her, but he didn't know whether he could. He ignored her question. 'Does the name Brandon Styles mean anything to you?' he asked. There had to be some connection between Belle and this company.

'No, nothing. Why?'

'He's named as the director.'

There was a pause. 'Why would someone I don't know set up a company I've never heard of with me as the shareholder?' Belle said. 'Jesus Christ. Why can't people leave me alone?'

'You're seriously telling me you know nothing about this,' Jesse asked.

'Nothing at all,' she said.

'You'd better be telling the truth, Belle,' Jesse said.

'I understand you won't believe me, but it's true.' She sounded authentic, but he didn't know her well enough to know how good an actress she was. 'It's late. I'm sorry you don't believe me.' She hung up.

Jesse sat tapping his fingers on his leg. His gut told him to trust Belle; logic told him the opposite. But Daniel was right —who ended up owning the company was a secondary issue. His family not owning it was the primary concern.

His thoughts turned to Grace—where she was and how she was being treated. He hadn't heard anything from the Broker since Daniel had sent over the signed pages, meaning that the forty-eight-hour window had pushed Grace's release back to six o'clock the following evening—a day and a half that would stretch for eternity.

His plan of getting Grace back before stopping the deal had evaporated. Martin Baxter was a literal dead end, and

Jacqueline was still in a coma, which meant he was no closer to understanding why she had made Baxter the protector. He sighed. It didn't matter; without the protector, there was no way to stop the deal. All he could hope for was Grace's safe return.

How had he allowed her to be drawn into this? How had he allowed her to be in danger? He raked his hands through his hair and rocked backwards and forward. He couldn't wait for Grace to be released—he had to find her.

He worked through the risk of the Broker learning that Jesse was looking for her. The deal had been signed—the Broker had what he wanted. If he'd always planned to release Grace, he would release her now. If he had never intended, she might already be dead. Jesse shuddered.

His phone beeped, and he snatched it up from the table. The Broker had replied.

She will be released on Wednesday at 6 pm.

Nearly two days that would stretch for eternity.

Jesse scratched his chin. The timing wasn't a coincidence. The Broker knew about the protector and the window for the sale to be vetoed. But why was he still worried about the veto if the Broker had killed Martin Baxter? He typed his reply.

Release her now.

There was no immediate response, so he sent another message.

How do I know she's still alive?

He rubbed his forehead and considered where the Broker would have taken Grace. It was unlikely he would have kept her in his own home. She would likely be able to identify the location after they released her. It was much more likely she'd been taken somewhere else. The same hangar where the Broker had taken him was a possibility, but the best hope was the address of Brandon Styles, the director of the company controlled by Belle. He'd start there and then try the hangar. He didn't have a plan beyond that, but at least he'd be doing something.

He stood up, ready to go, before forcing himself to slow down. He couldn't risk going alone, and he wasn't going to talk to the police about Grace because he believed the Broker's threat to kill her if he found out. His relationship with Cameron was stretched, but he couldn't think of anyone else to call. He reached for his phone just as another message arrived.

This time, the Broker had sent an audio file. Jesse's heart thumped as he clicked on the play button.

Grace started talking.

'It's 9:12 p.m. on Monday. Yesterday was the men's final at Wimbledon.'

Jesse listened as she read out the score. The message ended immediately after she finished recounting the score. His hands were trembling as he checked the match result. It was exactly as Grace had said. She was still alive.

Jesse dialled Cameron's number.

'Hello?' Cameron's voice was strained.

'It's Jesse.'

There was a pause. 'I didn't think you'd be talking to me.'

There was no hint of a celebration of signing the deal.

Jesse bit down on his thumb, his teeth sliding off the nail into the flesh. He cleared his throat. 'I need your help, Cam.'

'I wouldn't recommend it,' he responded.

'We're all in a difficult position. This is your sort of thing,' Jesse said.

'I don't know.' Cameron sounded like he was facing the count and struggling to get off the canvas.

'If you want to make things up to me, Cam, you can do this.'

'Really?'

It was a risk, but Cameron was the only person he trusted who could help. 'Yes. Really.'

'Okay. Thanks, Jesse. Tell me what I can do.'

Jesse took a deep breath. 'I need you to be my bodyguard.'

35

NOTTING HILL

10:15 PM

JESSE WAS WAITING ON THE PAVEMENT ABOUT HALF A MILE FROM Brandon Styles's address when Cameron pulled up in a car. He unwound the window and beckoned for Jesse to get in.

'I borrowed this from a customer. Thought it best not to be in my car.'

'Good. Did you find some bolt cutters?'

Cameron grinned. 'Yeah. I raided the toolbox at one of my gyms. I'm fully kitted out.' He started to drive down the road. 'Now, will you tell me what this is about?'

Jesse had known there would always be a moment when he'd tell someone about the Broker. He just hoped he wasn't making an error of judgment in choosing his cousin.

'Someone blackmailed me to make sure the company was sold.'

'Jesus? The same guy who played me?'

'I don't know. Whoever it is, I think they caused my parents' accident, and they've kidnapped my girlfriend.'

Cameron immediately pulled the car over to the roadside, turning to look at his cousin. 'Christ, Jesse. Are you serious?'

'Yes. They also abducted me and held me in a hangar. They threatened me. Then they sent me a text saying they had my girlfriend, Grace, and that they'd kill her if I didn't get the deal done.'

Cameron was staring at him. 'My God. You haven't told anyone? Not even the police?'

Jesse wondered whether it could be a test. If he'd called this wrong, this was the moment that he'd have Grace's blood on his hands. 'No. You're the only person I've told,' he said.

Cameron swallowed. 'But the deal's done now, right?'

'Yes.' He paused. 'They won't release her until tomorrow at six o'clock. Whoever this is, I think they've already killed two people to get this deal done. I can't just wait. I have to find her.'

'Killed two...' Cameron's eyes were wide. 'Who else did they kill?'

'I don't want to get into that right now. No one you know.'

'Right.' Cameron ran his hand through his hair and blew out a breath. 'What do you want me to do?'

Jesse showed him the address on Google Maps. Cameron nodded and set off on foot while Jesse waited in the car.

Cameron opened the driver's door fifteen minutes later and slipped into the seat.

'I don't think she's there,' Cameron said. It's a regular office. It's locked up. We could come back in the morning and go in, but from what I could see through the window, there's nothing suspicious.'

'Could there be another room out the back?' Jesse asked.

'Yes. But it's a busy road, and other offices are on the floor above and both sides. It's not impossible, but I don't think she's there.'

'Okay. Next, we try the hangar I was taken to.'

Cameron paused, and then he nodded. 'Let's do it.'

36

LONDON

11 PM

THIS TIME, JESSE LEFT CAMERON IN THE CAR, PARKED OPPOSITE the hangar. Cameron had his phone on his lap, and there was always the car horn for backup.

Jesse walked along the path between two silver, metal-framed buildings, out of sight from anyone around him. The door to the hangar was padlocked shut. He looked around to confirm there was no one else there. He lifted the bolt cutters and jammed the jaws on the chain. He grunted with the strain, but after a few seconds, the blades snapped together, and the chain dropped to the ground. He took a moment to listen for any movement from inside. His heart was thumping against his ribs, and his palms were sweating. Satisfied no one was in the hangar, he reached out and turned the handle before swinging open the door. He looked inside. Bile rose to his throat as he inhaled the industrial smell, which triggered his experience of being tied to the chair and blindfolded. He blinked rapidly and tried to push the memory away.

Grace wasn't there. The energy drained from Jesse's body. He hadn't realised how much hope he'd been investing in his first attempt being successful, but she wasn't there, and he had no idea where she might be. He looked around the hangar and spotted a small door at the back and a ladder leading up to a mezzanine level. He was halfway up the ladder when his phone started vibrating. It was Cameron.

> Someone's coming—single guy in a truck.

Jesse froze. Should he climb back down and try the back door? He wasn't sure he had time—another buzz.

> It looks like he's heading to you. Or the next building.

It would become clear in a few more seconds. He climbed up the ladder knowing he couldn't then be seen from the ground floor. Grace wasn't on the mezzanine level, either. He crouched down and waited. The visitor could spot the broken padlock any second now. His phone buzzed again.

> He's parked.

> Gone into the next building.

Jesse let out a slow breath. He typed out a reply.

> She's not here. Tell me when it's safe to come out.

A reply came straight back.

> Wait until I give you the all-clear. I've got an idea.

What the hell, Jesse thought, but he had no choice other than to sit tight. After waiting five minutes, he made his way down the ladder. When he reached the ground floor, he stood still, listening for something that might give him a clue about what was happening outside.

He swallowed. What was Cameron doing? Jesse walked quietly to the back door. There were bolts at the top and bottom of the door and a key in the lock. He reached up to the top bolt. There was a bit of resistance, but he slid it open with a little effort. He did the same with the bottom bolt. He turned the key, trying to be as quiet as possible. Then he closed his eyes briefly, muttered a silent prayer, and opened the door.

He scanned his surroundings. Behind the hangar, there was a small yard area and a footpath. Beyond the path was a wire-link fence. Jesse slipped out and turned up the pathway between the hangar and the one Cameron had said the guy had gone into. He could hear voices. One of them was Cameron. Jesse dodged back into the shadows, standing still so he could hear.

'Alright, thanks, mate.' That was Cameron. 'I'll try that. Sorry to interrupt. I'll leave you to get on.'

Jesse missed the reply, but he heard footsteps. He ducked back along the path and rounded the corner to the back of the hangar, but the footsteps didn't come any closer. He walked along the back of the building and turned up the path on the other side. His phone buzzed.

Come back to the car. Quickly.

Jesse broke into a run. He hesitated as he reached the road, glancing both ways, but he could see Cameron waving to him. He sprinted across the road and around the car to the passenger door and jumped in.

'Duck down,' Cameron said.

'What's going on?'

'I think I know where your girlfriend is.' The car lurched forward.

'What? Where?'

'Oh shit.' Cameron slammed on the breaks. 'Where are the bolt cutters.'

'On the floor, by the padlock.'

'Okay. Wait here. And stay down.'

'What are you—'

Cameron was already out of the car. Jesse could see him in the wing mirror. He picked up the bolt cutters and was walking back when there was a shout. Cameron snatched open the door and threw the bolt cutters onto the backseat. The car was moving before his door was shut.

'That's unfortunate,' Cameron said.

'What? What's going on?'

'I told that guy I was doing a favour for the owner, and I think he bought it. But he's just seen me with a pair of bolt cutters.'

'Where are we going?'

'Your man's got another lockup, a smaller one, further down this road. Number twelve. Down here on the right.'

'Jesus. You think Grace's is there?'

'We're about to find out.' The car veered to the right, and Cameron stopped outside a hangar with a fading green paint job. 'This is it.' He pointed to the hangar with the number twelve painted on the front. It was smaller than the other building. 'We'd better hurry, though. The neighbour's coming this way.'

They leapt out of the car, Jesse carrying the bolt cutters.

'Give those to me,' Cameron shouted. He placed them on the chain and carved through it in one swift movement.

'Hey.' The neighbour waved at them, moving fast. They had no more than thirty seconds until he was with them.

'Leave him to me,' Cameron shouted.

Jesse nodded and yanked open the door. Again, the lock-up was empty. Jesse looked towards the ceiling. 'Damn.' The word echoed around the room. There was no other level, no mezzanine, and no other doors. He could hear Cameron and the neighbour arguing, but the volume was decreasing. There were footsteps, and then Cameron and the neighbour walked into the hangar.

'No prisoner?' the neighbour said. His voice was flat as he studied Jesse.

Jesse walked over to the man. 'Please, you've got to help us. The man who rents this,' he waved at the lock-up, 'he's dangerous, and he's kidnapped my girlfriend. If there's anything you know that could help…' He trailed off, seeing the doubt in the man's eyes. 'Please,' he said.

'Are the police involved?'

Jesse made a split-second decision. 'Not yet. It hasn't been twenty-four hours, but this guy is violent.' His voice cracked. 'I can't wait. If the police get involved, they'll want to know everything.' The man was rubbing his face. 'They're going to want to speak to you and ask you lots of questions.' Jesse pushed out a deep breath. 'I'm just trying to find my girlfriend. Please help me.'

The man chewed his lip. He didn't look delighted to have been wrapped up in anything that might involve the police. He sniffed, and then he started talking. 'Okay, look, you never heard this from me, okay? I've never met the guy, and I swear I don't know anything about a kidnapping. Sweet Jesus. He left me an envelope with the cash for a month's rent for the two lock-ups. He gave me a name, too. Brandon Styles. If you're telling the truth, I'm guessing that's not his real name.'

Jesse's heart thumped against his chest. Brandon Styles was the name of the director of the mysterious company that Belle controlled—the Broker's pseudonym. It wouldn't be his real name, but he now had a direct link between the Broker and the transaction. The net was tightening.

'Anything else?' Cameron asked.

The man shook his head. 'That's all I know.'

Jesse pulled out his wallet. 'I'm sorry about the padlocks.' He handed the man a fold of twenty-pound notes. 'This should cover it.'

The man waved him away. 'Keep your money. The locks are his problem, not mine. All I want you to do is to clear off and forget you ever met me.'

Jesse climbed into the car and slammed his back against the passenger seat.

'I'm sorry,' Cameron said. 'But at least we have a name. That's something.'

Jesse twisted round to face his cousin. 'I guess he may have used the same name to rent somewhere else.'

'Couldn't she be in a hotel or his house?' Cameron was frowning.

'How would he keep her quiet unless he's there with her? He'd have to get her inside somehow, too. It's not impossible, I guess, but it's not easy. If this goes according to his plan, Grace goes free. The last thing he wants after that is her being able to trace him.' He shook his head. 'I don't think she's at a house.'

'Not even a mate's place.'

'It's the same issue. You'd need to be a good friend, and good friends are a connection.'

'Unless he's paid someone enough cash.'

'Maybe.' Jesse scratched his chin as he thought of the Broker disguising his voice. 'I don't think he'd risk it. I know a lock-up's a cliché, but it's a cliché for a reason. Low footfall, they're secure, and no one cares what you keep in them.'

'Okay. We have a name, and we're looking for a lock-up. What do we do now?'

'We phone all the providers, say we're Brandon Styles, and want to extend the term on our rental.'

Cameron was immediately busy on his phone. 'I've got twelve within four miles of here. Most of them open at eight o'clock tomorrow morning. I'm sending you the list. We'll call them all tomorrow. You start at the top, and I'll start at the bottom.' A beat and a grin. 'Just like in life.'

TUESDAY 16 JULY 2024

37

JESSE'S HOUSE, WAPPING, LONDON

8 AM

JESSE BARELY SLEPT. EVERY TIME HE WAS ON THE VERGE OF dropping off, he pictured a dead body lying on the floor of Baxter's house. He didn't know what Baxter looked like, and in each version of his dream, the dead body had the face of a different person who was close to him: Grace, Chloé, and both of his parents. Even Cameron had a cameo role.

Jesse rolled out of bed and rubbed his eyes. His head started to thump, and his throat was sore. He pushed himself up, walked to the bathroom, splashed water on his face, and headed downstairs. Cameron was already in the kitchen, talking on the phone with a cup of coffee in his hand. He pointed to the table with a steaming mug of coffee and a list of phone numbers. Jesse typed the first number into his phone and hit the dial button, listening to Cameron on his call.

'Yes, hello, my name's Brandon Styles. I have an account with you. Yes, Styles. No record? I must be confused; I was sure it was you guys.'

He was about to call number four on his list when

Cameron started waving at him. His cousin ended his call and nodded at him.

'I've found it,' he said. 'Styles has another place, three miles from the others.'

'Is whoever you spoke to going to be there to meet us?' Jesse asked.

'I don't think so. Their arrangements didn't feel overly formal.' He looked at his phone. 'We should be there in fifteen minutes. The problem will be identifying which one it is. I couldn't get them to tell me that without making it obvious I didn't already know.'

Jesse swallowed a mouthful of coffee. 'Well done, Cam. Come on. Let's get going.'

38

LONDON
9AM

THERE WERE THIRTY SEPARATE LOCK-UPS, FIFTEEN ON EACH SIDE of the road. Next to each one, there was enough space to pack a car or a small van.

'Okay,' Cameron said. 'What now?'

'I want you to drive slowly along the road,' Jesse said.

'You going to use your nose to smell her out.' Cameron grinned.

'Sure. Either that or I want to see which one has the same padlock as the other place. He used the same type on both.'

Cameron started rolling the car down the street while Jesse stared out the window. Number eight was the first one that looked like a possibility. By the time they reached the end of the row, they had identified three with similar locks. One of them, number twenty-two, had a car parked next to it, so Jesse would leave that one to last, which left numbers eight and eleven as his first two tries.

'Turn around and pull up at number nine,' Jesse said.

A few moments later, he stepped out of the car and walked purposefully towards number eight. When he was only a couple of yards away, he could see that the padlock was a similar but different design. He spun around and strode over the road toward eleven. This time, the padlock was a match. There was no car parked nearby other than Cameron's. Jesse swallowed. He was following a hunch; if he was wrong, he could face breaking and entering charges, but if he was right...

He stopped outside the door. Was there anything in Cameron's joke? He wouldn't be able to smell Grace's perfume after so long. His nose twitched. He could smell disinfectant. It wasn't much to go on, but if Grace had been kept in the same place for days, the Broker may have swilled the place with disinfectant.

Jesse made up his mind. He turned and signalled to Cameron, who was immediately out of the car and walking over with the bolt cutters.

'You've got a good lawyer, right?' he said as he secured the cutters around the chain.

'The best in the business,' Jesse replied.

'Okay, then.' Cameron grunted with the effort, but the blades sliced through the chain.

Jesse yanked open the door. The ammonia stung his eyes as he stepped inside.

He saw her immediately. Grace was lying on the floor. She had a chain clamped around her foot and a gag in her mouth. The space was empty apart from a chair and a bucket in the corner. Jesse sprinted across the floor and squatted down next to her.

'Grace. God, are you alright?'

She blinked as she came around. She nodded slowly but looked far from alright.

'Did you see who did this? Did they hurt you?'

He gently eased the gag from her mouth before wrapping his arms around her. His eyes fell on the chain, and he let go of her to retrieve the bolt cutter. The best he could do was to cut the chain close to the clasp on her ankle. Gingerly, she got to her feet.

'I don't know who he is. He always wears a balaclava.' Her face was drawn, but he couldn't see any cuts or bruises. 'He hasn't spoken a word to me.'

'Did he hurt you?' Jesse tried to stay composed, but his arms were starting to shake.

She shook her head. 'What's going on, Jesse?' Her voice sounded slurred.

He didn't have the answer yet. 'It's over, Grace. You're safe now.' He heard his cousin walk inside the hangar.

'Jesse?' Cameron said. Then he registered Grace. 'Jesus Christ.'

'Can we get out of here?' Grace asked, slowly getting to her feet.

Jesse snapped into action. He guided her outside and into the backseat of the car while Cameron climbed back into the driver's seat.

'I'm going to get some of my guys to come and camp out here.' Cameron said. 'With a bit of luck, we might catch the guy.'

Jesse wasn't so sure. The Broker had intended to keep Grace there until Wednesday evening. He'd need to be confident he wasn't traceable, so why risk returning to the lock-up?

'This is my cousin, Cameron,' Jesse said. 'He helped me find you.'

'Thank you,' Grace said by way of introduction. 'What did you mean by *some of your guys*?'

Cameron grinned. 'I own a few gyms. Some of the train-ers, they're like my family.' He flicked a glance at Jesse. 'Well, nearly like family. I've got a couple of them meeting us when we get back to Jesse's office.'

'We're going to the office?' Grace turned to look at Jesse.

Jesse nodded. 'I think it's the safest place.' He'd ruled out going to the police. The Broker was still out there, and he couldn't risk doing anything more until the deal was done.

It would all be over by six o'clock tomorrow night. He just had to keep Grace safe until then.

39

HOUSE OF MARCHAM OFFICES, SHOE LANE, LONDON

10: 00 AM

Jesse called Ben to explain that he was authorising Cameron, along with Dave and Olivia, the trainers from the gym who'd agreed to be informal protection for Grace, to access the client suite at the House of Marcham office.

Cameron drove in silence, with Jesse and Grace sitting in the back, catching up as best they could.

'How long did he lock you up in there?' Jesse asked.

'He took me on Thursday evening. I'd booked Friday off work. I was planning to go away for a long weekend. I drove to the supermarket to buy the stuff I needed. He must have followed me and got into my car. It was dark. After I put my shopping in the boot, I got in the car. I felt a scratch on my arm. I knew then there was someone else in the car, but I blacked out almost immediately. I woke up in the hangar.' She brushed her hair from her face. 'I was so scared, but I was also angry. I still am.'

'It wasn't you who responded to my WhatsApp message on Thursday night?'

Grace shook her head. 'No. It must have been him.' She

clasped her hands on her lap. 'What's happening, Jesse.'

He ran his hands through his hair and took a deep breath. So much had happened since he'd last spoken with her; he didn't know where to start.

'The man who took you wants to force a sale of House of Marcham.'

Grace blinked. 'What? But who is he? He must know that your parents wouldn't ever sell?'

Jesse bit down on his lower lip. 'My parents were in a car accident. On Thursday. Dad died, and Mum's in intensive care.'

Grace's hand flew to her mouth. 'Oh God, no.' She reached out and pulled Jesse towards her. 'I'm so sorry, Jesse. That's so awful.'

'I think the same man was responsible for the accident. He'll do anything to get what he wants.'

Grace was shaking her head. 'Shouldn't you go to the police?'

'Not yet,' Jesse replied. 'I will as soon as it's over.'

'What do you mean?' Grace asked. 'How will it ever be over?'

Jesse could feel his heart beating against his chest. 'We've agreed to sell the company.'

'What?' Grace was blinking, searching Jesse's face for some answers.

'The sale completes at six o'clock tomorrow evening. They'll have what they want, and there'll be no reason to threaten us anymore.'

Grace didn't immediately respond. The silence stretched to ten seconds, then twenty, before she spoke.

'And what then? They're allowed to get away with everything they've done?'

He frowned. 'I don't want to risk anything happening to you.'

'Something's already happened to me.' Her voice sounded hollow, and she was shaking. He reached out to take her hands, and she flinched before squeezing his fingers. 'I'm sorry. I...' She trailed off, releasing one of her hands to brush away the tears in her eyes.

The car slowed, and he looked out the window to see they'd arrived at the office. The car tilted as Cameron drove down the ramp to the underground car park.

'It's okay, Grace,' Jesse said.

They were meaningless words, but he said them anyway. He slipped his hand around the back of her head, his fingers softly tangling in her hair, and pulled her towards him. 'You're safe now,' he whispered in her ear. 'I won't let him hurt you again.'

Grace sniffed and nodded. She leaned her body against him, her arm across his chest. The car turned off the ramp into the basement. Jesse glanced at his reflection in the car window and blinked. The face looking back at him was barely recognisable.

Ben, Olivia, and Dave from Cameron's gym were waiting for them. Olivia had brought some of her clean clothes for Grace to change into. Ben led the others to the executive suite, and Jesse headed to Chloé's office. He forced himself to think. Grace was safe, but there were still over thirty hours until the deal was completed. Martin Baxter was the only one who could have stopped the deal, and Baxter was dead.

Jesse sat down at the desk and grabbed a pen and some paper. He started to write the names of everyone who knew about the potential claim against the company: the purchaser, anyone working with the purchaser, the Broker, Jesse, Chloé,

Cameron, Belle, and Daniel Kane. Then he added his parents' names—he couldn't be sure they knew, but it seemed highly likely. He stared at the names, but nothing clicked.

He circled back to motive. Why would the Broker kill Martin Baxter? The simple answer was the Broker killed him because he knew Baxter could stop the deal. If Jesse's parents had visited Baxter and told him he could veto the deal, maybe Baxter tried to make a deal with the Broker and, in so doing, signed his death warrant.

But there was another possibility. Jesse had wondered whether Martin Baxter was the one with the claim against the firm, in which case, the Broker would not only have guaranteed the sale would happen, but he also wouldn't have to pay the claim. One hundred million additional reasons to want Baxter dead.

Jesse scratched his head, trying to recall what Daniel had read out to him.

'*The youngest living descendant of Arthur Baxter, who has attained the age of twenty-one.*'

Martin Baxter was in his early fifties. Jesse's body fizzed. What if Martin had children? Any agreement Martin had made with the purchaser would belong to his estate, and if he had children, that payment would be theirs. Jesse's heart thumped against his chest. If Martin had children, they might now be in their twenties, which meant it was possible one of them would be the protector—they could still stop the sale.

There had to be a way for him to find out if Martin had family. Jesse forced himself to calm down, but a plan to save the company was beginning to take shape. He glanced at the time. It was less than thirty-two hours now. Not very long, but maybe just long enough.

He located the telephone number he needed—for once, the online telephone directory had delivered.

'Hello.' The woman on the other end of the phone sounded half-asleep.

'Hello, Hattie. It's Jesse Marcham.' He waited for the name to click in her memory bank.

'Oh, you. What do you want?' He could hear suspicion in her voice.

'I was hoping you could help me. I wanted to speak with Martin Baxter about a legal matter. I wondered whether he had any children?'

'It's Marty. Not Martin.' She said the full name in a mock posh accent. 'He didn't have any kids. Now stop poking your nose in other people's business. Let the poor bloke rest in peace.'

'Hattie, please—' But the line had already gone dead.

Jesse swallowed. Damn. Baxter had no children. He'd been the last protector, and he was unequivocally dead.

It was over. He'd saved Grace, but the company sale was unstoppable.

———

JESSE WALKED around Chloé's office and stopped in front of the shelf, which displayed every perfume that the House of Marcham had produced. *Distraction* was the most recent addition, although there was plenty of space for future launches. Jesse couldn't help but wonder whether he was looking at the finished collection.

He shook his head. They may have lost the family company, but Grace was safe, and although there had been no other choice than to sell, that didn't mean they couldn't do anything.

Grace was right—the Broker couldn't be allowed to get away with what he had done. Jesse needed to piece it together, work out who the Broker was, and build the case against him. He needed enough evidence to send him to jail. Maybe he could even get the company sale voided, but to do that, he needed to know the secret behind everything that had happened.

He reached out and picked up the first bottle on the shelf, *Evocation*. Then he laughed and shook his head. Why hadn't he thought of it before? The starting point was obvious; he just hadn't been paying attention.

He walked out of Chloé's office and toward his mother's room. Her assistant, Angie, was sitting at her desk outside Jacqueline's office. She stood up as soon as she saw Jesse approaching.

'Hello, Jesse. Is there any more news?' she asked.

'I'm afraid not.'

'It's so awful. I can't believe it.' She was as composed as always, but she'd worked with his parents for many years, and Jesse knew that her professionalism was masking a genuine distress. 'What can I do for you?'

'I'd like to look at the notebook, please.'

Angie looked surprised. 'The notebook?' She managed to catch herself. 'Yes, of course. I'll get the key. Shall I meet you in the boardroom?'

'Thank you. That'd be great.'

She nodded and slipped away from behind her desk. Jesse walked across the floor and pushed open the wooden door to the boardroom. He headed over to stand in front of the glass case that displayed the leather-bound book. To the untrained eye, it didn't look like much, but to the company, it was the most important book in the world. The book was opened to the pages where the first ever House of Marcham perfume recipe was recorded in fastidious script—the foundations of the Marcham perfumery business inked for posterity.

Jesse knew all the recipes by heart. His parents and Kath had changed them as little as possible, and it was clear that every drop manufactured, bottled, and sold was thanks to Alfred Marcham. Jesse knew, too, that some of the more unusual ingredients of *Evocation* were on the next page, away from prying eyes.

The wider display curated the history of their firm's history and photos of the wider Marcham family through the generations. He lingered on the picture of his parents, Richard holding the first production bottle of *Evocation* and Jacqueline displaying a replica of the original. The two bottles looked virtually identical.

Angie walked across the room, holding the silver key that opened the display case. He stood aside whilst she unlocked the front panel. Then she ducked down and unlocked one of the wooden cupboards beneath the case.

'What's in there?' he asked, frowning.

'Oh, sorry.' Angie looked up at him, her hand resting on the door handle. 'I assumed you'd want to see the other documents, too.'

'I didn't know there were any.' He couldn't recall his parents mentioning any other artefacts. Angie cursed under her breath. 'What's wrong?' he asked.

'They're not here.'

Jesse's shoulders tensed. 'What do you mean? Have they been stolen?'

'Oh no, nothing like that. Chloé was looking at them a few weeks ago. I imagine she hasn't put them back yet.'

Jesse gave a slight nod but said nothing. Chloé had been looking at them a few weeks before all of this had kicked off. She'd also secretly met with Global Fragrances. What had she been doing?

'Did she say why she wanted them?' He kept his voice neutral.

Angie shook her head. 'Not really. She was interested in the company backstory, I think.' Angie stood up and handed Jesse the key. 'I don't recall her saying anything specific.'

'Okay. Thanks, Angie. I'll lock it and return the key when I'm done.'

Angie nodded and left the boardroom, closing the door behind her.

Jesse picked up the notebook and gingerly turned the book over in his hands. There were no inscriptions on the outside of the book, nothing hinting at what it contained. He opened it and started to read the first page. It was densely covered with small, neat writing. He turned a page and found more of the same. On the third page was a perfume recipe, the first of many. As he flicked through, he noticed some pencil sketches among the recipes. There were designs for what appeared to be shoes, clothes, and jewellery.

Perhaps his parents had missed a trick. Maybe the House of Marcham could have been an international fashion house. He paused. Maybe they *did* have other plans. Perhaps this small book was a blueprint for a future of entrepreneurial endeavour. Ahead of its time, waiting for the ancestors who would bring everything to life. Perhaps the book was even more valuable than he'd first thought.

He closed the book and studied the front and back cover

and the spine, squinting to see whether there was anything he had missed the first time, but there were no personalised markings whatsoever. He rubbed the back of his neck. He'd been sure that he'd find something.

Just then, his phone buzzed with a text from his sister.

No change in Mum's condition.

Jesse pictured his mother, still in a coma, in her hospital bed. Tears prickled his eyelids. God, he needed her to pull through even though if she did, Jesse would have to tell her they'd sold her company. He buried his head in his hands. He took a moment to compose himself and then called his sister.

'Hi, how are you?' he asked.

'I can't cope with this—always waiting for an update from the hospital. It's awful.' Chloé sniffed. 'Rosie and Elaine have been wonderful, though. They take it in turns to call me every few hours.'

'Yes, they've been great.' The silence stretched between them, and he balled his free hand. 'Angie said that you had some old family documents.' He heard his sister sniff and swallow down the line. 'I'd like to have a look at them.'

'Why?' There was a catch in her voice.

'I'm just interested.' He paused, squeezing his hand again. 'Do you have them?'

'Yes, but not here. They're in my office.'

'I'm in the office now.' He left it hanging. There was still something in her tone. A hesitancy. He bit down on his lip.

'They're in my desk drawer. I think it's locked,' she said. He forced himself to wait. Chloé sniffed again. 'I'll email security. They'll unlock it for you.'

'Thanks, Chlo.'

———————

JESSE LOOKED up to see Ben walking towards Chloé's office. He beckoned for the security guard to come in.

'Boss, I've got the key for you,' Ben said.

'Great.' Jesse took the key and bent down to unlock the drawer.

'Good news that you found Grace.'

'Yes.' Jesse glanced up. 'I'm sorry, I probably overreacted earlier.'

'No problem. Is that everything, boss?'

'I think so, Ben,' he said. 'Thanks again for your help.'

Ben flashed a thumbs-up before leaving. Jesse was numb as he opened the drawer, reached for the box, and opened the lid. He stared at the second notebook momentarily before he depressed the clasp to slide the cover back and release it. He'd never even heard of a second notebook, but it made sense. Albert Marcham may have filled many other notebooks.

The book smelled musty, and again, there were no external markings. There was a slight creak as he opened the cover. Frowning, he turned a few pages before realising he was holding the book upside down. He smiled to himself. With the change of perspective, Alfred Marcham's penmanship was instantly recognisable. It was the same careful, overly stylised writing as in *the* notebook: the loops, swirls, and the dash rather than a dot sitting atop the letter *i*.

Anxious not to damage it, Jesse turned the pages slowly, drinking in the words. It was immediately apparent that this was a very different type of recording. The original notebook was like a scientific journal, crammed with ideas, some developed in later entries and others merely outlined concepts.

Most pages of the first journal contained sketches or diagrams, whereas this one was dense with prose. If book one covered the sciences, the sequel focused on the humanities.

Something else became clear very rapidly: Alfred Marcham wasn't the author of the notebooks; they had been written by a man named Art Baxter. It couldn't be a coincidence that two Baxters were linked with the firm. They had to be related.

Putting the notebook aside, he removed the document wallet from the bottom of the box and unfolded the paper. It was a contract. Jesse's heart thumped as he read it.

The contract showed that the rights to all the original perfumes had been assigned to House of Marcham. The agreement was dated shortly after the firm had launched, and the name of the man who had assigned the rights was a third Baxter—Harold Arthur Baxter. Harold must be a descendent of Art, and given the dates, he was likely also Martin Baxter's father.

The Marcham family story was a lie.

Arthur Baxter had created the perfumes for Marchams of London, yet when House of Marcham had launched, the Baxter name had been wiped from history. Not the House of Marcham, but the House of Art.

Yet, that wasn't the most remarkable thing about the contract. That honour was reserved for the price that the House of Marcham had paid to acquire the rights to all the perfumes. The prize-winning perfumes had been awarded a collective value of one pound.

Those perfumes and their story were at the heart of House of Marcham's success but the family business had been built on a lie.

The Marchams must pay. Or, as the Broker had said, *repara-*

tions will be paid. Jesse shivered as he recalled the word.

Jesse photographed the contract before repacking the notebook and the document wallet in Chloé's desk drawer. He felt lightheaded. The industry was no stranger to secrets and disputes concerning the origin of perfumes. Some people claimed that the recipe for Chanel No. 5 was stolen from a competitor's laboratory. Others dismissed it as a myth, and no one seemed to care much about it. It certainly hadn't stopped a bottle of the perfume from selling somewhere around the globe every thirty seconds.

The revelation would be embarrassing because much of the firm's appeal was built on heritage, on the family bloodline. Jesse flinched. *Legacy*, his new launch, would be a fraud.

But why were the buyers convinced the revelation could support such a significant damages claim? Jesse had a burst of conviction—his parents knew the truth when they launched House of Marcham. So why had Jacqueline only made a deal with Martin Baxter in the last couple of weeks?

Jesse tried to imagine what would have happened when his parents planned to launch the business. They would have read the journals and evaluated their strategy and the risk that using the same perfumes would mean they needed to pay the Baxter family compensation. How had they convinced Harold Baxter to give up everything for one pound? There was no good answer to that question.

Bile rose in his throat as another thought hit him. Chloé had read the second notebook and the contract. She already knew. He opened his online work diary and created a new meeting invitation, adding Chloé as a participant. His sister's availability appeared on screen. He hovered the cursor over a meeting already blocked in her diary. The title confirmed it was a meeting with the rest of the finance department. Jesse chewed his lip. Was it spying if it wasn't her private diary and Chloé knew all her appointments were available for anyone in the firm to see?

He started to page through the diary, quickly eliminating most entries. They related to the launch of *Distraction* or were regular business meetings or social events such as *dinner with L.* He paused over a mid-morning meeting. *Project Sunrise.* Jesse didn't know what that was, and he'd never heard her or anyone else at work mention it. He looked at the previous week. Two more meetings about the same project, and three the week before. He checked the attendees, but Chloé had been flying solo. Jesse sat back in the chair. For over a month, Chloé had been working on a project involving many meetings, and she hadn't even mentioned it to him. He switched to the firm's document management system and typed *Project Sunrise* in the search bar. Nothing. He tried just *Sunrise.* Again, nothing. Could she have met with Global Fragrances more than once? He tapped his fingers on the table.

Jesse's phone ringing snapped him away from his thoughts. It was an unknown number, and his knuckles whitened as he clutched his phone.

'Mr Marcham, this is Detective Constable Mayfield. We'd like you to come to the station to make a statement.'

Jesse's heart rate kicked up, and his legs trembled. He glanced at the time. 'Today?' He coughed to clear the croak in his voice.

'Now, ideally.' Mayfield was measured.

'Okay.' Jesse briefly closed his eyes. 'I should be able to get to you by midday.'

'Very good. You know where we are?'

'Yes,' Jesse replied.

'We'll see you then.'

40

POLICE STATION
12 PM

Jesse sat still, trying to ignore the lingering scent of lavender air freshener. The interview tape was already recording.

'Jesse Marcham,' he said, trying to keep his voice even.

'Thank you for coming in today,' Detective Sergeant Roberts said. 'We want to ask you about your relationship with Mr Baxter.'

'I don't have a relationship with Mr Baxter or his family.' His mouth was dry.

Detective Sergeant Roberts turned over the piece of paper on the desk. 'Your family owns House of Marcham, the luxury perfumery business, correct?'

'My parents founded the business.'

Roberts narrowed her eyes. 'You mentioned previously that there is currently a transaction involving the company and that Mr Baxter was also involved.'

Jesse cleared his throat. 'An offer was made to buy the company. The offer was accepted yesterday.'

'Yesterday?' The Detective Sergeant raised her eyebrows.

'Interesting. Can you explain precisely how Mr Baxter was involved in this sale?'

Jesse forced himself to take his time. 'We were informed by the purchaser that they had made a deal with someone who I believed to be Mr Baxter.' The police officers both looked at Jesse impassively and waited. 'They said he had a valuable claim against House of Marcham.'

'A claim?' Roberts made a note on her pad. 'And what was the nature of this claim?'

'They haven't told us,' Jesse said, which was the truth but perhaps not the whole truth.

Detective Sergeant Roberts looked at Jesse without saying anything momentarily, tapping her pencil on the pad. 'I assume you know the deal terms they agreed with Mr Baxter?'

'I don't know what they agreed with Mr Baxter, but the purchaser reduced their offer price due to the claim.' He paused. 'The adjustment was for one hundred million pounds.'

Mayfield let out a whistle, which earned him a glance from his boss.

'Who is the purchaser?' Roberts asked.

'It's a Jersey-based company called Scent Holdco Limited, controlled by a man named David Crosby.' Jesse held the Detective Sergeant's gaze.

'Thank you. We'll look into Mr Crosby. Perhaps you could explain what you intended to say to Mr Baxter?'

'I suspected he wouldn't be receiving the right amount.'

'The right amount being how much, Mr Marcham?' Roberts smiled at him.

'I didn't have a number in mind, but I thought he should

know about the deal being made.' Jesse tried hard to concentrate on the details.

'You thought he wasn't getting a fair deal?'

'I had no idea what would be fair, but I thought it was possible he wasn't getting the full payment.'

'What difference would it make to you, Mr Marcham?'

Jesse took a moment to think. 'None, directly. However, even though we've agreed to sell the company, it's still important. I wouldn't like to see my family's name dragged through the mud if there was a subsequent dispute.'

'I see.' Roberts rested her pen on the desk. 'I'm sorry to bring this up, Mr Marcham, but I understand your parents were recently involved in a serious road traffic incident.'

Jesse blew out a breath. 'That's correct.'

'And the offer to buy the company was made after the crash?'

'Yes.' Jesse's mind was scrambling.

'And during what I can only imagine must be a period of great personal stress, you and your family agreed to sell the company?'

'Yes.'

'Yes? Is that all you have to say?'

Jesse paused. 'Family businesses are complicated. I'm sure ours is no different in that respect. Sometimes decisions are made for reasons that aren't obvious to an external observer.'

There was a shared glance between the two police officers. Detective Sergeant Roberts tilted her head as she appeared to evaluate his answer. 'I see.' She picked up her pen. 'Do you think Mr Baxter could have been murdered as a result of his involvement in this deal?'

Jesse blinked and concentrated on his breathing. 'I don't know,' he said.

'We have a witness who saw a man entering Mr Baxter's house last Wednesday.'

'Okay?' There was a pinch at the base of his neck.

Detective Sergeant Roberts sat back in her chair with her gaze fixed on Jesse. 'The description of the man matches your father.' The air left Jesse's body as though he'd been sucker punched. 'Do you have any explanation for why your father would have visited Mr Baxter?'

'No.' Jesse's response was strangled. 'My father's dead, and my mother's been in a coma since Thursday.'

'Indeed. I wasn't suggesting that your father was a suspect in the murder, but the visit suggests that Mr Baxter may have been more involved with your family than you've suggested.'

Jesse gritted his teeth. 'I heard the name Martin Baxter for the first time yesterday.' His throat was tight. 'I guess it's possible my father, or even my mother, had met Mr Baxter, but I'm afraid I don't know anything about it. They never mentioned him to me.' Jesse's head was spinning.

The Detective Sergeant tapped her pen on her pad once again. 'Thank you, Mr Marcham. I think that'll be all for now. If we have any further questions, we'll be in touch.'

Jesse pushed back his chair. Detective Constable Mayfield stopped the tape and walked over to open the door. Jesse decided to chance his arm. 'Martin Baxter was entitled to a payment from the purchaser of my family company. That entitlement would pass to his children if he had any.'

Detective Sergeant Roberts was impassive. 'Detective Constable Mayfield will escort you out,' she said. It was clear she wouldn't be answering his unspoken question.

A minute later, Jesse was standing outside the police station. He switched on his phone, which beeped immediately.

> I warned you about talking to the police.

Jesse started to shake as he scanned the road. Was he being watched right now? The message had arrived the minute he stepped out of the police station. It could've been sent while his phone was off, but regardless of when it was sent, the Broker knew Jesse had spoken with the police. There was a second beep.

> You may have Grace back, but you can't protect her forever.

Jesse's hand trembled. Another beep pushed his heart rate through the roof.

> You and your family will pay if the deal isn't completed tomorrow night.

He felt his knees buckle, and it was all he could do to stop himself from falling. If he'd thought it was over, he was wrong. He steadied himself, took a deep breath, and typed a reply.

> I didn't say anything about you. They interviewed me about Martin Baxter's death.

He hit sent and stood for a minute. Then he typed another message.

> The deal will complete. Leave Grace and my family alone.

He waited to see if there would be a reply. After a few minutes without a response, he pocketed his phone and headed to Chloé's flat.

41

CHLOÉ'S FLAT, BATTERSEA POWER STATION

1: 30 PM

THE ROUTE FROM THE NEW UNDERGROUND STATION TO CHLOÉ'S flat had been christened the Electric Boulevard as part of the new Battersea Power Station development. The road was lined with double-height flagship stores of luxury brands, a new high street that could have been curated especially for his sister. Chloé had put down a deposit for her apartment the moment the project was announced, and she'd finally been able to move in a few months ago. Five buildings had been designed as distinctive flower-like structures and the residences above the stores stretched up to flank the roof garden complex. The pitch was built around luxury living, right up Chloé's diamante-studded street. It had surprised no one that his sister had asked to be involved with the firm's negotiations to launch a new House of Marcham store in the heart of Electric Boulevard.

Jesse heard some movement from inside, and a few seconds later, Chloé opened the door. She was wearing pyjamas and a dressing gown, thick and warm enough to try and keep the real world away.

'Hi, Chloé.' Her face was blotchy, her eyes bloodshot. She didn't say anything, didn't shape for a hug. She just turned and walked back into her living room. He followed her and sat in one of the chairs opposite the sofa she'd chosen to sit on. She had chunky socks on, folding her legs beneath her and pushing her hair away from her face, tucking it behind her ears. She wasn't wearing perfume. Not today. Perhaps for the first day since childhood.

'How are you doing, Chlo? Is Larry still here?'

A shake of the head. 'He's gone to New York.' Her voice was a whisper.

Jesse moved immediately to the sofa and hugged her. A flash of anger shot through him. Why couldn't Larry have stayed? She needed his support. Chloé said something, but her words were muffled. 'Say that again,' Jesse said.

'I ended it.'

He blinked. He didn't ask the obvious question, knowing she would tell him when and if she wanted to. 'I'm sorry, sis.' He rubbed her back.

'I don't want to talk about it,' she said. 'Not yet.'

Choosing a conversation topic was like navigating a minefield, but his sister had the right to know about what their parents had done with the trust. It might even help her.

'Okay, well, it turns out that Mum and Dad anticipated all of this,' he said. He figured it was a neutral enough opener. No blaming. No gaming. She pulled away from him, and he saw the furrow deepening on her forehead. A slight shake of the head. She seemed to be trying to compose herself. He switched tack. 'I don't know if it helps, but several things had to happen for us to sell the company. Your vote alone wasn't enough to sell the company.'

'I know it needed three votes, Jesse,' she said.

'It's more complex than that.' He cleared his throat. 'This isn't on you, Chlo.'

'Yes, it is.' Jesse leant forward, straining to hear what she was saying. 'Stop, Jesse. Please, stop talking.' Tears were now running down her face. 'It was me.' He stared at his sister, trying to understand what she was saying. She brushed the tears from her cheeks and lifted her head to meet his gaze. 'This is all my fault.'

Jesse slumped into the sofa. He shook his head, trying to get his thoughts to fuse. 'You'd better explain, Chlo.'

Chloé was nodding, but her breathing was ragged. He stared at her. He could barely recognise her as the confident, competent young businesswoman with the ambition to take over as the CEO of the family business.

'It was never meant to happen like this.' She pushed herself up from the sofa and started to pace around the room. A glimpse of the old Chloé, rising from the dead. She took a deep breath. 'A couple of months ago, I approached Mum and Dad about a buy-out. I'd been thinking about the future. *My* future. I've never made a secret of the fact that I wanted to be the CEO. I spent the last few months developing my plans for the business and expanding into new lines, cosmetics, and fashion. To transform us into a future rival to Hermès or Byredo.'

Jesse let it sink in. He wasn't surprised by her ambition, but the scale of it was impressive. Hermès was still family-owned despite having spent most of the last decade fighting against LVMH's minority shareholding and had come out the other side of the tug-of-war purring. An expansion into cosmetics made some sense, too. A thought fused. Global Fragrances, the company Chloé had secretly met with, had a cosmetics and personal care arm.

Chloé was still talking. 'I researched our company's history and found some clothes designs in the original notebook. I was so excited. I arranged some exploratory meetings with private equity houses.'

'Project Sunrise?' he asked.

Her eyes widened. 'You knew?'

'No. I didn't know.' He shivered at the thought of selling to private equity. Coco Chanel had sold out to a venture capitalist, retaining only ten percent of her eponymous firm. Then Marilyn Monroe said she wore nothing else in bed besides five drops of No. 5, sales rocketed, and now Coco Chanel's lifelong regret had a ten-billion-dollar price tag.

Chloé sniffed before carrying on. 'The PE houses loved it. They all had the spiel of *maintaining our heritage as a luxury family business while helping us expand our global footprint.* They were drooling over the recent sale of a minority stake in Coty and saying we could be the next Byredo.'

Jesse didn't say anything. Everyone in the industry knew the story of François Coty famously dropping a bottle of his *La Rose Jacqueminot* onto the floor of a Parisian department store that had refused to stock his creation. The scent drove customers to the tills, demanding to buy the perfume. Twenty-five years later, he was worth more than thirty million dollars. Fewer people knew that Coty's ex-wife was granted ownership of most of his fortune after their divorce and that when Coty Inc. was sold to Pfizer, she stipulated that no member of the Coty family could ever again be involved in the company. He shuddered. Not the legacy he'd wish for House of Marcham.

Chloé blew her nose. 'They liked our story. They loved my ambition.' She pushed her hair away from her face. 'And I got caught up in it. They showed me financial projections.

Their leverage would magnify the return on our equity. In five years, we could IPO or sell out. We'd make tens of millions, retain a core stake in the business, and be the leaders of one of the world's leading luxury companies.'

'We?' he asked. 'It sounds like a solo project.'

'I was going to tell you. I nearly have, so many times, but I wanted to wait until all the pieces were in place. I wanted us to do it together, Jesse. The idea of us working together to build that success was seductive.' She glanced at him. 'It would've been like the early days of House of Guerlain.'

When Pierre-François Pascal Guerlain died, the house was left to his two children: one as the master perfumer and the other as manager of the business. Thus, a long tradition of the master perfumer's role being a family affair was cemented. But Jesse knew that fairy-tale story had faded.

'Look how that ended,' he said.

'Selling to LVMH isn't bad,' she responded. 'And *Jicky* and *Shalimar* are quite the legacy.'

'They were both created when Guerlain was still in family ownership,' he replied.

Chloé lowered her head. 'I don't want to argue. I'm trying to explain.'

'So, what happened?' he asked.

'I took it to Mum and Dad, did this big pitch. They told me to read those other documents, which made it clear that Art Baxter was the creative force behind everything and that we had no rights to anything other than perfumes.'

Jesse massaged his temples and then stared at his sister. The reminder that what he'd only just discovered for himself, she'd known for weeks, hit him hard.

Chloé lowered her gaze. 'Don't look at me like that. I'm not proud of myself.'

'Okay,' he said, trying to change his expression.

'Mum and Dad told me to forget it—we shouldn't use anything in the notebooks. When I asked about the agreement for the assignment of the perfumes, Dad told me that there were special circumstances.'

'Did he tell you what they were?' he asked.

She shook her head. 'No. He just told me to forget about my plan, and that's what I was going to do.' She closed her eyes and took a moment to steady her breathing. 'But then someone contacted me and said they wanted to talk.'

'Who?' he asked, immediately thinking of the Broker.

'Martin Baxter.'

'Jesus Christ.' Jesse kept his voice even. 'You spoke with Martin Baxter?'

She lowered her head even lower and mumbled something.

'I can't hear you.'

Chloé lifted her head and cleared her throat. 'Yes. He told me he was Harold Baxter's son. We met in a bar in the West End. I thought I'd be able to negotiate with him. We discussed the past, our family history.' She folded her arms tightly across her chest. 'I said that given his father had agreed to assign the rights to the perfumes, perhaps Martin would consider the other stuff.'

'What did he say?'

'He asked me lots of questions about what had happened. He said he hadn't known anything about it until recently. He kept asking why his father had only been paid one pound. I told him that all I knew was that there were some special circumstances.' Chloé sniffed. 'He said he needed time to reflect on our discussion, but he'd be in touch.' Tears were welling in her eyes as she continued. 'That was the last I heard from him. He never answered his phone when I called.' She reached out to take Jesse's hand. 'You have to believe me. At that point, I assumed he'd walked away. I knew my deal was dead.' She tucked a strand of hair behind her ear and carried on speaking. 'Then the protest happened, and Cam turned up talking about his deal.' Her body started to shake. 'That's why I pushed to meet whoever was behind it. I thought Baxter had tried to broker a deal himself.' Jesse flinched at the word *broker*.

'How did Martin Baxter know to contact you? Did you mention his name in your pitch to any of the financial investors?'

'No. I didn't know about him. Even Harold Baxter, I only ever discussed with Mum and Dad. They told me they hadn't told anyone else about him. Only the three of us knew. Martin refused to tell me who had told him.' She flexed her hands. 'Do you think we could find him?'

He let out a slow breath and tried to clear his head. 'You don't know, do you?' he asked.

'Know what?' Her face was blank.

He tapped on his phone and found the news story. 'Martin Baxter was murdered.'

'Oh my God.' Chloé's hand clamped over her mouth.

Jesse passed his phone to his sister. He'd read the article so many times he knew it by heart.

Her eyes widened, and she shook her head. 'That's not him,' she said.

'What? That's definitely him. The police will have approved the picture.'

She shook her head again. 'That picture,' she tapped the screen of his phone, 'that's not the man I met.'

———

JESSE RUBBED HIS FOREHEAD. 'I'm afraid it gets worse.'

'How could it be worse?' Her voice was shaky.

'The police have a witness who claims they saw Dad at Baxter's house the evening after our family meeting,' he said. 'Did Dad say anything to you about going to see Baxter?'

Her shoulders heaved. 'No. I only had that one discussion with them about Harold Baxter. They never mentioned his name again.'

He believed her, but there was still a problem. Nothing she'd told him explained why she'd agreed to the sale.

'Chlo.' Her head tilted slightly in his direction. 'I know there's something else you're not telling me. I want to help.' His mouth was dry. 'But you need to tell me what's going on.'

'I have told—'

'You haven't told me everything, but you need to.' He walked over to his sister and bent down, stroking her hair with his hand. 'Please, Chlo. Please tell me.'

He waited, and after what felt like two rotations of the earth, she lifted her head, wiped away the tears that had streaked her face, looked at him, and nodded.

'They have a video,' she said.

Those four words made his head spin and his stomach sink. 'Of you and ... Larry?'

Chloé shook her head. 'No.' She closed her eyes. 'Not Larry.'

Jesse blew out a deep breath. 'Okay. Does Larry know?'

'No.' Her fringe was covering her face. 'I was going to tell him, but in the end, I couldn't do it.'

'Did someone threaten to send him the video?'

'Yes, unless I didn't vote for the deal. And not just Larry. They said they'd make it public. I couldn't...'

'Who? How did they threaten you?'

Chloé sniffed. 'I had a phone call. This voice.' She shuddered. 'It sounded robotic.'

Jesse said nothing for a moment. Struggling to find the words. 'What happened?'

His sister took a deep breath. 'I went for a drink with Larry one night last week after work. We'd arranged it as a date night. He was flirting with the waitress in the bar. Low-level stuff, nothing serious, but I asked him to stop.' She paused and scratched her forehead. 'He left early to go back to his place; he was annoyed with me. He said I was overreacting. I stayed for another couple of drinks. It's a bit of a haze. I remember a guy leaving the bar before me, holding the door open. And then...' she trailed away.

'And then what?' he asked.

'I don't remember anything else.'

He blinked. 'Do you remember who the guy was?'

'No.'

'Or anything that happened after that?'

'No. I woke up at home the next morning, alone. I thought I'd just passed out. I didn't think much about it, but I was sent a video. It was on a USB stick, in an unmarked envelope, pushed under my door. I was stunned when I watched it. It's definitely me.' She hung her head. 'And two guys. You can't see their faces. They took turns to record.'

'Jesus, Chlo, you need to go to the police.'

She bit her lip. 'I know, but what can they do?'

'You have to report it.'

'It would destroy Larry.' She buried her head in her

hands. 'It will destroy me, too.' Her words were barely a whisper.

'If he doesn't support you reporting this, you're better off without him.'

'But I was cross with him. I was drunk. Maybe I led someone on.'

'No way. Don't think like that, Chlo. You didn't consent. It doesn't even sound as if you were capable of consent. You were raped.'

Chloé started to breathe rapidly. 'I can't remember anything. I woke up. I was still wearing my suit. Apart from my jacket. I was in the same clothes as the video.' Jesse put his arm around her shoulder. 'And the video...' She took a moment to compose herself. 'I look like I was consenting. But it doesn't make any sense. I don't remember it at all. I don't want to go to the police, Jesse. Not yet. I just want to pretend it never happened.' She took in a gulp of air. 'If Mum wakes up, I just can't...'

There was no way that Jesse could go to the police without Chloé's blessing. He didn't know much about rape investigations, but the very little that he'd heard hadn't been positive for the victim. His blood was boiling. She rested her head against his chest, and he held her tight. He didn't know what else to do, but after a few minutes, she was asleep.

———

JESSE EASED himself up from the sofa before walking into the kitchen and calling Grace.

'Hi.'

'How are you feeling?' he asked.

'Much better for not being chained to a post, worse for being locked up in this office.'

'I'm sorry. Obviously, it's your decision, but I'd be much happier if you stayed there until tomorrow night.'

'I will, but I don't want to hide after six o'clock tomorrow.'

'I understand.' Jesse swallowed. He looked back into the dining room, glancing at his sister. He lowered his voice. 'He's blackmailing Chlo, too. That's why she agreed to sell.'

'I guess that shouldn't come as too much of a surprise. Poor Chloé.' The words were delivered as a sigh. 'Is there anything we can do?'

An idea had been scratching in his mind. 'I'm not sure,' he said, but at the same time, the idea was building momentum. He hadn't seen the videotape, and she had no memory of the incident. Jesse believed every word she had told him, but that didn't mean the tape was authentic. He could hear Grace's breathing down the phone.

'Let's just get through the sale,' she said. 'Then we can decide what to do next.'

'I'll do whatever you want,' he said.

'I know you will.'

The call ended, and Jesse returned to the living room. He sat back on the sofa next to Chloé and put his phone on the table beside him. He struggled to keep his eyes open—he hadn't slept properly for days. Just as his eyes closed, his phone beeped.

He sat up and reached for his phone. The message was a reply from the anonymous emailer.

WE NEED TO MEET

He stared at the message. The Broker communicated with him by text, but the email messages differed in style. The

Broker's messages were explicit and threatening, whereas the emails were vague. He typed his reply.

Where and when?

He shivered as he hit send.

Chloé twitched next to him, then rolled her head towards the arm of the sofa and returned to sleep.

42

DANIEL'S LAW FIRM OFFICES, NEW BRIDGE STREET, LONDON
3 PM

Jesse was in a taxi on his way to Daniel's law firm offices. He would've preferred for Chloé to come with him, but she had wanted to stay at home. As the taxi sped towards New Bridge Street, Jesse checked his messages. Olivia had confirmed that Grace had eaten and was now asleep.

His thoughts turned to the entanglement of the Baxters and the Marchams; two families with complex histories. He tilted his head as a new thought wriggled into his mind. Hattie had said that Martin didn't have children, but what if she was lying? Or was wrong? What if he had a child who didn't visit? Jesse grabbed his phone.

After twenty minutes of searching the internet and social media, Jesse finally had a breakthrough. Martin Baxter was on X as @baxthesax. Among the forty-seven people he followed was an account with the handle @chazparker5329. That account followed a collection of people similar to Martin Baxter's account.

There were six accounts that Martin followed that Chaz-Parker didn't. Jesse chewed his lip. Of those six, five followed

Martin. The one account that didn't was for a man called William Jackson. Jesse scrolled through William Jackson's timeline. Nothing had been posted since 2019, but his followers included one other Jackson. Jesse quickly found the Facebook account for Diane Jackson. She was a prolific poster, and her timeline unrolled her life story.

Diane Jackson had been in a relationship with Martin Baxter, and she'd left him when their child was three years old. William Jackson was now twenty-four, and according to his mother, he hadn't had anything to do with his father for twenty years.

Jesse smiled. He had discovered Martin Baxter's estranged son. He had unearthed a living protector, a man nobody knew existed.

Now, he just had to find him.

The taxi was pulling up at Daniel's offices. Jesse jumped out of the black cab, signed in at reception and was directed to the tenth floor. Daniel was waiting for him in a conference room, his laptop on the desk. He shook Jesse's hand and waved to the chair opposite him.

'Any update from the hospital?' he asked.

'No change.' Jesse lowered himself into the chair. How much should he share with Daniel? He'd always trusted him implicitly, partly because his parents had always done so, but the more secrets he'd unearthed about his family, the more cautious he'd become.

Daniel looked at him over the top of his computer screen. 'We're scheduling the completion meeting for tomorrow afternoon,' he said.

Jesse chewed his lip. 'Will David Crosby be there?'

'I'm not sure. His lawyer said it might just be her. He

doesn't like to spend too many days in the UK,' he said. 'For tax reasons.'

Jesse rolled his eyes and nodded. 'I need you to help me find someone.'

'Who?'

'William Jackson.'

Daniel looked blank. 'Who is he, and why do you want to find him?'

'I'd rather not say, just at the moment.' Daniel's eyes narrowed. 'Will you help me or not?' Jesse asked. 'I need his home address.'

Daniel sighed. 'I'd feel better if I knew what was going on.' That makes two of us, thought Jesse, but he kept quiet. Eventually, Daniel nodded. 'I'll get someone on it.'

Minutes later, Jesse walked out of the lift and over to the reception desk. He waited, tapping his fingers on the visitors' book until the receptionist finished her call.

'Just returning my visitor pass.' He placed the slip of paper on the desk.

'Thank you, sir. Would you mind just signing out, please?'

'Sure.' Jesse grabbed the pen, checked the time, and inked it in. He glanced at the names listed above his. He blinked and looked again. He'd not spotted it earlier.

Name of visitor: ID Lowe
Visiting: Daniel Kane
Time of arrival: 11:30 am
Time of departure: 12:30 pm

Isabelle Diane Lowe. Jesse chewed his lip. Daniel hadn't mentioned it. Jesse pushed through the revolving doors and headed to a quiet spot around the corner from the building's main entrance. Seconds later, he was speaking with Isabelle.

'Twice in twenty-four hours,' she said. 'What have I done to deserve this?'

'I wanted to speak to you about Daniel,' Jesse said.

'Daniel? Why?' There was a rise in her vocal pitch.

'I wanted to ask you what you discussed with him.' Jesse chose his words carefully, conscious she could hang up at any moment.

'You were there. You heard everything he said and no doubt more. If you recall, I left before you did.'

Jesse tried to keep his voice even. 'How about when you met with him this morning?'

'How do you—' He could almost hear her thinking. She was silent for a few seconds. 'Did he tell you we met?'

'No, of course not. Look, there's a lot going on that you don't know about—none of it good. I'm trying to work out how to piece the pieces together.' He paused. 'What did you talk to him about?'

Belle sighed. 'I'm not telling you, but I'm not picking on you; I haven't told anyone. It's a private matter.'

'You aren't making it easy for me to trust you,' he said. 'Or to trust Daniel.'

'I'm sorry, Jesse. For what it's worth, there's no reason for you not to trust Daniel.'

'And you?' he asked.

There was a pause for a few seconds. 'Perhaps you should get to know me for yourself rather than believe everything you've been told,' she said. 'Bye, Jesse.'

The line went dead, and he let out a deep breath. He'd always had Belle down as the driver of the friction between the families, but although she hadn't answered his question, he was beginning to reevaluate her. His innate suspicion was fading.

He was still holding his phone when it started ringing. It was an unknown number.

'Jesse Marcham,' he said, aware of a tingling in his hands.

'Hello, Mr Marcham, this is Doctor Hathaway. I have some better news for you. Your mother has made significant progress over the last twelve hours. We're hoping that we can bring her out of her coma soon, provided she continues to make progress.'

Jesse blinked as tears welled in his eyes. 'That's fantastic news. Thank you. I'm in London. Do you think...' He started walking towards the main road.

'It'll likely be a few days before we're ready. We'll keep you updated, Mr Marcham.'

'Okay. Thank you, Doctor.'

Jesse stood still on the pavement. Pedestrians streamed around him, someone cursing him for stopping suddenly. He stared into space. Tears started to flow down his face. His mother's recovery was more than he'd dared hope for, but that wasn't why he was crying. He knew it wouldn't be that night or even that week, but at some point, he'd have to tell his mother that they'd sold her company and, what was even worse, that her husband was dead.

43

HOUSE OF MARCHAM OFFICES, SHOE LANE, LONDON

8 PM

JESSE WAS WORRIED ABOUT CHLOÉ, BUT HE COULDN'T BE IN TWO places at once, and right then he needed to be with Grace. He was just a few hundred yards away from the office when a soft chime announced a new email. He glanced at his phone to see that it was a message from Daniel.

TO: Jesse, Chloé, Isabelle, Cameron

SUBJECT: Completion meeting for the sale of House of Marcham

Dear all,

A meeting with the purchaser has been scheduled for 4 p.m. tomorrow.

The deal is due to be completed tomorrow at 6 p.m., but we could agree to an earlier completion.

I await your instructions.

Daniel.

He saw that Belle had already responded, asking to have the meeting earlier in the day. But why was Daniel pushing for a completion earlier than required? There were twenty-two hours to stop the deal, and Jesse needed every minute to convince William Jackson to help him—assuming he could find him in time. He chewed his lip as he typed out his reply.

Keep the meeting at 4 pm, please.

A few minutes later, he walked into the private suite at the office. Grace was asleep in the bedroom, and Jesse perched on the side of the bed and stared ahead at the wardrobe. He blinked as a memory scratched into his mind, and he walked over and opened the door. The safe was bolted to the wardrobe floor, exactly where he remembered it. He tried the door, but it was locked, and the safe required a four-digit code. He tried the year the company was formed, his parents' years of birth, and his and Chloé's years of birth, but none of the combinations opened the safe. He walked back out of the bedroom and called security.

'Hi. It's Jesse. I need you to open the safe in the private suite.'

'Hello, sir.' Jesse didn't recognise the voice. 'Mr Marcham, I mean your father, had a strict policy that only he should have access.' The security guard was struggling for his words. 'We were told no one should be given the code. Even Mrs Marcham.'

The hairs on the back of Jesse's neck stood up. 'My father's dead,' he said, swallowing hard. 'So, I need you to open the safe.'

There was a moment of hesitation when the security guard tried to work out the new world order. 'Yes, sir. Hold on. I'll get you the code.' Jesse waited. 'It's the four digits, 2805, sir.'

'Thank you.'

Jesse returned to the bedroom, squatted down, and typed in the code. The door popped open, and Jesse pulled out a bundle of brown A4-sized, sealed envelopes. He gathered the envelopes and walked back into the living area. Before he could open any of them, a chime announced a new email.

WEDNESDAY 9 PM.

OUTSIDE BRIXTON TUBE STATION.

I'LL FIND YOU.

Unless it was a double bluff, the sender didn't know about the company's sale and its timeframe. Jesse didn't know who they were or whether they could help, but he was running out of options.

That's too late. Same venue. 1 PM.

He didn't have to wait long for the reply.

OK.

Jesse scratched his temple. He hadn't heard from Daniel about Willian Jackson. He dialled the lawyer's number.

'Hi, Jesse,' Daniel said. There was a touch of distance in his voice.

'Hi. Have you found that address for me?' Jesse asked.

'Hold on a minute.' He heard the lawyer talking to someone else. It sounded as though he was still in the office. A few seconds later, he was back on the line. 'Yes, hold on. I'm just being sent it. I'll ping it over to you.'

'Thank you.'

'No problem. My assistant said the address is in Brixton. It should hit your inbox any second, now.'

'Okay, thanks, Daniel. See you tomorrow.'

Jesse read the email, typed the address into Google Maps and studied the map of Brixton. William Jackson lived less than a five-minute walk from the rendezvous point suggested by the anonymous emailer.

Jesse shook his head. He'd been searching for William Jackson, yet it seemed William Jackson had wanted to meet Jesse all along.

JESSE SAT in his father's favourite chair and opened the first envelope. The only markings on the envelope itself were the initials HAB. He peered inside. It looked like photographs. He tipped the envelope, and the pictures slid onto the table. Some were picture-side down, but Jesse only needed a cursory glance to know that the pictures were of an older man having sex with a younger man—how young was hard to say.

Neither of the men was Richard Ford. Jesse shivered as he put the photographs away. HAB was almost certainly Harold Arthur Baxter. Whether he was the older or younger man didn't change much. Harold was married and had a son. That would have been enough ammunition for Richard.

Jesse knew he was looking at the reason his father had secured the rights to the perfumes for nothing. The *special circumstances* were that he'd blackmailed Harold Baxter.

He opened his phone and logged into the government website. A few minutes later, he'd confirmed that Harold had been dead for over six years and his wife had died only a few months ago. If Harold thought he had taken his secret to the grave, he was wrong, but at least he'd spared his wife from learning the truth. Jesse wondered whether that was a price worth paying.

He sighed as he looked at the other envelopes before selecting one at random. Like the first envelope, it was marked with initials—TJ—the two letters everyone in the industry used to refer to Taylor Jones, a legendary current-day perfumer. Jesse knew what the photographs would be before he saw them. What he didn't know was what price his father had extorted to keep them private.

Jesse flicked through the other envelopes without opening them—six in total. Two was probably enough to make someone a serial blackmailer, but six was beyond doubt. His thoughts were interrupted by Grace walking into the living area.

'Are you coming to bed?' she asked.

Jesse looked at the stack of envelopes. Now, he knew the basis for the claim against the company. He knew William Jackson was the key to both the claim and potentially stopping the deal, but he still didn't know who the Broker was. He also had to face the fact that he had never really known his father.

'No, sorry. You go back to bed,' he said. 'I've got some decisions to make.'

WEDNESDAY 17 JULY 2024

44

BRIXTON
11:45 AM

JESSE WAS STANDING ON A STREET CORNER CLOSE TO WILLIAM Jackson's house. He felt catatonic. Today was the day the House of Marcham would cease to be owned by the family. He thought of his mother, of how he would have to tell her the news when she was strong enough. They wouldn't be able to keep the truth from her for long, but he wasn't sure she would ever actually be strong enough.

If someone had told him the day before that the sale of the company would be a secondary issue on this day, he would have laughed at them. But the truth was the discovery about his father had dominated his thinking overnight and that morning.

Richard Ford was a serial blackmailer. His death would ensure that he never faced jail. Perhaps that was a blessing. How would Jesse have dealt with the issue if his father were still alive? He had no idea. How should he deal with it, given his father was dead? He had no more idea than if he were still alive, but he would have to decide before meeting with William Jackson.

Jesse had spoken to Chloé that morning but hadn't mentioned the photographs he'd discovered or William Jackson. Chloé didn't want to come to the completion meeting, and Jesse had made her promise she wouldn't answer the door to anyone until after the deal had been finalised.

A grey Skoda pulled up alongside him, and Cameron practically vaulted out of the driver's seat. He had his shades on his hair slicked back. They exchanged a fist bump.

'You ready for this?' Cameron asked.

'Yes.' He was going to call on William Jackson unannounced. 'Any chance you've got another foot soldier?'

'Haven't you got one of your perfume guys to do the job?' Cameron asked.

'They're all too busy training for their next cage fight,' Jesse deadpanned.

Cameron grinned. 'What do you need?'

'I'm texting you the address of that office in Notting Hill you checked out when we were looking for Grace. Ideally, I want photographs of anyone coming or going.'

'Okay. I'll sort it.' He pointed over the road. 'Is that where we're going?'

Jesse nodded. 'Knock after three minutes.' He started to cross the road and turned to call back over his shoulder. 'If I don't answer the door, you might have to break it down.'

———

JESSE RANG the doorbell while Cameron stood out of sight, ready to start the countdown. After a few seconds, he heard footsteps approaching the door. The security chain was slipped into place, and the door opened. He tapped his watch —three minutes and counting.

A woman in her mid-twenties with blonde hair peered through the gap. 'Yes?'

'Hello, I was looking for William Jackson,' Jesse said.

He hadn't considered William might have a wife, girlfriend, whatever. He'd viewed William entirely from the perspective of being Martin's son. Jesse realised that he knew absolutely nothing else about him.

There was hesitation before she spoke. 'Who are you?'

'My name is Jesse Marcham.'

The woman blinked and seemed to refocus on his face. 'Jesse Marcham?' She shrugged.

'I'm an acquaintance of his father,' Jesse said.

'His dad?' The woman snorted but stood staring at him. 'Wait there.'

She closed the door and walked away. A couple of minutes later, the door opened again. The woman had removed the security chain and was standing to one side. She shuffled on the spot. Jesse wondered whether William had told her what he'd been up to. 'Come in. Go straight through to the kitchen.' She looked at him as he entered the house as if she didn't fully trust him.

Jesse nodded his thanks and headed down the corridor. He heard the front door close. The kitchen door was ajar. He glanced into the room. It was empty, except for three white chairs surrounding a small table. He pushed the door open and walked towards the table.

'Will's just coming,' the woman said from the hallway.

Jesse walked over to the back door and glanced out of the kitchen window. He could see Cameron's car parked opposite it, but his cousin wasn't inside it. Almost a minute had passed when William walked in. Jesse stared at him as he straightened himself up. There was a tug at his memory. He didn't think he knew the guy, but there was something familiar about him. He was solidly built with stubble and messy hair, but not in a stylish way. He looked as though he didn't care how he looked.

'You're William Jackson?'

'Yeah.'

He was struck by the guy's lack of confidence. A keyboard warrior with caps lock fully depressed. 'You've sent me some emails,' Jesse said. 'Well, you wanted to meet, so here I am.'

'What's going on, Will?' the woman asked. She stood in the hallway outside the kitchen, keeping her distance.

'Martha, this guy,' Martin pointed at Jesse, 'he's a multi-millionaire. I thought he could help us.'

'Help us, how?' the woman asked. 'Is he a friend of yours?'

Jesse shook his head. 'We're not friends.' Just then, Jesse heard a noise coming from the next room. A toddler's crying filled the air. He looked at William. His left eye drifted off to the left, but both eyes momentarily filled with tears.

'That's my son, Neil,' he said. 'He's three years old. He's the most important thing in my life.' The man was balling his hands, his white knuckles showing. 'I'd do anything for him.' Jesse waited. 'He'll be lucky to make it to his fourth birthday. He needs medical treatment. It's only available in the US, and it costs hundreds of thousands of dollars.'

Jesse bowed his head. 'I'm sorry,' he said. This wasn't going how he'd imagined it would go.

'Look around you, Jesse. Do you see anything here worth that kind of money?'

'Actually, I do,' Jesse said, spotting his opportunity.

William laughed a hollow laugh. 'It's not funny.' His voice was scratchy. 'My son is going to die.'

'Maybe, but not for want of the treatment he needs.'

William scowled. 'What are you talking about? Are you going to pay?'

Jesse shook his head. 'No. But someone else can get the money you need to pay for everything your son needs.'

'And who's that?' William was staring at him. Hard.

Jesse met William's gaze.

'You,' he said.

———

'WHAT THE HELL are you talking about?' William threw his hands in the air. 'I've just told you I haven't got that sort of money.'

'I came here to talk to you about your father.'

William twitched, but after a few seconds of silence, he spoke. 'My father was killed two days ago.'

'I know. I'm very sorry.'

William shrugged. 'We weren't close. I hadn't seen him since I was a little boy.'

'Fair enough,' Jesse said, still searching for something to hook William. 'I don't know who killed him, but I do know why.'

This time there was a flinch. 'Go on.'

'He was killed for money.' If Jesse had been flailing around until then, he'd suddenly hit the jackpot.

'What are you talking about?' William said sharply. 'My old man wasn't worth anything.'

'You're wrong. When he died, your dad was owed millions of pounds.'

'What the hell are you saying? Why would he be owed anything like that amount?'

Before Jesse could answer, there was a knock on the front

door. At the same time, Jesse's watch started beeping. Martha moved towards the hallway.

'Leave it,' William said.

'That's my security,' Jesse said. 'If I don't answer the door, he'll break it down.'

William's shoulders rose and fell with his breathing. 'Okay. Answer the door. But tell him you don't need any security. You're not in danger here.'

Jesse nodded and jogged down the hall. He swung open the door to find Cameron standing on the doorstep. 'It's all fine.'

'That's good.'

He saw a glimmer of disappointment in his cousin's eyes. 'You can wait in the car. I'll be as quick as I can.'

He closed the door and walked back into the kitchen. 'When my parents created House of Marcham, they made an agreement with your grandfather.'

'What?'

'One of your ancestors was a man called Art Baxter.'

'Yeah, I know about him.' William's reply made Jesse blink. 'He worked for your family. I wanted to talk to you about him. I came close once or twice, but you were either with your girlfriend or your sister, and I wanted to talk to you alone.'

The connection clicked. 'You were in the wine bar last week.' William didn't confirm it, but he didn't deny it either. 'You've been following me.'

Martha gave her husband a quizzical look. 'Will, what's this all about?'

William sighed. 'I was going to tell you, Martha. Honestly, I was. I wanted to sort it first.'

'Sort what? What's going on?' Martha stood still, arms

folded across her chest.

'Those diaries, the ones Mum gave me, were written by Art Baxter. I read them. He worked for the Marchams nearly two hundred years ago. He was a loyal employee.'

A shiver ran down Jesse's back. Of course it made sense that there were more notebooks.

'You have some of Art's diaries?' Jesse asked.

'Yeah. I figured they might be the only thing Mum ever got from Dad that's worth something.' William shuffled on the spot. 'That's why I wanted to talk to you. I thought you could help.'

Jesse frowned. 'How?'

'I've read your website. You make a big deal of the family heritage. Well, Art was part of it, wasn't he? His diaries must be worth something to you.' William's conviction seemed to wither under Jesse's stare. 'I hoped you'd buy them, you know, do the right thing.'

'I don't want to buy the diaries,' Jesse said, 'but there's something else. Your grandfather, Harold Baxter, owned the rights to all the early perfumes that House of Marcham sold —the bottles, the perfumes, the names—everything. All the details were in a journal my parents had in their possession. When they launched their company, your grandfather demanded compensation from my father.'

'Sounds like he had a point,' William said.

Jesse nodded. 'He did. I have a copy of a contract signed by your grandfather assigning all the rights to House of Marcham.'

William pulled on his ear. 'How much was he paid?'

'Nothing,' Jesse said.

William shook his head. 'I don't understand. Why would my grandfather have given them away?'

Jesse didn't answer immediately. The cache of photographs flicked through his mind, along with the additional envelopes—the seedy portfolio of a serial extortionist—his father's legacy.

'My father took advantage of your grandfather. My mother only learned the truth ten days ago. She spoke with your father and tried to put things right.'

William's eyes were wide. 'How?'

'House of Marcham is being sold against the family's wishes. Anyone who can stop the sale could be paid millions.' William frowned, and Jesse pushed on. 'The only person who can stop the sale from going ahead is you.'

Martha sat down in the chair next to Jesse. 'Are you serious about Will being able to stop the sale?'

Jesse nodded. 'It's complicated, but yes. He can.' He paused and looked at them. 'I have a plan. But I'll need your help.'

———

MARTHA WAS SITTING on the sofa, Neil still asleep, lying beside her, his head on her lap. William was standing, a trickle of sweat running down his face. Jesse, perched on an armchair, held his breath. He had explained the role of the protector.

'I don't know what to think,' William said. He glanced at his wife and son.

Jesse studied him. What he was asking him to do wasn't easy. He'd explained about the Broker, a man who had already killed to get what he wanted. He'd have understood if William had decided to walk away, but the prospect of funding his son's medical care was a huge lever.

'It's a lot to take in.' William rubbed his forehead. 'I want to discuss it with Martha. Can you give us some time?'

'Of course. Take your time.' Jesse stood and walked towards the door. He hesitated and turned to face William. 'Would you mind if I had a look at Art's diaries?'

William looked at his wife, who shrugged. 'I'll go and get them for you,' Martha said.

————

THE DOOR CREAKED OPEN, and Jesse looked up from the diaries to see Martha's pale face poking into the dining room. He'd been absorbed in the lives and loves of Art Baxter.

'Can I talk to you?' she asked.

'Yes, of course.'

She shuffled in with her hands balled by her side. 'I don't want William to get into any trouble.' She glanced around the room.

'I understand.' His shoulders were tight.

'I listened to everything you said about agreeing to give Will his fair share, and we've discussed it.' She shuffled on the spot. 'He said he'll do it, the veto. But I know my husband, and well, he can be hot-headed. So, I'd say it was fifty-fifty.' Jesse swallowed and waited. 'I love him, but I must do what's best for Neil.' Martha was building up to something. 'And I got to thinking, what if it doesn't work out? What if Will doesn't veto, the deal happens, but the purchaser doesn't pay him?'

Jesse nodded. 'If that happens, I will personally pay your son's medical costs.' He saw her flinch. 'I understand that you don't know me, and you don't know if you can trust me, but I want you to speak with my lawyer, Daniel Kane. I'll tell him to expect your call. He will draft a contract for me to cover the costs.'

'Thank you.' She unfolded her arms and crossed them the other way.

'I need you to provide some documentation to Daniel. We need to confirm that Will is who he says he is.'

'Okay. I'll speak to your lawyer.' Then she nodded and walked out of the room.

———

JESSE WALKED TOWARDS THE CAR, dialling Daniel's number. Cameron was leaning against his car, holding two cups of coffee.

'Hi. Where are you?' Daniel asked.

Jesse ignored the question. 'I need you to do something else for me before the completion meeting.'

There was a very slight hesitation before Daniel spoke. 'Yes, of course. What is it?'

'I need certified ID documents for William Jackson, Martin Baxter's son. I'm texting you the contact details for his wife, Martha. She's with William now, and she'll let you have any documents you need if you can send a courier to collect them.'

'You want to be able to prove he's the protector?' Daniel had made the mental leap immediately.

'Yes. I need you to draft the veto document, too.'

'Leave it with me.' A few seconds passed. 'Do you think he will veto the deal?'

The one hundred-million-pound question. 'I don't know. He said he would, but he's unpredictable. I don't think we'll know for sure until we get to the meeting.'

Daniel sucked in a breath. 'Okay,' he said.

'There's one other thing. Martha Jackson's going to call you. I've agreed to meet the medical costs for their son, Neil, if William ends up with nothing and the sale goes ahead. I need you to agree the contract with Martha.'

'Okay. I hope you know what you're doing. Anything else?'

'Yes.' Jesse balled his free fist. 'Yesterday, when I left your office after our meeting, I saw the visitors' log.'

There was a moment of silence. 'It's not what you think.'

'Then why don't you reassure me by telling me what you discussed with Belle?' Jesse replied.

'You know I can't tell you what I discuss with other clients. I'm sorry.' Daniel sounded sincere, but Jesse still wasn't sure he could trust him. The lawyer carried on speaking. 'If I have a potential conflict in acting for two separate clients, I have to let both clients know and, in some cases, cease to act for one or both of them.'

'Is this your way of telling me there's a conflict.'

'No, this is my way of telling you I don't think there's any conflict.'

Jesse ended the call and slipped his phone back into his pocket. He had his trump card to stop the deal, but he wasn't ready to play it because he still didn't know who the Broker was.

Most importantly, he couldn't predict what the Broker would do if he did manage to stop the deal. Cameron's friends were guarding Grace, but Jesse also needed to ensure that Chloé was safe. Now, he was potentially exposing William, Martha, and Neil.

The Broker had already killed to prevent the veto from

being exercised, so Jesse couldn't risk blocking the deal until the Broker had been caught.

Right then, all he had were theories and some credible leads, but ultimately, what was credible didn't matter. It only mattered what he could prove. And right now, he couldn't prove anything.

————

CAMERON HANDED Jesse one of the takeaway cups and leaned against the door. 'How did it go?'

Jesse shrugged. 'Hard to say' He took a mouthful of coffee. 'William's agreed to come to the meeting.' He took another sip. 'Any news from the Notting Hill address?' Jesse asked.

Cameron slipped his phone out of his jacket pocket. 'Let's see. No. Nothing. I'll chase up my guy.'

Jesse tapped his fingers against his leg. 'Cam, I'm going to tell you something, but I need you to promise me that you won't ever breathe a word of this to anyone.'

'Okay.' He removed his shades.

'Chloé's being blackmailed. Someone made a sex tape, and they've threatened to share it.'

'Jesus. Poor Chloé.'

Jesse swallowed. 'I know. I can't get my head around it. She doesn't remember any of it.'

'What? How come?'

'She must have been spiked. She was out at a bar with her boyfriend, now ex-boyfriend, Larry. Have you met him?'

'Not properly. He was at Chlo's birthday party a couple of months ago, but I didn't get to speak with him.'

'Well, they argued when they were out, and he left and went home. Chlo stayed and had another couple of drinks.

She remembers talking to some guy. The next thing she remembers is waking up the following morning, in her flat, by herself.' Jesse took a deep breath. 'It could have been Larry or someone else in the bar who spiked her drink.'

'But it wouldn't be Larry, would it?' Cameron said, 'I'm not being funny, but why would he do that? It doesn't make any sense.'

'Yeah, you're right,' Jesse said. 'It wasn't him in the video, either. A few days ago, she was sent the video. It was recorded in her bedroom, and she had no recollection of it.' He rubbed his hand over his mouth. 'What's even more puzzling is that the video was deliberately shot or edited so you couldn't see the men's faces.'

'Men?' Cameron's pupils were like black points. Jesse didn't feel the need to clarify that detail. 'It sounds like someone made a deepfake.'

'What?' Jesse tilted his head.

'A deepfake. They shot the video of the men with a different woman, and someone used the tech to make it look like Chloé. It's like photoshopping a video.'

Jesse remembered Chloé telling him that she'd looked as though she was consenting. It couldn't have been Chloé because she was out cold, but a deepfake would explain it. 'Wouldn't Chloé be able to tell it wasn't her?'

'Not necessarily. They're sophisticated these days.'

'What would they need?' he asked. 'Images of Chlo and her apartment, as well as the original video?'

'It would help, for sure,' Cameron said.

'That would take us back to Larry, again?' Jesse chewed his lip.

'What do you know about the guy?'

'Not much. I've never actually met him. Chlo really liked

him. He took off to New York when she finished with him.'

'I'm probably being paranoid, but I can ask someone to keep an eye on his address,' Cameron asked.

'I'll have to get the address from Chlo. Thanks, Cam.'

'Of course,' Cameron said.

Jesse called Chloé, but there was no answer. He tried to keep himself calm. 'She's probably asleep. I don't know his address,' he said.

'Anyone else who would know? Do you know where he works?'

Jesse shrugged. 'In finance, but I don't know which firm.' He tried to think what he knew of Larry. 'I don't know much about him.'

'There must be something,' Cameron said.

'He bought her a Rolex for her twenty-first.' Jesse couldn't see how that would help.

Cameron straightened up. 'Do you know where he bought it?'

Jesse thought back. 'Yes. Chlo said he bought it from Highland Jewellers. It's a Lady-Datejust.'

Cameron was searching on his phone. 'What's Larry's surname?'

'Blackwood,' Jesse replied.

Cameron gave a thumbs up and held his phone to his ear. 'Hello? Fliss, did you say? Fliss, I'm hoping you can help. I bought a watch from your shop a few weeks ago. A Rolex. A Lady-Datejust.'

Cameron let out a laugh. 'Well, yes and no. It's been stolen, and I need a copy of the receipt for the insurance claim. My name's Larry Blackwood. Would you be able to email it to me, please?'

Jesse frowned, but Cameron was speaking again.

'No, sorry. I've changed my email.' Cameron sighed loudly. 'I can't access that email account anymore and I'm out of town for a few days. Could you just send a duplicate to my home address?' He sounded slightly tetchy. 'You *have* got my home address on the system, I take it?' There was a pause of a few seconds.

' Yes, that's right, 124 Courtenay Street, Kennington. Excellent. Thank you, Fliss.'

Cameron ended the call and smiled at Jesse. 'Bingo,' he said. 'I think it's unlikely Larry's involved. I'd imagine Chloé's apartment was marketed online. It'd be easy for anyone to access videos of the bedrooms. I've seen her post some stuff on Instagram, too.'

Jesse flexed his hands. Someone had set out to destroy his sister, and when he found out who it was, he would enjoy watching them pay. 'Yeah, you're probably right,' he said. 'Even so, I'd feel better if someone could keep an eye on his address.'

'I'll sort it,' Cameron said. He chucked his coffee cup into the nearby bin and checked his phone. 'I've just been sent the first photos from Notting Hill.' Cameron was scrolling through the pictures. Jesse swallowed. Were they about to uncover the true identity of the Broker? 'I don't recognise anyone.' Then he froze. 'Jesus Christ.' He was scowling at the screen.

'What?' Jesse said.

Cameron handed Jesse his phone.

The man entering the Notting Hill building, the registered address for Brandon Styles, was someone Jesse recognised immediately, someone he'd known for years and a man he trusted implicitly.

Daniel Kane.

Cameron whistled. 'Do you think Daniel's involved?'

'I don't know,' Jesse tried to force his mind to think as he looked at the photograph. 'Can you get your guys at both addresses to add me to the WhatsApp group?' He airdropped the Notting Hill photos to his phone and then passed Cameron's mobile back to him. 'I want to see any photos and hear about developments the moment they happen.'

Cameron nodded as he tapped on his screen. Jesse saw the notification for the two new groups appear on his phone.

Jesse turned to face Cameron. 'I'm going to take William to the completion meeting. I'll take Martha and Neil with me, too. They can stay in the suite with Grace until this is over, but I need you to watch Chlo.'

'On it,' Cameron said.

They exchanged a quick fist bump, and then Jesse stepped out of the car into the road and waved at an approaching black cab. He asked the taxi driver to wait while he collected the other passengers and then walked back into William Jackson's house.

His head was spinning. Daniel would be at the meeting, hopefully with the documentation that Jesse had requested and no doubt Belle would be, too. Jesse could still hear her protestations clearly in his head, protestations that burned with conviction. The funny thing was that Jesse wanted to believe her; he really did, but he couldn't take that final step. Not when she'd met with Daniel, and then Daniel had been seen at the registered offices for Belle's company.

There was another complication.

Only four people other than Jesse knew that William Jackson had the power to stop the deal. Three of them were Martin, Martha, and Cameron.

The fourth was Daniel Kane.

45

HOUSE OF MARCHAM OFFICES, SHOE LANE, LONDON

4:04 PM

Jesse hesitated outside the boardroom. The door was solid wood. 'Let's do this,' he whispered to himself. Then he turned the chrome handle and pushed open the door.

The formal table was set in the centre of the room, with twelve chairs around it—the perfect number for a jury. Belle was sitting in the chair at the head of the table. Sitting next to her was a woman who looked every inch like a corporate lawyer who charged by the minute and holidayed by the hour. Daniel Kane was standing drinking a cup of coffee, almost as if he wasn't prepared to cede ground.

Jesse walked over and stood next to Daniel, looking out the window down onto the London streets. 'I need to talk to you,' he said.

Daniel nodded and turned to face the room. 'I'm sorry, but I need a few minutes with my client. We'll be as quick as we can.'

They walked out of the boardroom, and Jesse led them into a room around the corner. As soon as the door closed, he pushed his phone under Daniel's nose. 'This is a picture of you at an address which links directly to a man I believe to be guilty of kidnap, murder and blackmail.'

Daniel's reaction was impressively muted. 'It's a registered office address used by a company formation agent.'

'What does that mean?'

'What's going on here, Jesse? You've been treating me with suspicion for the last few days. I don't understand why.'

'You're working for Belle.' Jesse stared at the lawyer.

Daniel let out a deep sigh. 'I'm helping her with something, but I can't tell you what it is without her approval.' He set his jaw. 'If I did tell you, would you trust me again?' Jesse nodded. 'Okay. Let me go and speak with Belle. I have no idea whether she'll agree, but I'll ask. I'll be as quick as I can.' Daniel walked back out of the room.

Jesse's phone started ringing.

'Jesse, it's Rosie.'

'Is it Mum?' he asked, his heart rate jumping. 'Has something happened?'

'No, there's no change with your mother. I wanted to speak to you about something else. It's a bit sensitive, and I may be way out of line.'

'I'm sorry, Rosie. I'm up against a deadline. Is it quick?'

'I'm calling about the deadline. I'm on my way to the meeting, but I wanted to speak to you beforehand.'

'You're coming to the meeting? Why?'

'I'll get straight to the point. Isabelle told me about the arrangement for House of Marcham to be sold to a company she apparently owns. I've done some digging, and I think my ex-husband is involved.' Jesse didn't say anything. 'Stephen Lowe is a dangerous man. He may seem calm on the outside, but I saw the very worst of him during our divorce.' There was tension in Rosie's voice. 'I don't want my daughter to get hurt.'

Jesse closed his eyes. His mind was too crowded. To make matters worse, Daniel walked back into the room. Jesse held up his hand to indicate he needed a couple more minutes on the phone. The lawyer nodded and took a seat in the corner of the room.

'Is there anything specific?' Jesse asked.

'He had a private investment company called SHBL Capital. Sell-high, Buy-low. He's set up SHBL Scent Limited to do this deal. That man will do anything to get what he wants, and I mean anything.' Jesse shivered. It sounded like a description of the Broker. 'I should be there in ten minutes.'

'Okay. We'll see you shortly.' He stared at his phone for a few seconds after the call had finished before turning to Daniel. 'What did Belle say?'

'She wouldn't authorise me to tell you. It's not personal. It's a sensitive issue, and she doesn't want anyone to know, so you'll just have to trust me.'

Jesse started to pace the room. Daniel had never done anything else to raise suspicion other than be in a position to know everything that was going on.

'Your parents always trusted me, Jesse.'

'Not enough to tell you everything, apparently.'

Daniel smiled and tilted his head. 'They haven't always confided in me, but they have always trusted me, and you can trust me, too. I've done everything you asked me to, even without you explaining what was going on.'

Jesse said nothing. His mind was cycling through Daniel, Larry, Stephen Lowe, and Belle. It was like a crazy, life-changing game of Cluedo.

'Rosie Ford is coming to the meeting.'

'Rosie. Why?' Daniel asked, his forehead creased.

'She thinks her husband is manoeuvring to become the ultimate owner of House of Marcham. She warned me about him. She's worried about Belle.'

Jesse still hadn't heard from Cameron. He should have arrived at Chloé's flat by now. Where was he? He hit dial, and Cameron answered immediately.

'I'm there. I've rung the doorbell, but there's no answer.'

'I told her not to answer the door to anyone.'

'I've called, but her phone is switched off,' Cameron said. 'I'm sitting in my car with a clear view of the entrance. I'll be able to see if she comes in or out.'

Jesse swallowed. 'Try her again. Maybe she was in the shower or something.' A hollow feeling was growing in his stomach. 'Let me know when you find her.'

He ended the call and turned to Daniel. 'Until I get confirmation from Cam that Chlo's okay, I'm not letting William in the room, and this deal goes ahead. Do you understand?' he said

Daniel nodded.

'Good. Well, I guess we'd better get back in the room.'

Neither of them spoke as they walked back into the Boardroom. Jesse pulled back a chair and sat down.

India Starling spoke first. 'We were expecting Chloé and Cameron, too.'

'They'll join later,' Daniel said.

India shrugged. 'Very well. In that case, let's get started.' She was straight into her Harvard-measured stride. 'As I'm sure you're all aware, the deal completes at six o'clock this evening. We wanted to take this opportunity to advise you of the changes that will take place immediately after the transfer of control.'

Jesse interlinked his fingers and waited to hear about the brave new world. 'Please go ahead.'

'Once the deal completes, the purchaser will immediately enter into a separate contract to sell on the company,' India said, which was news to precisely nobody in the room. 'There are certain conditions of that second contract that my client has agreed to.' She cleared her throat and started to read from a sheet of paper she held in her hand.

'Condition one. If Jacqueline Marcham, Jesse Marcham, and Chloé Marcham have not resigned by six o'clock today, they will be given notice of immediate termination.' India's voice was emotionless, but she was just a hired hand.

Belle stared intently at the lawyer as if she was in a trance.

'Condition two: To the extent that any formal relationship exists between Scent Holdco Limited or any entity associated with Scent Holdco Limited and Cameron Marcham, such relationship will terminate at six o'clock today.'

Jesse was pleased that Cameron wasn't there to hear that his role had been solely to act as a stalking horse and then a show pony. Now, he was being led out to the knackers' yard.

'Is that all?' Jesse asked. He frowned at his phone—still nothing.

'It's a condition of the onward sale that we make you aware of these upcoming changes; please let me finish.' India didn't meet Jesse's eyes as she spoke.

There was a knock on the door, and Jesse walked over to open it. He caught a trace of Rosie's perfume as she entered the room.

'Mum,' Belle said, standing up in surprise. 'What are you doing here?'

'I thought you might need some support,' Rosie said as

she pulled out a chair next to Belle and sat down. She looked at India. 'I'm sorry to interrupt.'

India looked confused. 'I'm sorry, I'm not sure it's appropriate for you to be here.'

'It's okay with me,' Jesse said. Belle was staring at him.

India nodded and glanced at her notes. 'I was saying that my client is obligated to notify the sellers of certain changes.' She looked at Rosie. 'Would you like me to repeat the first two?'

'Oh, no, thank you,' Rosie said. 'Please continue as if I wasn't here.'

'Very well. The third confirmation is that all relevant checks have been performed to establish that the new company owners will have the unfettered ability to change the company's name. They will be exercising that right immediately.'

'What?' Jesse couldn't help himself. There was tension in his jaw.

India looked up from her script before continuing. 'A press release will accompany the name change to explain the reasons for it.'

Jesse pushed his chair back and swept his arm toward the lawyer.

'Okay. That's enough of this theatre,' he said, glancing at the clock on the wall. It was eighteen minutes past four. He couldn't think of a single good reason why he hadn't heard from Cameron yet.

India ignored him and pushed on. 'That brings me to timing. As you know, we have the requisite irrevocable votes in favour of the deal. Your lawyer has advised that the only remaining completion term is the potential exercise of the veto by the Protector.' She paused for a moment, glancing around the room. Jesse was standing now, glaring at India. 'I understand that the Protector was a certain Martin Baxter, who sadly is no longer with us. I would therefore propose—'

'That's not quite right,' Daniel said.

'I'm sorry. Mr Baxter was confirmed dead.' She smiled coldly. 'It even made the news.'

'We don't dispute that. I was making the point that there is still time for the deal to be vetoed.'

India frowned as she started flipping through a document on the desk in front of her. 'I don't understand Daniel. The trust deed doesn't provide any mechanism for appointing a new protector, and if the protector's deceased, then—'

'The deal doesn't complete until the veto period has expired,' Jesse said. 'Given that it's not far away, I'm sure your client will be happy to wait.'

'I don't know what kind of second coming you're hoping for here, but fine. We can wait.' India said

Jesse's phone vibrated. There was a message from Cameron.

Still no answer from her flat.

Jesse's pulse quickened. He looked up to see Daniel staring at him, no doubt wondering whether he was reading the text that would give the go-signal. He gave a subtle shake of the head.

William Jackson, their trump card, was outside the room, waiting for Daniel to call him in.

Jesse tried to think. What was his next move?

———

JESSE SAW the door handle turn before the door creaked open, and a visibly nervous William Jackson walked in. He nodded awkwardly and stopped just inside the room.

Daniel was walking towards him. 'We're not ready for—'

'I'm not waiting any more,' William said.

'I'm sorry, this is a private meeting,' India said, still seated, 'I'm going to have to ask you to leave.'

'I'm in the right place. My name is William Jackson.' He stared around the room, defiance visible in his stiff posture. 'I am the only son of William Baxter.'

The room erupted into a chorus of shouts. William stood still, his head jerking around, sizing up the audience.

'This is ridiculous,' India said, her voice carrying above the others.

The secret was out, but it wasn't how Jesse had planned it. He clenched his fists. He should have locked William in the other room.

'Is this for real?' India demanded. She'd turned to William now, looking for anyone who could tell her what was going on.

Rosie clutched Belle's arm while Daniel tried calming everyone down.

William pointed at Daniel. 'He has a pack of documents confirming my identity.' He walked over to Daniel's seat and riffled through his papers before taking a document wallet and handing it to India. 'Here you go. I'm telling the truth.'

India leant forward and rested her arms on the table. 'We'll need to confirm your claim, William, but let's assume for now that it's true.'

'I just told you. It's true.' William jutted his jaw.

India motioned for William to sit down opposite her. 'You may already know that your father was entitled to a payment from Scent Holdco upon completion of this deal. I'm sure my client would consider that you are entitled to a payment.'

William glanced at Jesse. 'That sounds interesting. I understand you dropped the price by one hundred million pounds because of the payment to my dad.'

Word perfect, thought Jesse. It was just a shame his timing was off. His head started to throb. He needed to find Chloé. There was no point staying here.

William pushed on. 'So, how much of that would you be paying me?'

Everyone was staring at India, and Jesse saw her twitch.

Daniel leaned forward. 'That should be easy to answer. India, I assume the payment in question is documented as a contractual term?'

India took a shallow breath. 'The payment is ten million.'

William Jackson nodded. 'Okay,' he said. 'To someone like me, that's a life-changing amount.' He scratched his head. 'I'm not a corporate person, but looking at the basic maths here, I don't understand the difference between the money you were going to pay my father and are now offering me and the one hundred million reduction in the company valuation.'

'I have limited authority to negotiate on behalf of my client.' India pushed the words out through gritted teeth.

'Don't listen to her,' Jesse said. 'You can't trust them.'

'No, it's okay,' William interjected. 'I've listened to you, Jesse. Now, I want to hear what she has to say. What can you increase the offer to?'

The spotlight swung to shine directly on India Starling. 'Twenty million,' she said. Not even a waver in his voice.

Rosie was pale, and Belle was shaking her head.

Jesse studied William. Twenty million pounds was a vast

amount of money, and William needed the money for Neil. Would he trust the mysterious buyer to pay the amount India said her client would pay? A man who had, on the face of it, reneged on the deal he had struck with William's father and could conceivably have been involved in William's father's murder. Jesse hadn't offered William twenty million, but he had promised to pay all his son's medical fees.

William was now pacing around the room. He stopped and stared out the window. 'I think I still have some time,' he said. 'I'd like to think about everything I've heard. I suggest we take a break and meet again in about an hour.' He turned to Jesse. 'Hopefully, all the shareholders will be here, and I can hear everyone's best offer. That way, we can sort everything out once and for all.'

Jesse didn't like the sound of that. The offer of twenty million pounds, with the hint of a better deal to come, had called more loudly than Jesse had hoped. But right then, he couldn't do anything about it.

There was a chance the deal wouldn't go through, and Chloé was in more danger than ever. He had to find her.

Jesse stood up without saying anything. He then walked around the table and out of the room. He closed the door behind him, spun around and sprinted towards the lifts.

46

BATTERSEA POWER STATION

4:58 PM

THE MERCEDES ROARED THROUGH THE STREETS TOWARDS Chloé's flat as Jesse studied the recent WhatsApp from Cameron's crew. He scrolled through the photographs from the photographer stationed outside Larry's home address on Courtenay Street, Kennington. The first three were deliveries being made. He swiped to reveal the next picture.

Larry was pictured leaving his house almost two hours ago—when Jesse was heading to the completion meeting and Cameron was driving to Chloé's flat.

A bead of sweat traced down Jesse's back. Larry wasn't in New York. Jesse checked the next photograph—Larry getting into a BMW. Then, there was a video of him driving the car down the road. Jesse couldn't be sure, but it looked as though Larry was heading southwest, which was the route to Chloé's flat. He managed to select the number to call his cousin.

'Hi Jesse, I'm park—'

'I think Larry's at Chloé flat.'

'Jesus. Really?'

'We need to find Chlo.' Jesse was shaking. 'If he's the Broker, he'll kill her when he finds out about William.'

'How far away are you?'

'Five minutes.' Every fibre of his body screamed at him to tell Cameron to smash the door down, but logically, Larry wouldn't do anything to Chloé until he knew the outcome of the deal. Jesse massaged his forehead.

'I think you should wait,' Jesse said. 'I'll try going in. He might let me in if he thinks I don't know who he is.'

'That's risky, Jesse.'

'I know, but you'll be right behind me.' His phone beeped. 'Hold on a second.' He switched to his texts. His mouth went dry. 'There's a message from the Broker.'

> If William Jackson stops this deal, Chloé
> dies.

A chill worked its way down his spine. 'He's got her,' Jesse said. 'And he knows about William.'

He heard Cameron swear under his breath.

'Cam, Larry will be watching through the window. I want you to drive away, make him think you've gone. I'll get my driver to follow you once he's dropped me off. Borrow his jacket, anything that might mean Larry doesn't immediately recognise you when you head back towards the building. I'll call you when I can. If I call you Daniel, then come immediately. If I don't call you within five minutes, come anyway.'

Two minutes later, Jesse was sprinting down the Electric Boulevard to Chloé's flat.

47

CHLOÉ'S FLAT, BATTERSEA POWER STATION

LARRY OPENED THE DOOR OF CHLOÉ'S FLAT. JESSE'S HEART RATE spiked. He had to act as though he had no idea who this guy was and pretend he didn't know he was a murderer.

'Who the hell are you?' Jesse asked.

The man was close to six feet tall, lean, and dark-haired. 'I might ask you the same question.' The man had an easy confidence as if he had every right in the world to be in Chloé's flat. 'Although I think I know the answer. You must be Jesse, right?'

Before Jesse could answer, the man thrust out his hand. 'It's Larry. It's good to meet you at last.'

Jesse glanced at the outstretched hand and ignored it. Larry was close enough for him to smell the dry, woody scent of Creed's Aventus—not the same scent as the Broker. He frowned.

'I thought you and Chlo had split up?'

Larry grimaced and slowly withdrew his hand. 'We have,' he nodded. 'Her choice, not mine.'

'What are you doing in her apartment?' He pushed past

Larry, walked into the living room, and then into the bedroom—there was no sign of Chloé.

'I came to return her key.' Larry followed Jesse into the flat.

'You could have posted it.'

'She hasn't returned my calls. I just wanted to speak to her.' He looked momentarily sheepish. 'I was hoping for one last chance to see if we could start over.'

'Where is she?' Jesse asked.

'I don't know. I only got here a few minutes before you.' Jesse knew he was lying. 'She's not here.' Which may or may not have been a lie.

'Have you checked the bathroom?'

'No, I'll—'

'You won't do anything, pal.' He blocked Larry's path, putting his hands on Larry's jacket. He could feel the man's breath on his cheek. He had to play this right. 'Look, I'm sorry, Larry. It's a difficult time, what with our parents' accident, everything that's going on with the company, and now Chlo's missing. I didn't mean to snap.'

'Yeah, I understand.' Larry smoothed out his jacket. 'I'm sure she's just gone to the gym or something.'

'I hope so.' Jesse's mind was still racing. 'Look, I need to make a call. It's crucial the company sale goes through. There's a meeting going on right now to finalise it all.' Jesse hoped he was preaching to the converted.

'No problem. I'll try texting some friends and see if Chloé's with them.'

'Great. Thanks.' He hit dial, and Cameron answered on the first ring.

'Hi Daniel, it's Jesse.' He glanced at Larry, who was busy

sending a message from his phone. 'We need to make sure that the deal goes through tonight.'

'On my way,' Cameron said. He ended the call but carried on talking.

'I want you to do whatever's necessary. Pay William Jackson from the trust if you have to.' He paused. 'Yes, exactly. Just get it done.' He slipped his phone back into his pocket and walked over towards Larry. 'Any luck with her friends?' he asked.

Larry was staring at his phone. 'Nothing, yet.' Larry avoided direct eye contact, but Jesse saw him glance in his direction as he walked down the corridor toward the front door.

Jesse slipped the catch on the front door and walked back towards Larry, noticing the tension in his face. Larry was about to make a move. Jesse stepped behind Larry and flung himself towards him, slipping his arms under Larry's and locking his fingers behind the man's neck. His opponent twisted suddenly. He was too strong, and Jesse struggled to hold him. He grunted loudly as Larry back-pedalled and slammed him into the wall. His grip slipped. Larry wrestled free from Jesse and reached towards his pocket. There was a glint as he brought a switchblade up in front of him. His expression was stone cold. Jesse was backed up against the wall when the front door swung open, and Cameron sprinted down the hallway. Larry turned around to face him.

'He's got a knife,' Jesse shouted.

Cameron didn't flinch. He swayed backwards as the knife slashed towards him, and then his hands clamped onto Larry's arm. He pivoted on his foot, his hips pushing into Larry's body. Larry was launched high into the air and landed hard on the ground. Cameron was on him instantly, disarming and pinning him to the floor.

Jesse staggered over and crouched over Larry. 'Where's my sister?' Larry's face twitched, but he said nothing. 'Where is she?' He punched the man in the ribs.

Cameron put his knee on Larry's back and pulled the man's arms behind him. 'Find something to tie him up with, Jesse.'

Jesse walked into the lounge, scanning around. He spotted Chloé's skipping rope, picked it up and took it over to Cameron.

———

JESSE HAD CHECKED EVERYWHERE in the flat. Chloé wasn't there. Judging by the pressure being applied to Larry's back, Cameron was enjoying keeping Larry under citizen's arrest. Jesse picked up Larry's iPhone and held it to Larry's thumb. The screen opened. Jesse checked his text messages, but no text had been sent in the last few minutes.

He scrolled through the different icons—nothing in email, Facebook Messenger, or WhatsApp. On the third page, he found the Signal app buried in a group of icons called Sports.

There was only one contact. Whoever Larry had messaged when he'd said he was texting Chloé's mates was recorded simply as X.

Jesse is here. He doesn't suspect anything. We're still on. He's telling Daniel to pay WJ.

There was no response.

The previous message Larry had sent simply said, *I've got her.*

X didn't have a name or a profile picture. Jesse scanned some of the messages, which dated back two years.

Larry: I had a drink with her tonight. Got her number.

X: Good. You need her to fall for you. Hard.

Larry: You sure you want me to do this? I'll have to sleep with her.

X: I want you to do whatever it takes. I want to know everything she's thinking. I want her to love you so much that when you dump her, she doesn't want to live.

Larry: I don't know. She seemed alright.

X: She's poison. She needs to pay. Just remember, the harder you screw her over, the better everything will be for you.

Jesse scrolled forward.

Larry: I've never met anyone like you.

X: And you never will.

Larry: When can I see you again?

Jesse had read enough. Larry may be the Broker, but X was the mastermind, and he still didn't know who that was. He pocketed the phone.

'Who's X?' he said to Larry, but the man didn't answer. 'You're only making it worse for yourself, Larry. I'm going to call the police. It's not looking good for you. So, you'd better start talking.'

Again, Larry said nothing.

'No one came out of the building whilst I was outside. Why would he come back here if he'd already taken her somewhere else?' Cameron scratched his head. 'I don't even think he'd have had the time.'

Jesse nodded. Chloé had to be in the building. 'There's an underground car park,' he said. 'I'll check that. Are you alright with him?'

'Yeah. Hey, Jesse?'

'Yes?'

Cameron pulled a set of keys from Larry's pocket and threw them to Jesse. Clutching the keys, Jesse took the lift from outside Chloé's flat's front door. His nose wrinkled at the sanitised air as he entered the car park. There were only two cars there. A BMW and a Maserati. He clicked on the key fob, and the lights flashed on the BMW. He ran over to the car and opened the door. Chloé was lying in the backseat with a blanket pulled over her, but she was breathing. She was alive.

He opened the back door and reached in towards his sister.

'Chlo. Chlo. It's me. Jesse. Are you okay?'

Chloé moaned and blinked her eyes. 'What? Jesse?' Her voice was thick and slurred. Her eyes flicked open and then closed again as she relaxed back down on the car seat.

Jesse walked around and opened the passenger door. He perched on the seat whilst he called Cameron. 'I've got her. She's okay, but she's been drugged. Have you still got Larry under control?'

'Don't worry. He's not going anywhere. Can you bring her up here?'

'Not easily. I'm going to call the police and then drive to the office.'

'What about Chloé?'

'She's coming with me. I'm taking Larry's—' His nose twitched at a familiar smell. Coffee, vanilla and cedarwood. Automatically, his brain ran the fragrance through his memory bank. He blinked. The scent was familiar. And it wasn't Larry's *Aventus*. It wasn't a masculine at all. But it also wasn't Chloé's *Evocation, Blue Belle,* or *Distraction.* Jesse frowned. He knew that he'd smelt it recently. Jesse forced his brain to work. He tried to recall who he'd been with and where it'd been.

'Jesse, are you still there?' Cameron asked, 'I think the signal dropped.'

'I have to go, Cam. I'm going to drive to the office in Larry's car.'

He ended the call and forced himself to breathe. His hands shook as he dialled the number and lifted his phone to his ear. 'Detective Sergeant Roberts, please? This is Jesse Marcham. I need to speak to her urgently about the murder of Martin Baxter.'

Jesse frowned at the glove compartment. He must have opened it when he reached for the dashboard. He leant forward and pulled out a bottle of perfume. *Bleu de Chanel*. He shivered. Larry had worn it literally to throw him off the scent.

'Hello, Mr Marcham. This is DS Roberts.'

The conversation took under ten minutes. Detective Sergeant Roberts was sending officers to Chloé's flat.

Jesse moved into the driver's seat. He had enough time to get to the office. Before he started the engine, he pulled out Larry's phone. It was still unlocked, but he wouldn't be able to change the passcode. It took him three minutes to photograph two years' worth of messages. He didn't want to read them but knew he'd have to. It was the only chance of uncovering X, and he was running out of time. When X couldn't get hold of Larry, they could panic. Jesse didn't know who X was or what they might do if the sale didn't go through. But he did know what they were capable of. He had to get back to the meeting. He had to sell the company and leave the police to try and find X.

He drove up the ramp onto the street, replaying his

options in his head. He didn't know William well enough to predict which way his decision would go. Art Baxter had been passionate, brilliant, and impulsive—his diaries made that clear. Jesse had to hope that William hadn't inherited those traits.

It was only as he pulled out onto the road that he had a thought which turned everything on its head.

48

HOUSE OF MARCHAM OFFICES, SHOE LANE, LONDON

5:23 PM

WILLIAM WALKED BACK INTO THE ROOM. EVERYONE ELSE WAS sitting in silence. William didn't say anything as he took his seat opposite India Starling. He didn't need to. He just had to wait for India to offer him more money. He knew her immediate offer of twenty million meant her client had authorised an even higher offer. He wasn't holding out for one hundred million. Twenty million was already a crazy amount, but if waiting for sixty minutes got him more, it would be the easiest money he'd ever make. And the most.

India placed her phone on the table and raised her head to look at him.

'Thirty million,' she said.

William smiled. Everyone was staring at him but before he could answer a phone started ringing.

'Excuse me,' Daniel said, picking up his phone. William glared at the lawyer. 'I see,' Daniel said. 'Yes, I understand.'

William waited until Daniel had finished the call. 'Who was that?'

'That was Jesse. He's on his way here with Chloé. There's

been a development. They should be here in the next ten minutes.'

'What development?' Rosie asked. 'What's happening, Daniel?'

William tried to keep his hands from shaking. He was so close. He looked at India. 'We have a deal. Thirty million pounds, and I walk away.'

India sighed. 'I think we should wait for Jesse and Chloé. I need to know what I'm dealing with.'

William swallowed. Then he raked his hands through his hair. 'Just agree to my deal. What can Jesse Marcham say that will change anything?' He'd wanted his voice to carry authority, but even he could hear the hint of desperation.

'That's a good question,' India replied. 'I guess we'll find out soon enough.'

———

BY THE TIME Jesse parked outside the office, Chloé had come around and was sitting up in the backseat. He sat next to her and closed the car door.

'The video you were sent,' he said, 'I don't think it's real.' Chloé gasped. 'It's a deepfake.' His voice was thick.

'Is that ... Can they do that?'

'Yes. Someone would just need images of you to dub over the original video.'

'Oh my God, I'm so relieved,' she said. She was quiet for a few seconds before speaking again. 'Do you know who did it?'

Jesse took a deep breath. She didn't know about Larry. He started to talk.

———

He'd only had time to give her the highlights, but they were enough to leave her shell-shocked. He helped her out of the car, and together, they slowly made their way into the building. Jesse kept his arm around Chloé as they ascended in the lift. She reached out to squeeze his hand as they approached the boardroom.

He reached for the door handle to hold the door open for Chloé. He followed her into the room.

'What's going on?' Belle asked as soon as they stepped inside. 'Jesus, Chloé, you look dreadful. Are you okay?'

'I've been better. Someone drugged me.'

Belle's hand flew up to her face. 'My God.' Her eyes shot to Jesse, concern etched on her face.

Jesse scanned the room, still trying to solve the puzzle. He helped Chloé into her chair and walked behind Belle and Rosie.

Then it hit him. *Black Opium.* His body began to shake. He was sure his nose hadn't failed him, but the answer didn't make sense. Why would Larry's car smell of *Black Opium*?

Jesse's stomach pitched. He steadied himself by holding the back of the chair and then sat down. His mouth was dry as he looked directly at the person he now knew was responsible for the murder of his father. The person who had used Larry's relationship with Chloé to access information: Jacqueline and Richards' plans for the family, the notebook, the contract, Chloé's deal and the Baxters.

For the moment, Jesse said nothing. He typed two quick messages, one to Cameron and one to Daniel.

William Jackson was in full negotiation mode. 'Let's get this deal done. You can swap stories after. I've decided not to veto the deal.'

'It doesn't matter what you've decided.' Jesse said. He was exhausted, but adrenaline was fizzing through his body.

Daniel frowned at his phone and, without a word, left the room.

'Where's he going?' William asked, gesturing towards the door. 'This is ridiculous,' he added.

'You're not the protector,' Jesse said. 'You're a beneficiary of Martin Baxter's estate, that's true, but you're not the protector.'

'What the hell are you talking about? Of course I am. You told me yourself.' William was out of his seat.

'I was wrong, but the Protector is in this room.'

'What?' Belle looked baffled. 'Who is it?'

Did they know, Jesse wondered. He couldn't be sure, but he didn't think so. He cleared his throat before speaking. 'It's you, Isabelle.'

'What?' Belle pushed her chair back, but she leant forward and grabbed the edge of the table. 'What are you talking about?'

'Your great-grandmother was Victoria Selby.'

'What? Yes, I know that.' She shook her head. 'I don't...' She started again. 'She's your and Chloé's great-grandmother, too. So what?'

Jesse looked around the room. Everyone was staring at him as if suspended in time. He glanced at the clock. The deal would close in ten minutes unless Belle vetoed it. 'Victoria Selby was Art Baxter's daughter,' Jesse said.

Belle blinked. Then she blinked again. She opened her mouth and then closed it.

'You are all his descendants,' India said, massaging her head. 'You're all over twenty-one, which means that whoever is the youngest is the protector.' She shook her head in disbelief.

'Isabelle is ten days younger than Chloé—she's the youngest.' Jesse studied his cousin as she digested the news. 'So, it's up to you, Belle. Do you want to sell, or do you want to veto?'

Rosie was the next to speak. 'Isabelle already voted to sell.'

'True,' Jesse said. 'But there's something else she should know before she decides.'

'What about my thirty million?' William asked. 'We made a deal.' He stepped towards India.

'Don't do anything stupid,' Jesse said.

Belle leaned forward. 'What's going on, Jesse? What aren't you telling me?'

Jesse stood up and walked around to stand in front of the door. He cleared his throat. 'A man using the pseudonym Brandon Styles kidnapped and assaulted me. He blackmailed Chloé.' He glanced at his sister. 'He tried to kill our mother and murdered both our father and Martin Baxter.'

Belle lightly stroked her throat, her eyes distant, yet the worst was still to come. Everyone else was staring at Jesse.

The door opened, and Daniel walked back in, flanked by two security guards. All three stopped next to Jesse.

Jesse took a deep breath. 'Brandon Styles' real name is Larry Blackwood.' He saw his sister flinch. 'He was Chloé's boyfriend, but Chloé knew nothing about what he'd done.'

Belle's eyes flicked to Chloé. She was repeatedly pinching the skin between her thumb and forefinger.

'I'm sorry to have to tell you, Belle, but Larry Blackwood was working for your mother.'

Rosie was motionless, her expression stone cold.

'No.' Belle's voice was barely a whisper.

Jesse softened his voice. 'Your mother's been in a relation-ship with Larry for over two years.' He turned to face his aunt. 'Everything he's done, he's done because you told him to do it. We have all the messages between you. The police are arresting Larry as we speak, and they are on their way here to arrest you.'

Belle was shaking her head. 'My God, Mum.' Tears were rolling down her face.

'Take her to another room,' Daniel told the security guards. 'Stay with her until the police arrive.'

The guards walked over to Rosie, who still hadn't spoken. She stood up slowly and stared at Jesse. A shiver ran down his spine as he returned her gaze. She remained silent as she was escorted out of the room.

'I'm so sorry, Belle,' Jesse said. 'I really am.' He glanced at the clock on the wall. 'We have five minutes before the deal completes. I've spoken with both of our fellow trustees,' he glanced at Chloé, 'and I have a counter-proposal.' Belle stared at him. He tried to read her expression, but it was impossible. He pushed on. 'We don't sell, but we change the company's ownership.' Everyone was locked onto him. 'Sixty percent for Chloé, twenty-five percent for you, and fifteen percent for Cameron.'

'Hey, what about me?' William pointed at Jesse. 'What about my family?'

'The company will accept its liability to the Baxter family. The twenty-five percent allocation to Belle recognises that she is a descendant of Art Baxter. Neil Jackson is also a descendant of Art Baxter. The company will pay three million pounds annually to a trust for Neil over the next ten years. In satisfaction of the annuity, we would ask that William

Jackson waives all potential claims against both the company and the Marcham family.' William was frowning. Perhaps the maths was too hard. 'Thirty million,' Jesse said, hoping it would help. 'It's the same as the offer you were prepared to accept earlier.'

William nodded weakly.

Jesse waited for Belle. She had the most to process, and she alone had the power to stop the deal and save the family company.

'Who'll be CEO?' Belle asked.

'Chloé,' Jesse replied without missing a beat.

'What about you, Jesse?'

'Me?' He hadn't had much time to think about it. But the funny thing was, after all the months of frustration over the company's leadership when it came down to it, he hadn't needed much time. 'I just want to keep my job and for the company to recommit to always having an in-house perfumer,' he said.

Belle stared at him for a moment, then cleared her throat and scanned the room. 'I veto this deal in my capacity as protector. As a trustee, I agree with the new proposals. Daniel, I'll sign whatever you need me to sign.'

The paperwork had been drafted in the hope that Martin would sign it, but it would work for whoever was the protector. Belle picked up a pen and signed where Daniel was pointing.

Jesse slumped in his chair.

They'd saved the company. Finally, it was over.

———

JESSE WAS in the suite with Grace. They held each other tightly before Jesse relayed what had happened over the last few hours.

Chloé had opened a bottle of wine from the cellar and poured a glass for everyone. 'I think we've earned this,' she said.

'We sure have,' agreed Grace.

Chloé passed her brother a glass. 'I still owe you an apology,' she said.

'You don't owe me anything,' he replied.

'I do.' She winced and took a deep breath. 'I told *Scent* I was the favourite for the CEO role.' She stood there with her eyes closed. 'I'm so sorry.'

Jesse laughed. 'It's okay, Chlo. Forget about it. And besides,' he took a sip of the cabernet sauvignon, 'it turns out you were right.'

He was at peace with his decision, and Grace had accepted it without question, strengthening his belief that it was right for him.

Just then, the door to the suite swung open, and Cameron walked in. He hugged everyone before looking questioningly at Chloé.

'Help yourself to the wine, Cam. You don't need to ask. You're one of the family, now.'

'Belle accepted the deal, then?' he asked, looking at Jesse.

Jesse nodded. He'd called Cameron to outline his proposal on the drive over to the office. He hadn't known whether there would be a veto, but he'd wanted to be prepared.

'Although,' Jesse glanced at Chloé, 'there are a couple of details I haven't had the chance to cover off with our new CEO just yet.' Cameron frowned, and Chloé shuffled to the front of her chair. Jesse cleared his throat. 'I thought that when we secure the new premises in Electric Boulevard, we could install a Mad Cows Gym in the basement.' Cameron's eyes bulged. 'And I'm sure we could come to some deal on financing. Perhaps a joint venture?'

Cameron turned towards Chloé. 'I mean, that would be amazing. What do you think, boss?'

Chloé shook her head and rolled her eyes to the sky. 'Okay, fine.' She held out her glass towards her cousin. Her watch gleamed in the light. She paused before unfastening it and placing it on the table.

'That bastard deserves to rot in prison for a long time.' Cameron's white knuckles suggested he might also like to have Larry in the ring for a round or two before he was remanded.

'I still don't understand how he knew about the Baxters,' Chloé said. 'I told him about the meetings with the private equity funds but never about the Baxters. I only ever spoke about it to Mum and Dad. Maybe I talk in my sleep.'

'The shop told me he bought that watch in March, more than two months before your birthday,' Cameron said. Chloé frowned. 'Do you wear it all the time?' She nodded.

'Even in, for example, meetings with Mum and Dad?' Jesse asked.

Chloé closed her eyes and sighed. 'He bugged the watch,' she said, shaking her head. 'Unbelievable.' She stood up. 'Right, I'm going to head home. If we're heading up to Lancaster tomorrow, I need to get some sleep.'

The siblings had a long hug, and Chloé promised to get one of the firm's drivers to take her home. Jesse watched her leave.

'Poor Chloé,' Cameron said. Jesse nodded as he pulled

out Larry's phone and placed it beside the watch. The police would want to examine both. 'Well, I'm going to make a move, as well. Mum asked me to go to the hospital tomorrow, too. Is it okay if I join you for the journey up?'

'Of course,' Jesse said. They exchanged a fist bump, and Cameron walked to the door, leaving only Grace and Jesse in the room.

'I'm exhausted,' Grace said. 'I know I said I wanted to leave, but shall we stay here for one more night?' She yawned and stretched out her arms.

'Fine with me,' he replied as Grace walked towards the bedroom. 'There's just one more thing I need to do.' He pulled his phone from his pocket and clicked into the photos. He wasn't looking forward to reading Rosie and Larry's messages, but he needed to understand—or to find out whether that was even possible.

His hands trembled as he started to read. Twenty minutes later, he closed his phone. He'd read enough.

AUGUST

49

MANSION HOUSE, LONDON

JESSE'S MOUTH WAS DRY. THERE WAS A CHILL IN THE AIR, YET A bead of sweat trickled down his back. Grace was sitting on his left, and she reached over to squeeze his hand. He offered her a smile. Chloé was sitting on his other side. He wouldn't have wished for it to be any other way. There was silence in the church as everyone waited for him to stand and walk to where he would deliver the eulogy to his father.

Seventeen days after the accident, Jacqueline Marcham was brought out from her induced coma. She was transferred to the step-down unit to continue her recovery under close monitoring. She could speak, and the doctor hoped she would be discharged within the next few weeks.

Explaining to his mother that Richard had been killed was the hardest thing Jesse had ever done. Keeping his father's behaviour to himself was a close second.

Jacqueline had said she wanted Jesse and Chloé to proceed with the service for Richard. She wouldn't be there, but she'd find her own way to say goodbye.

Jesse looked out at the crowd. Next to Chloé, fidgeting in

his seat, was their cousin Cameron. One of the best things to have emerged from the ashes of his father's death and the fight for the company was that Jesse and Cameron had spent more time together than at any point since they were boyhood friends, and it hadn't taken long for them to fall back into their natural rhythm. Once the expectations around wealth and business had been scrubbed back, they simply had family and, more importantly, friendship.

If Cameron taking his place on the family front row was a surprise, the woman sitting next to him was a bombshell. Jesse couldn't fall back on a childhood friendship with Belle, but the last weeks had been like being introduced to a cousin he hadn't known existed. The first few days after Aunt Rosie had been arrested had been tough for her, but if Belle was anything, it was resilient. They'd always had that right about her. She'd already given evidence to the police to support the case against her mother and Larry Blackwood, and she'd told Jesse that she was determined to try to rebuild her relationship with her father. They'd supported each other in accepting the truth about Rosie.

Jesse's family filled the front row pew on the left. He glanced to the right and smiled. His extended family now spilt over to the other pew. William had Neil on his lap, and Martha sat next to them. Jesse still wasn't sure about William, but Martha and Neil were great.

Jesse unfolded the paper that contained his speech. He'd struggled to express how he felt. The words were stilted and awkward, and last night, he'd binned draft number seven and started again, trying a different perspective. It wasn't about loss. It was a celebration of what he'd found: what family had given him, what family still gave him, and what family would give him in the future.

He cleared his throat, ready to start, when Neil thrust out a chubby arm and pointed at him. The little boy looked genuinely delighted to see his new friend. The medical specialists in London had already reviewed him, and he was being flown to the US the following week to start his treatment. His main concern was how many cuddly toys he'd be allowed to take with him. Neil looked up at his mother and pulled on her arm. Then he pointed again and waved, 'Hello, Uncle Jesse.' Jesse gave the little boy a smile and a wave. Then he took a deep breath and began to speak.

'My mother can't be here, but she would be heartened to see so many of you here today to celebrate Richard's life. She'd be heartened, not because people came for Richard, or for her, but because you are here for each other.' He paused and wetted his lips. 'Just a few weeks before my parents' accident, they met with family—a family that was dear to them but, for various reasons, had drifted apart. In those meetings, they spoke of the bonds of family, the strength of family, and the importance of family. They recognised that they had perhaps lost some of that connection and wanted to do what they could to put that right.' He glanced at Belle, who was blinking hard.

'I know we are here to pay our respects to my father, but it's impossible to think of my father without thinking of my mother. They were always a team, and it will be hard for her to be without him. My father wasn't perfect, but everything he did, he did for my mother, and I know with total conviction that had he been told only one of them could survive the accident, he would have saved my mother in a heartbeat.' He paused and sipped water from the glass on the lectern shelf. 'I've learnt much about my family over the past few months. You'll have read the news, so you'll know it too—most of it, at least. Some of it has been shocking.' Jesse knew the audience would be thinking of Rosie Ford, with only him thinking of his father. 'But we adapt, we forgive, and we grow. I like to think that my father would agree.' Jesse swallowed the lump in his throat. 'I know he would embrace our newfound family members too.'

Chloé was dabbing at her eyes, and Cameron was chewing on his bottom lip. 'People used to say that my parents' legacy is House of Marcham. I think they have an even better legacy: family and friends. So, my thanks to you all. And on behalf of me, my sister, and my mother, I want to finish with these words.' Jesse's throat tightened, but he was nearly there. 'Rest in peace, Dad.'

Then he folded his piece of paper, slipped it into his pocket and walked back to his seat.

———

THE REMAINDER of the service seemed to be over in moments, and soon, the guests were filing out of the church to the outside reception area. Belle and Elaine stood together, and Jesse approached them, greeting them both with a hug.

'Lovely speech, Jesse,' Elaine said. She flashed a warm smile at Belle. 'Lovely to see you. I'll leave you two to catch up.' She rubbed Jesse's arm and walked away, following Cameron towards the exit.

Jesse looked at Belle. 'How have you been?'

'It's only a week since you saw me for lunch, Jesse.' She smiled. 'But I'm doing okay, thank you.'

Jesse had no idea how long it would take Belle to process what her mother had done. 'Did you visit your mother in the end?'

'No. And I don't think I will. I'm not sure I'll ever be able to forgive her for what she did, even though I now know why.' Tears shimmered in her eyes. 'She wrote me a letter.' She sniffed and dabbed her eyes with a tissue. 'I started to read it, but...' She shrugged.

Jesse thought back to his conversation with Rosie in Moor Park. He still found it hard to equate his experience of the warm, kind-hearted woman he'd spoken with that day to the woman who'd been behind everything. She'd told him she'd been influenced by her family growing up. That much was true, up to a point. The claim to have come to terms with the family's past had been brutally exposed as a lie.

'Why did you stop reading?' he asked.

'She started talking about Chloé. It was obsessive, and it was vile. I didn't want to read any more.'

Jesse wasn't surprised. He never wanted his sister to read Rosie's messages on Larry's phone, the evil spewing from their aunt. He hadn't asked his mother about Richard's other sister and didn't think he ever would. His mother had enough to cope with, and her memory was patchy. It was quite possible that she wouldn't be able to recall the traumatic details of her husband's childhood. It was even possible that Richard had never fully shared them.

Jesse had been forced to piece it together from the cache of messages between Rosie and Larry, supplemented by discussions with Belle. Belle hadn't known about her mother's twin, but when Jesse had told her, she'd searched the online newspaper archives. The local newspaper report she unearthed told of a tragedy buried in the family's wall of silence. Rosie's twin sister, Chloé, had died in a road traffic accident when she was eight years old. It was a hit-and-run. Chloé was with Rosie, and she had run across the road when she'd seen her big brother as they walked home from school. The photo of little Chloé could easily have been a picture of Rosie. They had been identical.

Belle had also told Jesse about research that suggested an identical twin who'd lost a twin had an increased risk of psychiatric disorder. Whether her mother would receive a formal diagnosis wasn't clear. What was clear was that the subsequent trauma had shattered the family. Neither Stephen Lowe nor Belle recalled any contact between Rosie and her mother. The close mother-daughter bond Rosie had described to Jesse was a sham.

Stephen had told Belle that Rosie's simmering anger towards her wider family began to define her. She saw slights and injustice everywhere she looked, and it worsened after Belle was born. On the day that Belle reached the exact age that Rosie's sister had died, Stephen found his wife passed out at the cemetery.

When Belle told Jesse the date, 28 May, Jesse realised why his father had chosen the security code 2805 for his safe.

All of Stephen's attempts to encourage Rosie into treatment were rebuffed. Later, she filed for divorce and petitioned the court for sole custody of their daughter. Her mania around her dead sister morphed into an unhealthy obsession with Isabelle, twinned with hostility toward Richard's daughter. The second Chloé never stood a chance with Rosie.

Just then, Daniel walked past. He waved to them both and kept walking, clearly not wishing to interrupt. 'You never did tell me why you met with Daniel?' Jesse said.

Belle smiled. 'I didn't, did I.'

'Don't you think you'd feel better if you told me?' he asked, matching her smile.

'You know, I think I would.' She still made him wait. Eventually, she laughed and started speaking. 'I went to him for advice about my mother.' Jesse said nothing. 'She'd always been intensely focused on me. Only child syndrome, maybe. I don't know. When I was younger, it was fine. She was always in my corner. For a while, it was better than fine. But as I grew up, it became more extreme, more intrusive. People who beat me fair and square started to have inexplicable bad luck. I could never be sure, but I suspected my mother used her money and influence to help me. Only, she was hurting me.'

'So what did you want Daniel to do?'

'Originally, I wanted advice. Could I get an injunction order; do something to stop her interfering in my life?' Jesse nodded. 'Afterwards, when you told me about the company being set up with me as a shareholder, I called Daniel and asked him to remove me. I couldn't stand the thought of being manipulated by anyone. I was sick of it. Daniel wasn't very hopeful but agreed to try.'

'Hence his visit to the company formation agent,' Jesse said.

'Sorry?'

'Never mind. It's not important. Did you tell Daniel about Brandon Styles? Or the deal the company had with the purchaser of House of Marcham?'

Belle shook her head. Jesse was silent for a while. House of Marcham and the Marcham family weren't Daniel's only clients. Belle had gone to him for help, and he'd responded. Daniel had just been doing his job.

Jesse looked around. They were the last people left inside the church.

'I think we should join the others,' Belle said, linking arms with Jesse.

'Good idea.'

They walked towards the crowd that had gathered outside. He blinked in the sunshine and spotted Grace laughing with Chloé.

'Go on,' Belle said.

'You're coming too,' he said, gently dragging her over to the others. Chloé and Grace were drinking champagne, each holding a spare glass. Belle and Jesse accepted the drinks offered to them.

'It's a shame mum's not here,' Chloé said.

'To Jacqueline,' Grace said, and they all chinked glasses, joining in the toast.

'Hold on,' Jesse said.

His nostrils were twitching. He'd watched Grace apply her perfume that morning and recognised the scent on Belle the moment they'd embraced in the church. He leant towards Chloé, closed his eyes, and inhaled. The perfume they were wearing was still at least a year from a formal launch, but Jesse had declared himself happy with the blend just the week before. He had also told everyone he had ditched the name *Legacy*. The world knew the truth about House of Marcham. It was time to be authentic, and he'd always wanted the name to have a bit of edge.

The three women were grinning and joined together in their plot. He didn't know whose idea it had been or how they'd snuck some of the perfume out of his lab, but all three were wearing his newest creation.

Secret by House of Marcham.

'You've got a great nose, Jesse,' Chloé said, nudging him in the ribs.

'I'd like to make a toast,' Belle said, raising her glass again. 'To House of Marcham—its past and its future.'

Jesse scanned the group, laughing together—a manifestation of their newfound intimacy. He shook his head and shut his eyes to savour that moment with the three women now closest to him, to bask in an emotional intensity worthy of only the world's greatest perfumes.

THE END

FRAGRANCE NOTES

FOR THE PERFUMES MENTIONED IN THE NOVEL

AVENTUS BY CREED

Top Notes: Apple, Bergamot, Blackcurrant Leaves, Pineapple.

Heart notes: Birch, Jasmine, Patchouli, Pink Berries.

Base notes: Ambergris, Musk, Oakmoss, Vanilla.

FIREDANCE BY RUTH MASTENBROEK

Top notes: Apple, Lemon.

Heart notes: Damask Rose, Leather, Cashmere.

Base notes: Oudh, Patchouli.

LE MALE BY JEAN PAUL GAULTIER

Top notes: Cardamon.

Heart notes: Lavender and Iris.

Base notes: Vanilla.

. . .

305 BURNING LEAVES BY CB I HATE PERFUME

Notes: The smoke of burning maple leaves – pure & simple.

BLEU DE CHANEL BY CHANEL

Top notes: Pink pepper, Lemon, Vetiver.

Heart notes: Grapefruit, Cedar, Labdanum.

Base notes: Sandalwood, Ginger, Frankincense.

BLACK OPIUM BY YVES SAINT LAURENT

Top notes: Pear Accord, Mandarin Essence.

Heart notes: Vanilla, Orange Blossom, White Flowers.

Base notes: Black Coffee Accord, Cedarwood Essence, White Musk, Patchouli.

DAISY BY MARC JACOBS

Top notes: Blood Grapefruit, Wild Strawberry, Violet Leaf.

Heart notes: Gardenia, Jasmine, Violet.

Base notes: Musk, Vanilla, White Wood.

ALSO BY NJ BARKER

THE HONESTY INDEX

A gripping thriller about a game of secrets and consequences.

Over one hundred 5-star ratings on Amazon.

"One of the best books I've read in a long time."

"I have never read a story like this one! Highly recommend."

"One of the best thrillers I've read - what a book!"

If Trent had never agreed to play, his friends would be safe...

PREPARE TO BE GRIPPED BY THIS INTRIGUING, PULSE-RAISING THRILLER FROM DEBUT AUTHOR NJ BARKER.

Trent Ryder's life was shattered by the fire that killed his parents and younger brother. The cause was never found, and the mystery has haunted him ever since. Now in his twenties, he and his old school friends receive a chilling invitation to a game—one that promises to finally reveal the truth behind the blaze.

But there's a catch. The game knows their darkest secrets. If they refuse to play or dare to lie, those secrets will be exposed to the world. Each friend must endure five questions and five pleas, and with every round, Trent inches closer to uncovering the answer he's been seeking. Yet the price for this truth is steep—brutal honesty about the past.

Can Trent stop the game before it destroys them all?

Are you ready to play?

The Honesty Index is a gripping psychological thriller, perfect for fans of T.M. Logan and Harlan Coben.

GENIUS CLUB

They were gifted
enough to be selected

Are they smart
enough to survive?

GENIUS CLUB

NJ BARKER

The new thriller from the author of *The Honesty Index*

A gripping, dark psychological thriller

"Draws you in and you can't put it down."
"Loved this book. Couldn't put it down. Would highly
recommend."
"This is a cracker of a story. It's like Frankenstein for the
modern age."

**They were gifted enough to be selected. Are they smart
enough to survive?**

PREPARE TO BE GRIPPED BY THIS INTRIGUING, PULSE-RAISING THRILLER FROM THE AUTHOR OF THE HONESTY INDEX, NJ BARKER.

Professor Matthew Stanford is a genius with numbers, but when it comes to people, he's always struggled.

As a teenager, he was offered a scholarship by the reclusive polymath, Benjamin Caesar, where he met a group of like-minded intellectuals, which became known as the Genius Club.

The now thirty-something prodigy still stays in close contact with the other participants, but when Matthew discovers his wife - also a member of the club - dead on the floor with an empty syringe by her side, his life unravels.

Authorities dismiss it as a tragic overdose, Matthew is certain something far darker is at play. When he uncovers unsettling truths about Caesar's motivation behind forming the club, Matthew realizes he and his friends have been part of a disturbing experiment all along. And now, they are being hunted down one by one.

Can Matthew outsmart a faceless enemy before he's next?

Genius Club is a dark psychological thriller perfect for fans of T.M. Logan, Alex Michaelides, and Michael Crichton.

ACKNOWLEDGEMENTS

I hope you enjoyed reading *The Family Secret*.

This story was inspired by music. I knew I wanted to write a thriller set in the world of family business. I was thinking through different industries that might provide a good background for a twisty plot when my playlist shuffled to an early 1990s favourite of mine: *Perfume (All on You)* by *Paris Angels*. For me, it is simply one of *those songs*. I must have listened to it over a thousand times since it was released.

So, the industry was chosen, and this thriller was born, living with the working title, *Perfume*. I had no idea there was already a famous thriller with that title, but that was a challenge for another day. The first major issue with the choice of industry was that I knew nothing about perfume and also had a terrible sense of smell. I spent the summer of 2024 researching the industry. *The Secret of Chanel No. 5* by Tilar J. Mazzeo, *Perfume: In Search of your Signature Scent* by Neil Chapman and *Essence & Alchemy* by Mandy Aftel gave me a fascinating insight into the perfume world, whilst *The Perfect Scent* by Chandler Burr was my standout favourite industry book.

Wanting to move beyond the printed page, I signed up for a fragrance customisation experience at *Floris* London with in-house perfumer Penny Ellis. The hours flew by, and I'm proud to say that a bottle of my very own scent (that sounds wrong; I helped to create my own perfume with expert guidance) sits on my shelf in my writing room.

I still have a terrible sense of smell, but learning about the industry was an eye-opening experience—there is an essence of magic and mystery running through it—and I hope I haven't taken too many liberties in creating my own version of the industry in my novel.

I'm delighted to see *The Family Secret* in print. It's my third standalone thriller, and I hope it's my best one yet. As with all my books, I want to acknowledge the support and help of a collection of fantastic people. In no particular order, my heartfelt thanks:

To special agent Jo, who has been a champion of my writing these last few years, super reader Sarah, and all at Bell Lomax Moreton.

To the Faber crew: Emma, Siobhan, Tonks, Zo, Vania, Robyn, Nicole, and Alison.

To my A* grade, beta-readers Susie, Andy, Kay, Mike, Elizabeth, and Alison.

To Ellie Hawkes, for her support and insightful structural and developmental edit. Anyone looking for editorial support do check out her elspells.com website.

To Jason Anscomb for my stunning cover. I love all my covers, but this one might just be my favourite.

To Ellie Pilcher, marketing guru, for her support and guidance pre and post-launch.

To the ROAR Book Blast team for loving books and for the social media support.

To Lucia, for the proofread.

To Claire and to James, for everything that I can't adequately put into words.

Finally, my thanks to you for reading my book. I'm forever grateful.

ABOUT THE AUTHOR

Nigel lives in Kent with his wife, son, and their two cocker spaniels. When he isn't writing, he's usually trying to recover a sock from Milo.

NJ Barker's website